Ellora's Cavemen

Seasons of Seduction

Volume II

Ellora's Cave
Romantica Publishing

Ellora's Cavemen: Seasons of Seduction II

Gillian's Island

Lani Aames

After a storm at sea sinks their boat, two couples are stranded in a small chain of islands called the Pirate Keys. Gillian's sprained ankle makes her unable to travel, so she and Brandt wait while Paige and Tony cross difficult terrain to find help.

Paige and Tony run into problems with both their mission and their relationship, but discover that nothing matters more than the burgeoning love they share.

Gillian and Brandt take advantage of their privacy to explore their deepest desires, and a centuries-old mystery draws to an unearthly conclusion on Gillian's island.

Devon's Vix

Rebecca Airies

After a single bite from a rogue vampire, Jessie Coulter discovers she's changing. If that wasn't bad enough, she's been marked for death by a fanatical anti-vampire society. Even then, she was certain she could handle it. But she couldn't handle Devon Knight's sudden reappearance in her life. She'd broken off her relationship with him when she'd learned he was a vampire.

Devon hasn't been able to get Jessie out of his mind. When he discovers she's in danger and transforming into a vix, he's determined to protect her. Even as danger gathers around them, desire flares. They'll have to confront their enemy and win or lose any chance at a life together.

Wendy's Summer Job

Charlotte Boyett-Compo

Wendy Cole has been given the boot by her evil stepmother and there will be no more college tuition for the budding actress. With her funds cut off and her credit cards frozen, the young woman knows she'll have to support herself.

Responding to a receptionist wanted sign in the window of an automotive shop, she comes face to face with hunky Drake Quinlan, co-owner of the shop. Darkly handsome with a killer smile to go along with a devastatingly well-honed body, he's just the kind of man for whom Wendy would love to work.

But there's a catch: Drake and his two brothers, Kyle and Lance, enjoy very intimate, sharing games that only certain, extraordinary women would be willing to play. The right woman is the one they are looking for and they've got their eyes on Wendy.

A delightful romp through the fertile imaginations of three delightful men who are seeking Miss Right. Only serious players need apply.

Chasing the Dragon

Megan Kerans

Captain Jade Ahnat is on a mission to acquire the rare Dragon's Eyes seeds from the only source—The Dragon. The seeds are the only cure for the Dark Sickness, the only way to save her sister and thousands of innocent people from agonizing death. Success will also bring Jade a promotion to general.

Raj Cad, The Dragon, has no desire to assist the United Planetary Federation that betrayed him and massacred his fellow warprinces. But once he sets eyes on Jade, he desires her enough to make her submission for twenty-four hours part of the price for Dragon's Eyes seeds. But after the day is up, can Jade be willing to give up the role her people and family expect of her in order to follow her own desires?

Viking's Pledge

Melany Logen

Mista is terrified of her master, the warrior Raynor. Yet he has never touched her in any way, only offered her his protection. When he returns from a six-month voyage, however, his lust is uncontrollable—and Mista finds him irresistible. But a slave is not a suitable wife for a warrior, and her longing for her native Ireland is more than she can bear.

Raynor will give her anything, including her freedom. As the time approaches for her to return to her homeland, though, Mista realizes she might have given up the only home she knows—or wants.

Taking It All

Cheyenne McCray

Lisa Peterson's life is *boring* and *average*—until she runs into a man. With her car. Instead of asking for her insurance card, he asks her out for a drink. What can she say, but yes?

Brad Akers is anything but average. He's sexy, witty, interesting, and a man with muscles in *all* the right places. Lisa experiences things she'd only dreamed of—turning over control and allowing herself to be bound and spanked for his pleasure and hers too. As he draws her deeper into his world of BDSM, she has no qualms about taking it all—especially if that means Brad.

An Ellora's Cave Romantica Publication

www.ellorascave.com

Ellora's Cavemen: Seasons of Seduction II

ISBN 9781419956690

Editorial Team: Raelene Gorlinsky, Pamela Campbell, Nicholas Conrad, Sue-Ellen Gower, Briana St. James, Denise Powers.
Cover design by Darrell King.

This book printed in the U.S.A. by Jasmine–Jade Enterprises, LLC

Electronic book Publication June 2007
Trade paperback Publication June 2007

Content Advisory:

S - ENSUOUS
E - ROTIC
X - TREME

Ellora's Cave Publishing offers three levels of Romantica™ reading entertainment: S (S-ensuous), E (E-rotic), and X (X-treme).

The following material contains graphic sexual content meant for mature readers. This story has been rated E–rotic.

S-*ensuous* love scenes are explicit and leave nothing to the imagination.

E-*rotic* love scenes are explicit, leave nothing to the imagination, and are high in volume per the overall word count. E-rated titles might contain material that some readers find objectionable—in other words, almost anything goes, sexually. E-rated titles are the most graphic titles we carry in terms of both sexual language and descriptiveness in these works of literature.

X-*treme* titles differ from E-rated titles only in plot premise and storyline execution. Stories designated with the letter X tend to contain difficult or controversial subject matter not for the faint of heart.

ELLORA'S CAVEMEN:
SEASONS OF SEDUCTION II

ହ

GILLIAN'S ISLAND

By Lani Aames

Chapter One

Somewhere in the Caribbean

ॐ

Gillian Alford sat close to the fire that Brandt had built before Paige and Tony went for help. She watched his muscles ripple as he gathered driftwood along the stretch of beach. Besides being a gorgeous hunk with sun-streaked blond hair, ice-blue eyes and a body to die for, Brandt could light a fire…inside her as well as with wood and matches.

"Are you comfortable?" Brandt asked as he set the bundle within easy reach. He dropped down beside her and checked the strip of canvas he had tied around her sprained ankle as a makeshift bandage. A battered tarp and a few broken pieces of the boat were all of the flotsam and jetsam that had washed ashore after the storm. "Are you sure you aren't in pain?"

"I'm fine, I promise." It was only a small lie to keep him from worrying. A sharp pain shot through her ankle occasionally, but as long as she didn't move her leg too much, it happened less frequently. Otherwise, she had come through their harrowing ordeal unscathed.

It was a miracle any of them had survived.

But, she decided as worry wrinkled Brandt's brow anyway, if she had to be stranded on a deserted island, she couldn't have picked a better hunk to be alone with. Handsome, strong, capable—Brandt Powers was everything she'd ever dreamed of in a man. They had been dating over a year, and for Gillian, it had been the happiest year of her adult life. She had fallen wildly in love with him and believed he loved her, but neither had said the words yet.

Gillian was too afraid of breaking the spell, afraid voicing the words would somehow jinx their relationship. She didn't know why Brandt hadn't said them. Maybe he thought actions spoke louder than words, not realizing she needed to hear them anyway, even though his actions were always those of a loving, caring, giving man.

Unwilling to rock the boat—pardon the pun, considering their predicament—Gillian had allowed their relationship to remain unchanged. She wanted more, but didn't know how to go about getting it without taking a chance of spoiling what she did have.

"I can't believe it." Brandt put a few more sticks on the fire then settled by her side on the dried-out tarp they had spread out on the sand. He leaned against the dead log they used for a backrest. "The first real vacation we've taken together and this has to happen."

Gillian patted his arm. "Think of it as an adventure. We all came out of it okay. Tony lost his boat, but we all could have lost our lives. And Paige and Tony are on their way to the other side of the island to get help. In fact, they should be in Pearl City by now."

"If we're on the island you think we are."

"I can't be positive, but I think this is Pearl Island. I spent all my summers, until I was fifteen, fishing with my dad around the Pirate Keys."

Brandt frowned. "That was over ten years ago. You haven't been back since."

"I know. That's why I jumped at the chance when Paige and Tony invited us to spend a week cruising the Keys."

She touched the waterproof pouch, fastened securely around her waist, that had miraculously survived the storm, the capsizing of Tony's cabin cruiser and her swim to shore. She had another reason to return to the Keys, but no one else knew about that, not even Brandt.

"I'm sorry about my ankle or we'd be with them. We'd be spending the night in a hotel room instead of here."

"It's not your fault," Brandt reassured her. "And it could have been a lot worse. We'll be all right until morning when help arrives."

Gillian nodded. "They wouldn't dare try to rescue us, by land or by sea, tonight. The terrain across the middle of the island is too dangerous to travel at night, and the rocks around the shore are too near the surface to circumnavigate in the dark. That's why this side of the island is uninhabited. We're perfectly all right here until morning. My dad and I used to camp out on the Keys all the time."

Gillian had made sure Paige and Tony understood there was no reason to insist a rescue team be sent that night. After they'd determined her sprained ankle was the worst injury any of them had suffered, their main concern was food. They'd eaten a hearty breakfast aboard the boat just before the freakish squall hit. On the island, Brandt and Tony had found and gathered a good supply of a variety of fruits and coconuts.

They had nothing to break the hard brown coconut shells, but the fruit was delicious and would prevent hunger and dehydration until morning when help would arrive.

Or until Paige and Tony came back across the island.

But Gillian was *almost* certain this was Pearl Island. Brandt was right. It had been a long time and she could be mistaken. Gillian didn't think so, though. The summers she'd spent with her dad were treasured memories that hadn't faded like some memories did.

Gillian brought out the map of the Keys and packs of matches from her waterproof pouch, careful not to reveal what else she carried. Tony had agreed their position was near Pearl Island when the sudden storm hit, and it was likely to be the island where they'd come ashore.

"Y'know." Brandt moved in closer to her and put his arm around her. "I'm not happy about what happened, but since we all came through it all right, I'm glad you and I have a chance to be alone for a while."

"Really?" Gillian grinned.

"Yeah. It's kind of nice here on the beach with the fire. No distractions. No Paige barging in every ten minutes. No Tony singing off-key at the top of his lungs. Just you and me."

"What did you have in mind to do with all this privacy?"

Brandt's free hand slid beneath her shirt and cupped a breast, his thumb slipping under the lacy edge of her bra. Her nipple tingled in anticipation of his touch. When he made contact, rubbing the taut tip, a delicious quiver threaded its way through her body to her very core.

Surviving disaster was a total turn-on, Gillian decided, and sex a way of celebrating *life*. She closed her eyes, enjoying the staccato thrum of her clit in response to Brandt's caress. Her pussy grew wet almost immediately, and she moaned.

"Oh, damn, I'm sorry, Gillian." Brandt jerked his hand away from her breast, ending the sweet torture.

Gillian's eyes flew open. "What?"

"I forgot about your ankle. Did I hurt you?"

"You weren't anywhere near my ankle." Gillian took his hand and put it back under her shirt. "But if you stop now, I might hurt you."

"Are you sure? I mean, it starts with a breast then it progresses to other parts of the body..." His voice turned low and sultry, and his fingers trailed over each place as he said the name. "The ribs, the hip, the belly, the pussy, the thighs—"

"Um, back up one," Gillian directed breathlessly.

"The hip?"

"No, silly. That wet place between the belly and the thighs."

His hand unsnapped her shorts and dove inside. When his fingertips nudged her clit, she nearly took flight.

"You mean there?" he asked in mock innocence.

"Oh, *yes*!"

His fingers swirled around the sensitive nub, and when Gillian's hips rose, they delved deep into her slit. With each thrust of his fingers, her hips rose higher, massaging her clit against the heel of his hand.

"Oh God, Brandt..." she moaned as her muscles tightened around him.

He, sadistic fiend that he was, suddenly pulled his hand free.

Nearly blinded by the building pleasure, but unable to release it, Gillian squirmed wildly. "What—"

Brandt removed her waist pouch and took hold of the waistband of her shorts and tugged them and her panties down, carefully pulling them over her injured ankle.

"A special night like tonight calls for a special fuck," he said.

"Hmm, you turn me on when you talk dirty," she murmured.

"Then you're going to really enjoy tonight." He leaned in close, his breath tickling her ear, and whispered, "I have an idea if you'd like to play along."

Chapter Two

ꝏ

Gillian's eyes widened and she held her breath. Neither of them was adventurous in bed or, until now, had ever expressed an interest in trying anything even slightly beyond the norm. Brandt was conventional in so many ways that she had never dared share her fantasies with him.

She exhaled slowly. "What did you have in mind?"

Brandt licked his lips. "Let's pretend I'm a pirate. My ship attacked yours, and I kidnapped you because I had to have you the moment I saw you. Then a storm came up and sank my vessel, drowning everyone aboard except you and me. Now we're stranded on this island, and there's nothing to stop me from taking what I want."

Gillian's breathing deepened as Brandt's scenario unfolded. She'd never role-played during sex before, but his fantasy of taking her by force dovetailed nicely with hers of being taken. The thought excited her, making her breasts ache and her clit throb.

Still, she wasn't going to be an easy captive. She placed both hands flat on his chest and shoved. "Get away from me, you dastardly brute!"

Brandt landed on his backside, a stunned expression on his face.

"Like that?" she asked.

He grinned. "Yeah, like that. Except we need a safe word."

"A safe word?"

He nodded. "If you're uncomfortable with anything I do or your ankle starts to hurt, we need a word you can say so I'll know you really mean for me to stop."

Gillian was surprised he knew what to do. "Have you ever done this before?"

"No…but I've been reading about it." He sounded a little embarrassed, although in the dimness of encroaching twilight and with his back to the fire, she couldn't tell if he actually blushed.

"Why didn't you tell me you're interested in stuff like this?"

"I don't know." He shrugged and ran a hand through his short-cropped hair, something he did when he was nervous. "I was afraid it wouldn't interest you or…or you'd think I was weird or something. You don't, do you?"

"No, of course not." But Gillian's heart grew heavy. How could they be so close, yet unable to confess their innermost thoughts and desires or even say *I love you*? When had they built this invisible wall between them? And why? "How about Aquarius? It's my birth sign."

"Aquarius," he repeated. "If I do something you don't like or something that hurts you, say Aquarius and I'll stop."

That meant if she said *stop*, he wouldn't. Gillian nodded.

"I don't plan to do anything too wild. Mostly, I'm concerned about your ankle." Brandt moved in closer and leered at her. "Ah, 'tis a shame to cover such buxom beauty."

When he reached for her shirt, her hands automatically flew to ward him off. She was surprised how easily she took on the persona of offended virgin.

"Don't touch me, you filthy beast," she cried out, then bit her lip to keep from laughing. Well, perhaps she wasn't as offended as she should be.

"Touch you? I'm going to do more than touch." Brandt grabbed her shirt, pulling it over her head. She didn't struggle with him, unwilling to risk tearing the only shirt she had with her. But something stirred deep inside her. What would it be like to have Brandt rip the clothes from her body in his urgent need to possess her?

With one flip of thumb and forefinger, the lacy cups of her bra fell free. Gillian crossed her arms over her breasts, feeling exposed to the hungry expression on Brandt's face. She had never seen Brandt look at her that way, as if he could devour her. What troubled her more was even though she was a bit uncomfortable beneath his stark gaze, she enjoyed the heat in his eyes and the lust on his lips.

Suddenly, he grabbed her wrists, forceful enough that she couldn't pull free, but not hurtful. Caught by surprise, she frowned. For a moment, his grip loosened and he waited. She remained silent. Brandt had done nothing so far to make her want to use the safe word.

His fingers tightened again. He spread her arms wide, uncovered her breasts and stared at them.

"You're beautiful when you're aroused," he murmured thickly. "Your pink nipples are already hard with desire."

Gillian's first reaction was to cover up again, and she tried to jerk her arms together. Brandt wouldn't let her.

"I know how to stop you from covering yourself while I take what I want." He released her long enough to remove her bra and used it to tie her hands in front of her.

"No, please don't," she whimpered, partly for effect and partly because of panic. She struggled with him in the role of captive, but also because of the unfamiliar sensations and restriction of movement. She had never been tied up before.

Gillian was now completely naked and completely at his mercy. Brandt could do anything he wanted to her. *Anything.* Brandt wouldn't hurt her, and she had the safe word. Otherwise, he could do anything at all.

Heat coursed through her at the possibilities, and she felt more moisture gather between her thighs. She wriggled in anticipation.

"You want me to fuck you, don't you?" He dropped the fake pirate accent, but his voice was gruff. He reached out and cupped her breasts, his thumbs making lazy circles over her sensitive nipples.

Gillian nodded.

He bent his head and took one nipple between his lips, sucking and running his tongue over it, while tweaking the other. Gillian moaned under his attention, the beat of her clit growing faster.

Too soon he pulled away and lowered his shorts. His cock sprang free, long, thick, rigid, and jutting from its nest of golden-brown curls. He tossed aside his shorts, and spread her legs wide, moving between them on his knees. When he touched her, she gasped, and her hips rose to meet him.

"You're so wet and ready." His voice was low, and she could barely hear him over the gentle sounds of the surf. "Are you ready for me?"

"Yes..." she whispered.

"Tell me you're ready for me."

"I'm ready for you, Brandt."

"Tell me what you want me to do," he prodded.

"I want..." She pushed into his hand again, rubbing her clit against the heel of his palm. His fingers delved into her, slipping in and out. She closed her eyes. "I want... Oh God, Brandt, I want you inside me. Now."

His fingers wiggled. "But I am inside you. Tell me what you want, Gillian."

Her muscles clenched around his fingers, and she could barely think. "I want...your cock inside."

"And?" he coaxed.

"Fuck me, Brandt." It wasn't a word she used, but it rolled off her tongue easily enough. "I want you to fuck me."

His hand withdrew, and she quivered at the loss of stimulation. "Oh, Brandt."

"Just a minute, sweetheart."

Her eyes fluttered open as he tugged a corner of the tarp over the log. Then he helped her up, careful of her injured foot, and set her on her knees.

"Lean over the log, Gillian," he ordered.

She did as he said, resting her elbows on the tarp-covered log. Brandt placed himself against her backside, and his warm hands slid over the curves of her hips, caressing each cheek until he reached her lower lips. She thrust backward, but his fingers were now elusive. She ached to continue what he'd been doing before.

"Brandt, please..."

"Please what?"

"Please touch me."

"Hmm." He laughed—short and meaningful. "But you told me not to touch you."

"Please," she said and writhed against him.

"How about this?"

Brandt rubbed the full length of his cock against her pussy. She immediately joined his rhythm, swaying back and forth so that the tip of his cock nudged her clit each time he drove forward. Intense pleasure built within her, riding along her nerves.

"Oh, yes..."

"I can't hold it much longer, Gillian. I have to have you now."

On his next move forward, he plunged into her slit and ground his hips against her, his balls swinging into her clit.

"You're so tight and hot," he groaned.

He drew back and rocked into her again and again, his balls tapping her clit. Her entire body was on edge and on fire, quivering with need. She rubbed the hard peaks of her nipples against the rough tarp and pleasure jolted through her.

A moan started deep in her throat and turned into a cry of surrender as she gave her body over to the hot burst that shot through to her toes. Brandt seized her hips, holding her steady, as he slid into her quick and hard. His groan mingled with hers as he came deep inside her.

Breathing heavily, Gillian draped over the log, and Brandt leaned over her, propping himself up too. She didn't think she could move, but she wriggled her rear and his cock slid free.

Brandt nuzzled her neck and planted a kiss on her shoulder. "Did you enjoy it?" he murmured against her ear.

"Yes, very much."

After they caught their breaths, Brandt helped her to her feet and untied her hands. He shook out the tarp and spread it. They lay together, letting the night breeze cool their heated sweat-soaked skin.

Gillian's ankle throbbed. Strange, but it hadn't hurt at all while she and Brandt were playing. And the pleasure was definitely worth a little pain now.

"Would you like to do that again sometime?" he asked quietly.

"Sure." She looked at Brandt, the firelight glinting gold in his blond hair. He looked at her and smiled. She nestled into his arm. "You know, I've had fantasies of my own. About being captured and tied up."

"Really? Why didn't you say anything before?"

"Same reason as you, I guess. But we can talk about them now, and try some new things."

He held her tighter and kissed her temple. "When we get home safe and sound. That took our minds off our situation for a while, but we're still marooned for the time being."

"Paige and Tony will be back tomorrow with help. Right now, I have something else I need to tell you."

Gillian trusted him with her body, her heart and her fantasies. Now it was time to trust him with her treasure map.

Chapter Three

ꟃ

Paige Douglas looked down into the deepest gulch or ravine, or whatever it was called, that she had ever seen and clamped her hands over her ears, but she could still hear him.

"Will you *shut up*!" she screamed.

"What?" Tony shouted at her, loud enough for the sound to penetrate her cupped hands. "You know I sing when I work."

"But you can't sing. Didn't anyone ever tell you that you can't carry a tune in a bucket?"

She glanced at him. His face fell and he looked as if she'd wounded him. She didn't think that was possible. She had ridiculed him enough times over the past few months that surely his feelings were hardened against her jibes.

"Aw, Paige."

She dropped her hands and plopped down on the ground, hugging her knees. Tears stung her eyes. She was cutting off her nose to spite her face, and it was as painful as if she hacked away at it with a rusty saw.

The first time she'd seen Tony Stompanato she'd fallen hard for him. They had slept together that night, and she'd loved the contrast of his long black hair, coffee brown eyes and olive complexion against her red hair—the box said *Tahitian Titian*—blue eyes and pale skin.

A one-night stand for sure, she'd thought at the time, because a twenty-two-year-old Italian stallion wouldn't want more than that with a woman old enough to be his mother. But one night had turned into two, then three. They couldn't stay away from one another, couldn't keep their hands off each other's bodies. Every time they fucked it was like lightning striking and the sky exploding. She'd finally realized they were *making love,* not merely screwing. There was a world of difference.

Falling in love for the first time at her age scared her. She never wanted to be that silly or vulnerable. Being in love made you do and say stupid things, and it made you dependant on someone else because you wanted that person to be in love with you too.

She glanced at him again through a glaze of unshed tears. Tony loved her, she knew that, but how long would it last? Tony was so young, exactly half her age, and one day he would fall for a younger chick and tell Paige to hit the road. The best thing she could do to protect herself was push him away before he broke her heart.

Tony proudly held up the vine to show her his handiwork.

Paige dashed away her tears. "Do you really think that's strong enough to hold us while we climb down into that ravine? If we do, by some miracle, happen to make it, how are we going to get up the other side?"

The ravine ran narrow but deep. Both sides went down nearly vertical and were relatively smooth. Maybe an experienced mountain climber could find hand and toe holds, but neither of them had climbed even the fake rock wall at the amusement park. Both were city kids, born and bred in a concrete jungle, their leisure activities confined to a city environment. If Tony hadn't won the cabin cruiser in a contest he'd entered on a whim, they would never have set foot out of the city.

"Hey, I learned how to tie knots when I took boating lessons," he said defensively.

Paige sincerely admired his caution and diligence. He had taken six months to learn how to operate and care for the cruiser. But trawling around the coast was one thing and going out into open sea another. Paige had insisted they invite Gillian and Brandt along. Tony and Brandt were best friends, and Gillian had grown up around the water and sailing and knew the Pirate Keys firsthand. It had paid off when the storm chewed up the cruiser and spit them up on one of the Keys. Pearl Island was Gillian's best guess.

Paige hoped she was right. There were a number of the tiny, inhospitable islets where no one lived. If she and Tony made it to the other side and didn't find any trace of civilization, she couldn't face crossing it again to where they'd left Gillian and Brandt.

"That doesn't make you Jacques Cousteau," she snapped.

Tony threw down the vine. "What the hell do you want from me, Paige? I'm doing the best I can."

"Well, your best isn't good enough!" The hurtful words kept pouring out of her mouth, and she couldn't stop them. "You should have sold that boat instead of trying to be something you're not. Just think what you could have done with the money."

"We, baby. I told you it belongs to both of us," he said quietly. "We've had more fun on that boat than anywhere else, and we've had a lot of fun in a lot of places."

That was true. She blushed, thinking of all the places, private *and* public, they had made out or fucked themselves silly. Tony was sexually daring and it was one of the things she loved about him. Over all the years and through all the lovers, it had always been in a bed and missionary position for her—with the occasional blowjob thrown in when she really liked the guy. Tony had opened up a whole new world of sensuality for her.

He was also right about the boat, but she couldn't let him know he was right about anything. Soon, he would get fed up with her sniping and they would part ways. That way, she was in control of when they split and wouldn't be blindsided.

"No climbing," Tony said, and picked up the end of the vine again. "We swing across."

She looked at him in horror. "Now you think you're Tarzan? You are crazy if you think I'm going to swing across on *that*! The vine won't be strong enough to hold us. It'll break halfway across, and we'll plunge to our deaths."

"Look, Paige, we don't have much choice. It took us a lot longer to get to this point than Gillian thought it would. It's getting late, and it'll get dark fast in here under the trees. We probably could use vines to climb down the ravine and up the other side, but we'll never make it before nightfall. Swinging across is our only chance if we want to get to the other side of the island while it's still light."

Paige shook her head. "You go on without me. I'll wait right here until you bring back help."

His jaw clenched. "I'm not leaving you, baby."

Baby. She should be calling him baby instead of the other way around. He was the one young enough to be her baby.

She swallowed hard and looked away from him. "I can't do it, Tony. I'm not going to break my neck. But you go on, Mr. Bigshot, prove what a macho man you are."

He didn't say anything, and she wondered what he must think of her. Then she heard movement and a creaking in the trees. She must have finally insulted him one too many times. He really was going to go without her.

She shot to her feet and whirled around.

Tony had one foot in a stirrup tied in the end of the vine and gently swung back and forth parallel to the ravine. His grin was broad and triumphant as he dipped to make his arcs a little longer and faster.

"See? It's holding me."

Sure it was...while he was safely over high ground. As soon as he arced over the ravine the vine would break and buh-bye Tony.

"C'mon, Paige." He started dragging his free foot to break. "We'll both swing awhile, and you'll see how safe it is."

She shook her head. He had come to a full stop and stood, one foot still in the stirrup, waiting for her.

Well. Maybe… It couldn't hurt to swing a little, could it? If they weren't in this stupid predicament, it might actually be fun. Paige took a step.

"That's it, baby," he coaxed.

"Okay, but just for a little bit."

He positioned her facing him, her arms around his neck. He gripped the vine with one hand and held her tightly with the other. He pushed off to get them started and each time they reached the rear apex, they dipped to push them farther and faster.

"That's enough, Tony!" she cried out as the ground passed to and fro in a blur.

"Don't look down," he said and continued to accelerate.

She looked up instead. Where the vine attached to the limb was so high she couldn't see it, but she heard the creak it made with each pass. Maybe, just maybe it would hold them.

"Paige, I'm sorry, but you have to hold on tight." He stiffened as if to prepare for her resistance. "I'm going to swing us around and across the ravine."

She tightened her grip on him, squeezed her eyes shut and nodded against his shoulder.

They continued to swing back and forth. She wasn't aware when he changed their course, but after a few more arcs, he said, "Okay, baby, this is it. We jump when I say *go*."

"I love you, Tony," she whispered close to his ear.

"I love you," he said. "Go!"

Chapter Four

ꟷ

Then they were freefalling and Paige screamed, she couldn't help it. They hit the ground hard with Tony on the bottom, taking her weight too. The fall broke her hold on him, and she bounced, landing on him again. She thought she felt the ground give, but she chalked it up to disorientation.

Tony lay still beneath her.

"Tony?" She climbed off and knelt beside him. "Tony, can you hear me?"

Panicking, she grabbed his shirt with both hands and shook hard.

"Don't you die on me, Tony Stompanato!" she screamed in his face. "You're the first man I've ever fallen in love with, and if you die on me I'll never forgive you!"

His hands clamped over her wrists, and he shook his head as if to clear it. "The *first* man you've fallen in love with? I'd better be the *last* man too!"

He yanked her closer and raised his head to kiss her. Their lips slid together and their arms surrounded one another.

She heard a rumble directly beneath them, and the ground trembled.

"Oh, baby, you make the earth move," he murmured.

"Tony, it's not me! It's—"

Before she could finish, the ground gave way and they were falling again. When they hit, Tony grunted, once more bearing the brunt of their weight. Paige bounced to the side and lay still in the crumbled dirt, humus and foliage that had fallen with them, cushioning their landing. She gasped for air in the darkness. She couldn't move, afraid it might cause them to fall yet again.

"Are you all right, Paige?"

She nodded, then realized he couldn't see her. Light slanted from the hole they'd fallen through, but it didn't reach them. "Y-Yeah, I'm okay, I think. Are you?"

"Yeah. Be still a minute."

She heard him strike a match, and a tiny flame flared.

"Gather up some of those dead leaves and twigs," he said. "We'll get a fire going."

Soon they had a small fire to see by and quickly assessed their surroundings. They were in a small cave, but the ceiling was high enough that even if she stood on Tony's shoulders she couldn't have reached the hole. Several tunnel openings went off in different directions, but they had no idea which one, if any, would lead them back to the surface. They decided it was best to stay right where they were until they could think of something to do.

"Brilliant idea, swinging across the ravine," Paige griped as she watched Tony feed the fire. The bits of wood and dried plants that had crashed through with them wouldn't last long.

"I told you, Paige, I'm doing the best I can. Why are you—" He broke off, clamped his lips into a thin line and shook his head.

"Why am I what?" she snapped.

"That."

"That what?"

He sucked in a deep breath. "Why are you always sniping at me about everything I do? You weren't like that in the beginning."

Paige froze. It had taken him months to question her about her attitude. What could she say?

"I don't know what you're talking about."

They sat in silence. She watched the firelight play over his strapping body. He was buff but not overblown. His long hair was tied back, and his dark eyes reflected the flickering flames. God, she loved him and wanted him and, yes, *needed* him. Life without Tony would leave her broken and bitter. And incredibly lonely.

"Maybe you don't," he said after a while. "Or maybe you do. Whatever. I just want you to know that nothing you say will drive me away. I mean it, Paige. I love you, and I'm in this until you can look me in the eyes and tell me you don't love me anymore."

"Oh, To-ny." Her voice broke on his name as sobs shook her body. He moved closer to her, but she tried to back away from him. He grasped her arms and wouldn't let go.

"Why are you running, Paige? What have I done?"

"Noth-ing." Her voice broke again, and she covered her mouth, wishing the tears would stop. They made her feel too defenseless.

"Then why?" His hand slowly trailed up her arm.

Her desire for him, always smoldering just beneath the surface, burst into flame in the pit of her belly. Her clit began to throb with an intensity that stunned her. To continue the charade she played, she should pull away. Tony leaving her now would hurt less than his leaving later, she reminded herself. She ignored the looming devastation at the thought of Tony leaving her at all.

He drew her closer, and she didn't resist. The bulge of his rock-hard cock pressed against her, and whatever was left inside her shattered with the heat of her need.

"Y-You still want me?" The question came out in a tiny, surprised tone.

"Always, baby," he growled softly. "Always."

On his knees between her legs, Tony's mouth covered hers in complete possession of her and her senses. He laid her on her back. Moisture from her pussy dampened her panties as his tongue swept over hers. His hands slid into the waistband of her capris, and his fingers dug into her butt cheeks, pulling her hips hard against him. He ground his erection into her pussy, massaging her clit through the layers of their clothing.

Paige nearly melted and almost gave in. Stuck in a cave with no way out and little hope of rescue, they didn't need to play games. She should just call a halt to the stupid criticisms, accept him and love him unconditionally for the little time left to them.

Not that easy, of course.

"Always," she whispered and hiccoughed. "If we make it out of here alive, always is a long time."

"I know. I'm looking forward to always with you," Tony murmured softly.

He rocked against her, and each time he bumped her clit, ripples of pure pleasure ricocheted through her, building her tension.

She gasped when he took hold of the waistband of her capris and panties and slid them over her hips, but she didn't have the strength to fight him. He sat back on his heels and lifted her legs, one at a time, to pull them free. Then he fit himself between her thighs again, spreading her legs wide, and reached for his zipper. His beautiful cock, bulging with thick veins, sprang free. The play of firelight enhanced his already impressive erection.

She stopped him with a hand to his chest. "I'm forty-four years old."

"I know that, baby."

"When you're forty-four, I'll be sixty-six."

"And you'll be the sexiest sixty-six-year-old ever." He moved in again, the enormous head of his cock touching the entrance to her pussy.

Her hips rose on their own even though she tried to resist. Somehow she found the strength to stop him with both hands on his chest this time.

"I'm too old to have kids. I don't want kids."

"We've talked about this before, Paige. I don't want kids either."

His hands left trails of heat as they slid down the insides of her thighs.

"Always means forever. You're young. You'll change your mind," she insisted.

"Just because I'm twenty-two doesn't mean I don't know what I want." He bent and placed a kiss on her belly. "Kids are okay. For other people. I like to go when I want, do what I want. I've never had the urge to be surrounded by screaming babies. You're making an issue out of something that's never been an issue. I know how old you are and I can add. It doesn't matter. Nothing matters except *this*..."

His cock plunged into her in one clean, hard stroke, and her hips absorbed the impact, rising to meet his. He filled her up perfectly. She slid her legs around his waist to hold him tightly. She never wanted to let him go when they fucked with such urgency, their frenzied actions in complete sync. They moved as one, as if they'd been made especially for each other and no one else. This time held an even greater significance. Their bodies seemed to know this time might be one of the last for them to come together if they didn't find a way out of the cave.

Her pleasure intensified and rippled through her, turning into a burning heat. Her inner muscles clenched around him, and she spiraled out of control. Head thrown back, he rode her hard, each striving thrust of his cock sending her closer to the edge until she toppled over with an outcry of relief and release. Her limbs turned to jelly as she strained into him, her back bowing with the effort.

"That's it, baby, that's it," Tony murmured to her. "I love you, baby. Don't ever doubt how much I love you."

Paige cried out again, this time in pure joy, and tears spilled from beneath her closed lids. She always felt loved when intimately entwined with Tony, and only later did uncertainty plague her. At that precise moment, she wondered how she could ever doubt him or what they shared.

Another soft sound escaped her lips as the final spasms waned and her body began to return to normal. Tony's hand slid up into her hair, cupping the back of her head, and his mouth covered hers. He groaned, his hips jerking into her, his rigid cock plumbing as deeply as it could inside her.

Then he tensed as he drove into her one last time and ground his hips against her. Another groan sounded deep in his throat and she felt the heat when he stiffened and his cock spilled its release.

When the last of his tremors ebbed, he dropped down against her, their sweat-slicked skin slipping and sliding together, and raised his head. Emotion filled his dark eyes—love for her and everything they experienced. Reaching up, he gently wiped away her tears.

"Nothing matters except that I love you, baby."

Paige wept as he moved around her. He lay beside her, their bodies curled together, her butt snug against his twitching cock.

"Go to sleep," he murmured. "We'll decide what to do in the morning."

But Paige couldn't sleep. She watched the fire dim and go out. When all was completely dark, not even the faintest light coming from the hole they'd fallen through, Tony tightened his arms around her.

"When we make it out of here and find help for Gillian and Brandt, we're going to talk about getting married."

Paige's heart pounded in her chest. "M-Married?"

"Yep." Tony's hand crept under her shirt and rested around her breast possessively. "I can't imagine loving anybody else the way I love you."

Paige smiled in the darkness and the tightness that had been in her chest for months uncoiled. "Are you sure, Tony? It'd break my heart if—"

"I'm sure, baby. Are you?"

She nodded against his broad chest and closed her eyes, contented. He'd finally convinced her, and he wanted to marry her. She could torture herself with what-ifs or she could relax and enjoy the ride.

Paige pressed a kiss to the inside of his arm. And relaxed.

Chapter Five

ꟷ

"You can't be serious." Brandt rose up and stared at her, his ice-blue eyes wide in disbelief.

They lay on the tarp, still naked, and Gillian turned over onto her stomach. She found her waterproof pouch and pulled out two folded pieces of paper. Flattening one of the sheets, she slid it in front of Brandt who flopped over too.

"This is a photocopy of the picture with the magazine article on Handsome Jack Black, the notorious pirate who sailed these waters in the late eighteenth century. It's a picture of a jewelry box he sent as a token of his love to Lady Margaret Worthington, but he was killed before he could return to her."

"Everybody knows the legend of Handsome Jack." Brandt took the paper and looked at it. "None of his treasure was found after he died. The old stories say he buried it on one of these islands, but most everyone believes he spent it as fast as he stole it. I've never heard about the jewelry box, though. Or Lady Margaret."

"I never heard about the box, either, but my dad told me all the stories he knew about Jack. One story was that Jack had left a woman back in England and he vowed to return to her a wealthy man. Dad never mentioned the woman's name, and I don't think anyone knew it until two years ago when the Worthington estate donated the box to the museum and revealed the story behind it."

"But what makes you think you know where to find Jack's treasure?"

Gillian heard the amusement in his voice even though he was doing an admirable job of holding back outright laughter.

"The more I looked at the picture, the more I thought the layout of the gems seemed familiar. I made a copy of it and studied it for months before it came to me."

Brandt ran his fingers over the picture, touching each gemstone in turn. "The islands."

"Yes! I wish I'd seen it as fast as you did." She slid over the second sheet, the map of the Pirate Keys. "Each jewel, and there are quite a few different precious and semiprecious stones, represents an island. If this was Jack's way of letting Margaret know where he'd buried his treasure, then the secret died with them. Margaret had been ill a long time and died about a month after Jack's death and a couple of months after she received his gift. She never had a chance to retrieve the treasure."

Brandt tapped the papers and handed them back to her. "Then there's no way to break the code, *if* there is a code. But if you're right, you've narrowed it down to this area and these islands. But you don't know which island? Or where on the island?"

"True," Gillian conceded. A twinge ran through her ankle, and she carefully shifted her foot into a more comfortable position. She gave the picture of the box to him. "But I think I know which island. Look at the jewels again."

Brandt squinted in the firelight, studying the picture for nearly five minutes. Gillian could barely contain her excitement as she waited for him to see what it had taken her nearly a year to discover.

But he shook his head. "I thought maybe the size of the stones had something to do with it, but they all look roughly the same."

"Within a few millimeters. That was my first thought too. I called the museum for the exact measurements. Then I thought about the worth of the stones—the more costly jewels representing the larger islands and so on—but that didn't pan out either. I came to the conclusion that while the pattern isn't random, the jewels Jack used are. Probably whatever he had on hand at the time."

"Then you're no closer to figuring it out." A stronger breeze kicked up, and Brandt reached for the edge of the tarp. He spread the free end over them to ward off the chill night air.

Gillian shivered and snuggled closer to him. "That's what I thought for a long time. But I kept studying the picture, hoping something would jump out at me. I even decided to have a replica made—with colored rhinestones because I can't afford the real ones. I called the museum again to verify the kinds of jewels Jack had used. That's when I knew the answer."

Brandt threw back his head in exaggerated death throes. "You're killing me, Gillian. What is it?"

Gillian laughed. "Jack used at least three of each kind of gemstones except one. There's only one pearl."

She watched his expression change from puzzlement to excitement as he realized what that meant. He snatched up the picture and map and compared them. "The pearl represents the island you think we're on, Pearl Island."

"It makes sense," she said. "The pearl is the only gemstone on the lid that's created and harvested in the water. Jack would associate the treasure he gathered at sea with the pearl. In Jack's time, no one lived on the Keys, although the pirates used them for hiding out. The name Pearl Island became official when the island was settled. I have a feeling Jack was the one who first called it that, after his ladylove, because the name Margaret means pearl. I don't think we'll ever know the truth about that, though."

"This side of the island is difficult to reach. It would be the perfect place to hide his treasure." Brandt didn't sound skeptical any longer. He looked up and down the beach while Gillian put the papers away in the waterproof pouch. The shadows of the rocky cliff blended with the graying water and the twilight that shrouded all. "Jack's treasure could be anywhere, even buried right under us. I don't think we'll be finding any booty tonight."

Gillian turned on her side and put her hand under the tarp. Her fingers danced along his body until she reached his cock, already at half-mast. She cupped his balls and felt them tighten. His cock grew to magnificent proportions. "That depends on what kind of booty you're looking for," she murmured suggestively.

She'd never heard anyone groan and laugh at the same time, but Brandt did, his hips surging to meet her palm and fingers.

"Mmmm, I'd rather explore your treasure chest," Brandt said. "But you can shiver me timbers and blow me down any time."

Gillian giggled.

How could she not love this man? His wicked sense of humor delighted her. His body made hers want to do things she'd only thought about in the most secret place in her mind. She scooted closer to him and wrapped both hands around his cock. Just touching its satiny surface sent a shiver of pleasure through her and made her hips surge toward him.

She massaged him, sliding her hands up and down his erection. A hoarse but satisfied groan escaped from Brandt, his cock hardening and lengthening with her continued touches.

He reached around where her hands connected with his cock and tangled his fingers in the soaked curls on her mound. She pressed toward him until he went deeper, sliding through her tender folds of flesh and over her throbbing clit.

Her hips thrust toward him again and her legs automatically spread. His fingers delved farther into her center, the heel of his hand kneading her clit.

Arms entwined, they stroked one another, their rhythms matching. Their mutual pleasuring made it almost as if their bodies joined in the ultimate intimacy. She loved the feel of his hands on her and inside her pussy, and she loved touching his strong, lean body and his hot, rigid cock.

Why couldn't she tell him how much she cared for him and the impact he had on her? His presence in her life and in her bed made living more enjoyable. She had never truly felt about any other man the way she felt about Brandt.

Brandt pushed his cock deep into her hands, and her pussy rose to meet his swirling fingers then fell when he withdrew only to rise once more as he drove into her grasp again. The tempo of their steady undulations increased until Gillian lost all sense of time and place and felt nothing but the intensifying knot of ecstasy ready to burst along her nerves.

When Brandt leaned forward and caught the tip of her breast between his lips, he suckled gently, pulling the orgasm through her body. Her hips quickened their pace even more and her breathing became fast and shallow. He drove harder into her hands, and their pleasure came at the same instant. It ripped through Gillian fast and furious so that her heart trip-hammered in her chest, then slowed to a lazy, lush ripple. She made only a small sound, a mewling moan, while his cock pulsed his release into her hands.

They lay together for a while, their bodies touching everywhere they could. Gillian listened to their breaths as her heartbeat slowed to normal. She pressed her ear to Brandt's chest and found his heart had returned to its slower tattoo also. Words of love and longing lingered on the tip of her tongue, but she didn't want to spoil the perfect moment in case he wasn't ready to hear them.

Chapter Six

ꟗ

Gillian didn't want to leave the warmth of Brandt's body next to hers, but when she opened her eyes and saw the glowing white form of a woman crossing the sand, she had no choice but to rise. She glanced back once at Brandt who remained undisturbed beside the fire. They had dressed again before settling down to sleep, so she followed the ghostly figure.

The moon rode high in the black velvet sky and enabled Gillian to find her way easily. She limped along the beach, pain darting through her foot with each step. By the time she reached the rocks where the woman in white had turned, her ankle throbbed continuously. Even so, she couldn't go back. She gritted her teeth and plunged ahead.

Using the rocks for support, Gillian threaded her way to the top of the cliff. There, another glowing figure waited. He was an extremely handsome man and dressed as a pirate. As soon as the woman saw him, she broke into a run. He waited, his outstretched arms ready to hold her. When they touched, the glow became a blinding white light, then dissipated to its former softness.

The man and woman embraced. He looked at her and tenderly touched her face.

"Margaret, my love." His voice, as soft as a sigh, carried eerily on the night air.

"Oh, Jack," she cried out.

The reunited lovers kissed, their passion as palpable as the breeze.

Gillian heard a noise behind her and turned to find Brandt approaching. He must have awakened in time to see her leave and followed her.

"It's *them*," Brandt whispered near her ear.

She nodded and moved closer to Brandt. His arm went around her protectively. Tears stung her eyes as she watched the lovers kiss and touch for the first time in centuries.

"She didn't know," Gillian guessed, her voice breaking with emotion. She'd always thought departed spirits would know everything once they reached the other side. "Maybe Margaret didn't know where to find Jack until the secret of the jewelry box was spoken out loud. She never knew it was a map. She must have been too ill to give it more than a passing glance."

Brandt held her tighter. "And maybe Jack was bound to this island because of the way he lived his life and unable to search for her."

The lovers parted and turned to face them. Lady Margaret stood close to Jack, his arm around her, their stance mirroring hers and Brandt's. Lady Margaret smiled fondly.

"Thank you," she called to them, her voice no more than a faint whisper.

Then Jack raised a hand, motioning for them to follow.

"Can you make it?" Brandt asked, his hand on her elbow.

"Try to stop me."

Brandt helped her as they followed the pirate and his ladylove down the other side of the crest. The two disappeared into the side of the cliff.

Gillian felt a stab of disappointment. "Where did they go?"

"Here." Brandt helped her move closer. "It's a cave."

With Brandt's help, Gillian limped into the cave. She expected total blackness, but the glow from Margaret's and Jack's ghostly forms illuminated the interior.

At the back of the cave, Jack pointed to a pile of small rocks which looked as if they hadn't been disturbed in over two hundred years. He made motions with his hands.

"He wants us to move the rocks and dig there," Brandt said and Jack nodded.

Together, Gillian and Brandt moved the cairn and scooped up the loose, sandy soil. A couple of feet down, Gillian's hand scraped a hard surface. When they cleared away enough soil, Gillian saw the top of a brass-bound trunk. Brandt tried, but couldn't lift the lid.

"It's locked. We'll have to wait to see what's inside." Brandt sounded as disappointed as Gillian felt.

Jack left Margaret's side and floated toward the rear wall, pointing to a small niche. Brandt joined him, reached in and brought out a large brass key.

"Here, Gillian." Brandt handed her the key. "This treasure is yours. You do the honors."

Gillian looked at Margaret and Jack. The pirate moved to his ladylove's side again and couldn't keep from touching her. She looked happy.

"No, the treasure isn't mine. Jack intended it for Margaret so it belongs to the Worthington estate."

Both Margaret and Jack looked surprised and shook their heads. Margaret pointed at Gillian. "Yours," Margaret said and Jack nodded.

Gillian took the key. Her fingers trembled as she tried to turn the key in the lock. In the end, Brandt had to help her. They tugged the lid open.

"Oh, my God," Gillian breathed.

The open chest was like something out of a movie. Piles of gold doubloons and tangles of jewelry, of every kind imaginable—necklaces, lockets, rings—spilled over the side. Gillian was looking at a veritable fortune in pirate treasure.

Jack stepped near the chest, his glowing hand reaching for a strand of pearls. The necklace shimmered with white light as soon as he touched it. He carried it to Lady Margaret and fastened it around her neck. The pearls matched the earbobs she already wore.

They looked at Gillian again and motioned toward the cave entrance. It was time for them to go.

Gillian and Brandt quickly closed the lid and smoothed the dirt over the chest again. By the time they finished, they could barely see. The light from the lovers was fading.

Outside the cave, Gillian waved to them as they vanished from sight.

"I'd never believe it if I hadn't seen it," Brandt said.

Gillian had to agree.

Brandt built a cairn beside the cave entrance so they could easily find it again. Then he swept her into his arms and carried her down the cliff, along the beach and to the tarp beside the dying fire.

Chapter Seven

ꝏ

When Paige awoke, she blinked her eyes open. She was able to see the interior of the cave quite well. Had Tony gotten up and built another fire while she slept? She snuggled into him, but the light bothered her. It wasn't a warm golden glow from flickering flames. It was cool and white and misty. She sat up, waking Tony in the process, and saw the cold, charred remains of their earlier fire.

"What's wrong?" he asked.

"The light. It's—" Her eyes focused on a ghostly pale figure emitting the misty glow. Her mouth worked, but no sound escaped her lips.

"Baby, what—" he cut off sharply.

Paige's voice finally broke free. "You see it too, don't you?"

"Uh-huh. But what is it?"

The apparition was dressed in pirate garb, down to the bandana around his head, gold ring in his earlobe and sword at his side, and he was almost as good-looking as her Tony. He bowed toward them slightly, then spread his hand toward one of the tunnel openings.

"He's showing us the way out." Tony scrambled to his feet, pulling up his trousers and fastening them.

Only then did Paige remember she was nude from the waist down. "Tony! Stand over here."

With Tony between her and the pirate, she quickly pulled on her panties and capris. He might be a ghost, but he was still a man.

Tony grabbed her hand and pulled her along, following the pirate. Paige stopped short at the tunnel entrance. The ghost, already several yards ahead, waited patiently for them to catch up.

"How do we know he's a good pirate? What if he's leading us to our deaths?"

Tony glanced down the tunnel, then back at her. "Baby, we don't have any choice. I don't have any idea how to get us out of here without blundering around these tunnels and getting lost." He looked toward the ghost again. "Besides, I think he's Handsome Jack, the pirate Gillian was telling us about. The way she talked about him, I don't think Jack would do us harm."

The ghost smiled and bowed again, as if to say Tony was right.

Paige didn't have a better idea about how to get out of the cave. "Okay, Tony. I trust you."

Tony grinned and squeezed her hand. "It's about time."

They followed the glowing ghost through what seemed to Paige like miles and miles of tunnels. The passageway curved and wound and dipped and rose, and she lost all sense of direction.

She grew apprehensive every time they came to a fork. What if Jack guided them away from the surface? What if he led them deeper and deeper under the island? What if he wasn't Handsome Jack at all, but a bloodthirsty cutthroat who didn't give a fig about karma?

Paige felt the air stir her hair, but didn't realize what it meant at first.

"We're nearly there," Tony said.

By the time Jack brought them through the opening and out onto the sand, his glow had begun to fade. He pointed in the direction they should go.

Paige called out, "Thank you!" just as he disappeared into nothing, a boyish smile on his handsome face.

"Gillian and Brandt will never believe this," she said with a shake of her head.

The night sky began to lighten as Paige and Tony raced along the beach and topped a hill. Below them, Pearl City spilled toward the sea. It wasn't exactly the metropolis Paige expected. She saw a few small, modern buildings, but the rest amounted to no more than a sad collection of ramshackle bungalows that had seen better days. A few lights winked here and there in windows.

It didn't matter, though. Houses and lights meant people, and that meant help was at hand. Paige started down the sloping path, but Tony grabbed her up in a bear hug, lifting her off her feet.

"We made it, baby. With Jack's help."

"Yeah, we did." She looked down at him. "We'll make it the rest of the way, won't we?"

"Into Pearl City? Sure." Then his brow smoothed as he realized what she meant. "You bet, baby. We'll make it all the way."

Paige melted into him, sealing the promise with a kiss.

* * * * *

Somehow, Gillian had slept again, but Brandt woke her and pointed to the water. A small rescue dinghy slowly wove its way through the treacherous rocks.

"Was it a dream?" Brandt asked as they waited.

"Could we both have had the same dream? Besides—" Gillian reached into her pocket and brought out a brass key. "I have this."

Brandt laughed and hugged her close. "Yesterday put everything in perspective for me. We could have died, or worse, I could have lost you. Then discovering that it took Handsome Jack and Lady Margaret two hundred years after their deaths to find one another…"

"Yes, it's incredibly sad," Gillian agreed.

"I don't want that to happen to us. I don't want to leave our souls restless and wandering so that we can't find one another on the other side."

Brandt cradled her in his arms and kissed her deeply, a kiss to rival that of Jack and Margaret's. Gillian was breathless when they parted.

"I love you, Gillian. You may not be ready for commitment or to take the next step, but I want you to know how much I love you. I won't let us end up like Jack and Margaret. I won't give up until we're married."

Gillian was almost speechless. Almost. "Is…is that a proposal?"

"Yes, it is. I know you're happy with the way our relationship is. You don't have to answer now."

Had she really been that distant? Did he really think she didn't want more?

"But what if I want to answer now?"

"I wish you'd wait and think about it. I don't want to hear your answer if it's no."

"Oh, Brandt, I love you. Of course, the answer's yes!"

He smiled and framed her face with his hands. "Are you sure, Gillian?"

"I've been sure a long time."

Brandt let out a long breath. "So have I. What's been holding us back?"

"Maybe the same thing that made us unable to share our deepest fantasies. Neither of us knew how the other would react." Gillian shook her head then glanced at the top of the cliff. "I'm glad Margaret and Jack are together again. I'm sorry it took them so long to find one another, but they taught us a valuable lesson. We need to grab hold of what we want now because we might not get a second chance in this lifetime. If something happened, I wouldn't want to wait hundreds of years to find you, Brandt."

Epilogue

ഇ

Three months later, the small double wedding took place on the uninhabited side of Pearl Island at the top of the cliff. The happy couples wore white, their clothing inspired by eighteenth-century fashion. The brides wore pearls, and the grooms were dressed like dashing pirates.

During the ceremony, Gillian felt the presence of Lady Margaret and Handsome Jack. When she and Brandt kissed for the first time as husband and wife, she sensed the star-crossed lovers' blessing for both newlywed couples to have long and passionate lives together.

Also by Lani Aames

Desperate Hearts
Ellora's Cavemen: Tales from the Temple I (*anthology*)
Enchanted Rogues (*anthology*)
Eternal Passion
Lusty Charms: Invictus
Moonstoned
Santa's Lap
Santa's X-mas
Statuesque

About the Author

Lani welcomes comments from readers. You can find her website and email address on her author bio page at www.ellorascave.com.

Tell Us What You Think

We appreciate hearing reader opinions about our books. You can email us at Comments@ElloraCave.com.

DEVON'S VIX

By Rebecca Airies

Chapter One

ꟃ

Jessie Coulter's booted feet sank into the plush tan carpeting of the elegant cream-walled hotel hallway. Stopping in front of a door, she swiped the keycard and then twisted the knob. She'd like to be home, in her large comfortable apartment, but that wasn't possible.

She was under orders. The latest attack on her had scared Steven enough to have him put guards on her and place her in protective custody. As commander of the Dallas unit of the Protectorate, Steven Carson took action when he became worried. Considering that the human agency dealt with the crimes committed by or against the numerous paranormal species, it was normally hard to rattle him. This latest attack had done more than that. No amount of talking had made a dent in his determination to get her out of danger.

Brushing a long strand of straight black hair off her cheek, she stepped to the side of the door. Unzipping her faded denim jacket, she sighed as she waited for one of her suited bodyguards to check the room. The blond man in a gray suit who'd been trailing behind her walked into the room. He stepped out, handed her the keycard and nodded to her.

Walking into the hotel room, she turned and locked the door. She reached out to adjust the thermostat and froze. The hair on the back of her neck stood on end and a fluttery sensation rippled through her stomach. *Oh hell.* She looked around the room, watching for the betraying shimmer of a moving cloaked vampire. Nothing in the room moved. *Vampire hunters and now a vampire—can the day get any worse*?

Taking a deep breath, she paced to the edge of the bed. Struggling to act like she didn't know a vamp was there, she tossed her small sack of clothing on the white blanket. If she reacted too strongly, the vamp would know she was more than human. A human would feel a little unease, but nothing more.

She tried to keep her hands near her hip and the gun hidden beneath the bulk of her jacket without being too obvious about it. It had to be a rogue, a vampire criminal. Vampires didn't usually go around using their abilities. It made some humans nervous and most of the paranormal beings tried to blend in with the normal population.

"You've already given yourself away, Jessamine. Even if you hadn't, Steven told me about you." The rolling voice seemed to echo in the room.

She gasped. It was worse than a rogue. That rumble was instantly recognizable. For months, she'd been avoiding meetings with Devon Knight, member of the Vampire Council and recently appointed liaison between the Protectorate and the vampires of this region.

Bringing him or any vampire into this wasn't needed or wanted. True, she'd been attacked three times. Vampire hunters from the Society of Pure Hearts had come after her with tools to kill a vampire two other times. Although most people accepted or at least tolerated vampires and other paranormals, fanatical fringe groups had been around since the paranormals had gone public with their existence. She had no idea why she'd been targeted. She didn't live the life of a classic vampire. She was out in daylight as much as she was at night, even if they were partly right.

Technically, she wasn't a vampire—yet. She accepted that one day she'd have to make the transition to full vix, a female vampire, but it wasn't necessary now. The drugs the medics gave her had kept the conversion rate down to under twenty percent.

The air rippled on the opposite side of the bed and then a familiar figure took shape in front of her. Blond, broad-shouldered and intimidating, Devon hadn't changed since she'd last seen him. He was still a predator.

She'd dated the man and come close to sleeping with him. Something about him had drawn her the moment they'd met in the trendy bar. Even now, it was hard to keep her hands off him if she was near him.

He wasn't pretty. His hard features, the deep brown of his eyes and his slightly bent nose didn't lend themselves to sweet and cuddly or even handsome, but he oozed sex appeal.

Devon had a body made for fighting and sex. She loved his hard, corded muscles and the smooth glide of his walk, not to mention his gorgeous ass.

When she'd been with him, she'd thought that he was human. Her jaw had dropped when she'd seen him walk into Protectorate headquarters with two known vampires. Generally, vampires and the Protectorate worked together to catch the rogue vampires. It was just amazing she hadn't seen him before that. She'd considered herself lucky to have found out there and not in bed.

She'd broken off the relationship that day. As much as she wanted him, she hadn't been prepared to take the risk. She'd had too many secrets to keep. Secrets he now knew thanks to Steven's panic.

"That's why you stopped seeing me and started dating Joshua Ryland. You didn't want to take the chance that I'd taste your blood and discover the truth." He cocked a golden eyebrow.

She shook her head, clearing it of the arousing image of his mouth at her neck. Dressed in a light gray t-shirt and blue jeans, he looked very casual. His stance belied that impression. Muscles tensed, his long legs braced to leap, he was ready for any move she made.

She gritted her teeth. Damn Steven—she'd told him that she'd be fine. She'd even agreed to stay in this hotel for a few days. Those fanatics hadn't even wounded her.

"What I do is my business. Get the hell out of my room." She clenched her hands into her fists.

"You know better than that. It stopped being your business seven months ago. You know the law. You were required to report the discovery of your reaction to that bite to the Vampire Council." He stepped around the bed, his long stride carrying him across the room in a few steps.

That law sucked and she'd intentionally ignored it. The council had only one policy when it came to women going through the change—full conversion. She wasn't about to give up her freedom because of a biological reaction to a bite. Luckily, compliance was basically the choice of the woman, because there were virtually no penalties that affected anyone but the female vix.

It had happened during a hunt for a vamp who'd left bloodless bodies behind him as he moved from city to city. She'd been cornered, bitten by the rogue vampire before the rest of the team arrived to help. Physically she'd been fine. She hadn't lost much blood and the wound was minor. It had needed only field treatment. Two weeks after the bite, she'd gone to the unit medic for required after-bite tests.

She'd never been bitten before, but she didn't expect the medic to find anything strange. Very few people could be changed into a vampire. Her world had shaken when she'd learned the results.

The blood test had been conclusive. She was changing. That one bite had begun altering her DNA. Shocked, she'd walked around in a haze for days after hearing the bad news. The medic had noted the diagnosis on her chart, but the responsibility to report it had been Jessie's.

"Yes, I really should have called the local fold of vampires and said, 'I was bitten recently and I'm turning into a vix.' I don't want to be a vampire. The drug cocktail I'm on keeps the change at bay. It practically stops the progression." Sarcasm and anger dripped from her words.

He strolled over and trailed his fingers across her rounded cheek. "You are a vix. Even if this hadn't happened, I was going to have the Protectorate test your blood for a reaction to vampire enzymes the next time you went in for a physical. I couldn't get you out of my mind. There's usually a reason for that."

"It's called lust." She tried to turn away from him. His touch felt too good.

"Is that so? I think it's more." He stepped closer and his hard body brushed against hers.

Their bodies had always fit well together. She was nearly six feet tall, but he was at least six inches taller than her. His hard muscles had seemed so right nestled against her curves.

Jessie drew in a shaky breath. He was so damn sexy, just looking at him sent her mind straight to the forbidden. And that's what frustrated her. No matter how many times she told herself that it was impossible, she couldn't get him out of her head. She still wanted him.

"I think you thought of me just as much as I did you." His head lowered and his mouth trailed across her jaw.

She'd thought of him every day. At night, he'd starred in hot, erotic dreams. "It was my decision."

She lifted her hands, intending to push him away from her. Her hands settled against his chest. Her chocolate brown skin seemed even darker contrasted against the gray of his shirt. His lips closed over her earlobe, biting gently. She drew in a quick breath and her heart slammed into a faster rhythm.

His hand lifted and cupped her full breast. Even through her t-shirt and the fabric of her bra, she could feel the heat from his large palm. When his thumb brushed across her hardened nipple, she'd almost swear that he'd somehow managed to slip his hand beneath both layers of clothing. Her hands froze and she couldn't force herself to push him away.

"You could have had a large amount of freedom—maybe a few years—if you'd reported the genetic changes." He cupped her chin and ensured she looked at him. "The council might have even let you slide on this non-reporting incident. A certain amount of shock and resistance is expected. But not when you've been attacked three times. They believe you're a vampire, Jessamine."

"I can't change that if I disappear or whatever you plan. Once they see me walking in the sun, they'll back off." She put her hands on her hips.

Every "vampire hunter" she'd ever encountered believed in those stupid myths. Hell, she sometimes wished that bit about a vampire bursting into flames if touched by even the lightest rays of the sun was true. They did have a slight sensitivity to it, but would get nothing more than sunburned and physically sick from prolonged exposure, much like a fair-skinned person. And silver didn't bother them. That's what made the rogues so hard to stop. Well, that and the freaky abilities they had.

"It won't work. Once these societies target someone, they don't give up. You're coming with me." His dark eyes narrowed and he seemed to be waiting for her to argue with him.

"So you're going to take me to a fold?" She took a deep breath. Her mind raced, searching for a way to escape or convince him that this wasn't necessary. Running would be useless even if he was across the room. Vampires moved too fast and they could leap an amazing distance.

"No, the council has decided to draw these people out, to make them act." He dropped a kiss on her cheek and captured her hand.

"How could they follow us? Steven made certain that no one could find me here." She raked her free hand through her hair. While she didn't believe this was as serious as he did, she'd like to have this settled.

"We're going to make sure they know exactly where you are. They'll make a move when they think you're vulnerable."

He released her hand to grab her jacket and bag from the bed. Curling an arm around her slender waist, he opened the door and urged her into the hallway.

She stopped and arched back to look up at him. "Why would they believe I'd suddenly be with a man I haven't even dated in months? And where are my two guards? Did you have something done to them?"

She hoped she didn't sound as panicked as she felt. No way could she hold out long if they were alone together. The chemistry between them had only grown while they were apart. She'd wanted to fuck him before she'd broken off the relationship. Now, it was like a fever in her blood.

"Who knows what spin they'll put on it, but they'll follow. As to your guards, by now Steven will have called them and told them they're not needed." He smiled and once again urged her down the hallway.

*****

Jessie tucked her jacket closer around her, still a little chilled after the brief walk to the hotel from the limo. She shot a glare toward Devon as he tugged her toward the reception desk. She'd never heard of the Les Jardins Hotel, but she knew just from the lobby that it was an exclusive, probably five-star hotel.

Devon chatted with the woman behind the desk, who leaned toward him, smiling and flirting outrageously. Fluttering her lashes, she handed him the keycard to their room. The too chipper woman behind the desk was yet another person who would remember them and their arrival in the dark hours of the morning.

Right now perky was the last thing Jessie felt. Devon had stuffed her into the limo and hadn't said a word to her for the entire ride across town. He'd been on the phone, making arrangements. She'd heard enough to know he was sending people to her apartment and had told someone else to "spread the word".

"Come on, Jessie-mine. Our room is waiting." He turned and smiled at her as his fingers twined with hers.

He'd been sending her seductive glances, holding hands and touching her. On so many levels, he was making his position clear. He was staking his claim.

With his hand at her hip, he pulled her against his side as they walked to the elevator. On the ride to their floor, his hand wandered up her rib cage. And his fingers stroked over the full outer curve of her breast. Her bra suddenly felt too tight and the fabric felt like sandpaper against her nipples. The elevator stopped smoothly and the doors swished open. Reluctantly, he released her. He led her down the gold carpeted hallway. Stopping in front of a door, he inserted the keycard. With a twist of the knob, he opened the door.

She stepped forward automatically, but stopped and stared wide-eyed for a moment. The furnishings screamed expensive luxury. The walls had been painted a very light golden cream color. A desktop computer sat on an ornate desk next to one wall and a top-of-the-line multipurpose printer sat on a small table to the side of it. On top of the table on the other side of the room, she saw a laptop computer.

"This isn't a normal hotel room." She walked over and opened a connecting door and saw the king-sized bed, deluxe surround sound system and wide-screen television. Aside from the technology, the furnishings looked antique.

"This isn't a normal hotel. Most of the businesses in this area are owned by vampires. This hotel caters almost exclusively to our kind. I asked for what I needed. I want to control this situation." He took off his coat and then went to work on the buttons of his tailored jacket.

In her black slacks, sweater and light denim jacket, she felt underdressed. "There's only one bed."

"We'll make love, but it won't be when you're exhausted. You won't be able to say that I caught you in a weak moment." He smiled, flashing his lengthened fangs. The hunter was definitely on the prowl.

A discreet knock on the door startled Jessie. Her heart slammed against her chest. She whipped her head around and stared at the dark panel of wood. *The fanatics couldn't have found them this quickly.*

"It's just our bags." He tossed a smile over his shoulder as he walked to the door.

He checked the small video screen at the side of the door before he opened it. He watched as the man unloaded their bags. Jessie went into the bathroom determined to try to relax. She took the band out of her hair and let it flow free.

Bracing her hands on the counter, she closed her eyes. The situation was impossible. She'd been living with the death threat. Devon's reappearance in her life as well as his knowledge that she was a vix had thrown her mind into chaos. She'd definitely lost control. Now she was waiting for the Society of Pure Hearts to come and find her.

She couldn't do anything about a lot of it. Cooperating in Devon's plan to stop the Society was in her best interest. When the threat to her life was gone, maybe she could find a way to get some more time. Maybe the vampire council would overlook the fact that she hadn't reported the transition.

Deciding that she needed sleep to think more clearly about this, she left the bathroom to see what was in those bags. With any luck, he'd arranged for some other clothes for her, because that little bag only had a single change of clothing. Hopefully, whoever had bought this clothing had gotten the right size.

Chapter Two

ꟷ

Devon pulled Jessie close. He hadn't gotten much sleep last night. She'd been exhausted, falling into a deep sleep almost as soon as she'd slid between the fine linen sheets. He'd slipped an arm beneath her and pulled her over next to him. She'd grumbled for a little and then settled closer to him.

She was so beautiful in the ivory shorty nightgown. Her dark cocoa skin gleamed against the silk fabric. He nuzzled her silky black hair, inhaling her sweet scent. The brush of her gorgeous ass against his cock had kept him in a constant state of arousal. When he had slept, he'd woken with his hands cupping her ample breasts and his cock nestled between the lush globes of her ass.

He dropped a kiss on the top of her head. He wanted to kiss her awake, to slip his hands between her thighs and stroke her until she woke on fire for him.

Taking a deep breath, he turned his thoughts away from sex to the attacks on her. He didn't know if she'd thought about all of the seeming coincidences in the assaults by the fanatics. There were just too many of them. The commander of her unit had seen it at last and moved to get her to safety.

Three attacks on a single woman by an anti-vampire society was no coincidence. They had targeted her. The Society seemed to know exactly where to find her at almost any time. Someone had to be feeding them information. Finding the person responsible for that was the Protectorate's job. Stopping the Society from getting its hands on *his* vix was his.

She wiggled a little, her body pressing back against his. A low sexy moan rolled from her throat and her foot slid along his calf. She tensed, remaining perfectly still for a moment. Her hands slid up to where his palms cupped her breasts, brushing over his knuckles.

"I thought you weren't going to take advantage of a weak moment." She looked over her shoulder. Her amber eyes glittered in the dim light from the large window.

He didn't see fear in her eyes. That would have held him back. He would've given her time if she was genuinely afraid. All he saw in those gorgeous eyes was nervousness.

"Taking advantage would have been slipping that lacy thong off you and stroking your clit until you woke begging me to fuck you. One day I'll do that. This time, you're awake and know what's going to happen." His right hand slid down and swirled over the silky nightgown, gathering the fabric.

Her hand slid over his, halting the movement. "What you think is going to happen. I know you won't rape me."

He smiled at her assurance. They'd had two instances where they'd come close to making love, but had been interrupted—once by his work, the other by hers. Both times they'd had difficulty tearing themselves away from each other. She trusted him, even if she didn't recognize it.

"You want me already. The scent of your arousal is becoming stronger even now." He slipped his hand beneath the gown, tracing her warm sensuous curves.

Her stomach muscles tensed beneath his palm. He slid his fingers up over her rib cage. A moment later, he was cupping her breast. He flicked at her long nipple with his thumb and enjoyed her gasp and the wriggle of her body as she pushed into his touch.

"Want doesn't mean I have to have it." Her fingers curled into fists.

"You can say no anytime." He dropped a kiss on her neck.

He pulled his hand back and slipped his other free of her body. There would be nothing sneaky about this seduction. She'd know exactly what he was doing.

He urged her onto her back and dropped a kiss onto her shoulder, just next to the strap of her nightgown. Pressing another to the dark creamy skin just above the silk lace on the swell of her breast, he leisurely explored the skin bared by the sexy lingerie. He deliberately trailed a path down the deep V of the neckline. Placing another kiss on the skin just above the lace, he began to explore the silk-covered mounds. Letting the heat of his breath filter through the sheer fabric, he kissed his way up one rounded breast. He smiled as she drew in a sharp breath. Letting anticipation build could sometimes be far more useful than a direct approach.

Her fingers threaded into his hair just as he closed his mouth on one hard, long nipple. He scraped his teeth across it, letting the wet silk add another tormenting layer of sensation to the mix.

She squirmed and tightened her grip on his hair, pressing him more firmly to her breast. His tongue flicked the taut bud. He knew what she wanted, but she wasn't getting it. Not until she asked for it. He licked and pulled at the distended nipple. His free hand roamed down her hip, trailing toward her inner thigh and then up to the thin strap of her thong. His fingers skimmed close to her pussy, but never quite touched.

"Devon!" She tugged on his hair.

He laughed. Taking her nipple between his teeth, he tugged. Her nails sank into his scalp, trying to pull him closer.

"What do you want, Jessie? Tell me and I'll give it to you." He raised his head to look up at her, ignoring the stinging pain in his scalp as her fingers tightened.

"I want you to suck at my breasts. I want you to touch me." She arched sinuously.

He dropped a kiss on the dark crest visible through the nearly transparent fabric. "Do you want this on?" With his lips he pulled the silk away from her skin for a moment.

She shook her head. "Take it off."

He urged her into a sitting position and skimmed the skimpy nightgown over her head. All she wore now was the ivory thong. She pulled him with her as she lay back against the soft sheets.

His lips closed around her dark nipple and drew it into his mouth. He suckled. His fingers closed around the neglected hard crest and tugged. She shivered and a low moan ripped from her throat. He pulled, tweaked and twisted the hard nub between his fingers, determined to take her higher.

His teeth lengthened, scraping against the full mound. He wanted to taste her, to feel her blood pumping into his mouth as his cock thrust into her pussy. He held back. She'd ask for this too. Her body would demand it.

He was rapidly coming to believe that this woman was his mate. And it wasn't only the fact that she was so damned sexy that his cock ached to be buried inside her. She intrigued him and he enjoyed being with her. She was intelligent and brave and stubborn enough for two people.

He gave her breast a last firm squeeze before he trailed his hand down her midriff to the triangle of ivory cloth covering her sex. His fingers brushed over the silk, stroking her plump folds through the fabric. He felt the dampness, knew she was already wet and slick with her juices. Before he was through, she'd want him more.

Her hips lifted, twisting when he found the hard bead of her clit. He stroked lightly, rubbing through the silk. She shuddered and pulled his head more firmly against her breast. He flicked at the nipple with his tongue, licking around the fat areola. He placed a kiss on the tip and then turned his attention to her other breast.

"If you don't stop playing and touch me, I'm going to shoot you when this is over," she threatened, her hand fisting in his hair.

"I'm touching you." His fingers feathered across the cloth-covered lips of her pussy. "What do you want?"

"I want your fingers in me." Her hand clasped around his wrist, pressing his fingers against her clit..

He smiled as he ran his tongue around her nipple. He tugged, ripping the bands of the thong. Pulling it free of her body, he tossed the ruined underwear away. He trailed his fingers across her sleek hairless mound, down the slick lips. The smell of her desire rose, an exciting, enticing scent that made his mouth water. He parted the folds and found her hot and wet. Flicking his fingers over her clit, he enjoyed her ragged groan and the sensuous ripple of her body. He wouldn't be able to hold back much longer. He wanted to feel that heat wrapped around him.

His fingers circled the hard nub. Her hips rolled, pushing up into his touch. Sliding down, his fingertips circled the entrance, pressing lightly on the sensitive tissue. He pressed two fingers into her slick pussy. With slow strokes, his hand pumped against her.

He raised his head and watched her. She was beautiful. Her golden eyes had darkened. He could see the slight flush of passion on her dark skin. And her lush lips looked even more enticing. She arched, her head tossing on the pillows. She angled her head, baring her neck. He couldn't stop the slow grin from curving his lips. Already her body was asking for his bite.

"Please fuck me." She pulled at him.

"They'd have to pull me off you this time." He moved between her thighs.

His cock pressed against the opening. Her slick juices scalded him as his shaft slowly entered her sheath. He threw his head back. She was so tight.

"You feel so good." He sank into her until she'd taken all of him. The rippling clasp of her inner walls pushed him toward climax.

She arched, her thighs gripping his hips. His balls tightened even more as he fought to hold back. He withdrew until just the head of his cock remained within her. Then he rocked forward. He set a slow grinding rhythm, determined to deny his pleasure as long as possible.

She writhed under him, her nails sinking into his shoulders. Her body bowed and little whimpers escaped her lips.

He lowered his head and nibbled on her neck. His tongue swirled across the pounding pulse point high on her neck. She moaned and held on to him. Her hips lunged up, meeting his downward stroke.

Her inner muscles clamped around his cock. He felt the seed churning and almost lost control. Gritting his teeth, he surged against her. He looked into her eyes and saw the hunger burning in her eyes. She would ask for it. Her body was practically begging for it.

She whimpered and tugged at him. "Please..."

"Tell me what you want." He scraped his teeth across her neck.

She shivered and arched her neck a bit more.

His hips pumped. He licked from the base of her neck to the underside of her jaw. Scraping his teeth just over the vein in her neck, he sucked at the soft flesh.

"Bite me!" She laced her fingers into his hair and pressed his mouth against her neck.

He swirled his tongue over the tender skin of her throat and then sank his fangs into the sensitive tissue. Hot sweet blood flowed into his mouth. She tensed beneath him and he felt her pussy clench around him as she came. Fire zinged through him as the endorphins pumped into her blood and flowed into him.

His release boiled through him, tightening his body. He pumped into her, desperate to grasp the pleasure. His cum spurted into her.

When the last tingling pulse of pleasure faded, he relaxed against her. Holding on to her, he rolled with her until she lay on top of him. She relaxed against him. He saw her eyelids begin to close.

"Don't go to sleep yet, my Jessie. I have some definite plans for you today. We've been apart much too long."

Chapter Three

ꙮ

Jessie watched her hand shake as she drew the brush through her hair. She couldn't believe she'd asked him to bite her. God, how she'd wanted it. She'd ached to feel his teeth sinking into her neck. When they had, lightning had blasted through her body. Hot electric pleasure had sizzled through her. She'd never had such an intense orgasm in her life.

She could still feel the reaction to that bite sizzling through her. Her body seemed overly sensitive. Just the brush of her hand over her thighs caused arousal to stir. She knew enough about vampires now to know that that bite had sent chemicals racing through her veins. The change would progress at a faster pace. And she didn't have any suppression drugs to slow it.

On top of that, he seemed determined to resume their relationship as if there hadn't been any break in it. She closed her eyes and exhaled heavily. Emotions whirled through her head in a confusing conflicting mess. She loved being with him. It was too easy to relax in his arms and just listen to her hormones. Her body ignited whenever he was near. Who was she kidding, the sex was amazing. It was the relationship that scared the hell out of her.

She put down the brush and then smoothed her hands along the expensive green material of the shirt and slacks. These definitely hadn't come out of any of the stores she normally shopped at. Even the sexy underwear in those bags looked out of her price range.

She slipped into black tennis shoes and then walked out of the bathroom. "Where are we going?"

"I thought we'd do the tourist thing this afternoon while they don't expect us to be out." He turned away from the window. His eyes ran over her body.

Tourist. She rolled her eyes. He didn't live too far from Dallas and was in the city at least once a month.

"You left a wide trail. They should already be here." She paced over to stand beside him.

"Ah, but we're vampires and they think we can't be out in sunlight. They'll be here before sundown, but not much sooner." He reached out and took her hand.

She had to admit he was probably right. The Society's faith in the old myths had been proven again and again.

She looked out the window. "So do you have plans for this tourist thing or are we just going to wander around in the freezing cold until we find something?"

"I thought we'd visit a few shops. We'll keep an eye on the time and make sure we get back before sunset. We wouldn't want them to see us coming back from our outing." He walked over to the bed and picked up a long, black coat and held it up to her.

He smoothed the thick fabric over her shoulders as she slid her arms into sleeves. She absolutely adored it and the gloves he held out to her.

Hours later, Jessie cuddled into Devon's side as they walked back into the hotel lobby. She felt tired, but relaxed. They'd munched on hot roasted nuts as they walked, talking and laughing. Some of the stores had been fun to visit. Others had some of the most beautiful items on display she'd ever seen.

The day had brought back memories of the first time they'd dated. He'd always seemed to find ways to make her smile and laugh. She'd been happy with him until she found out he was a vampire.

They trudged into the room. Jessie tossed her coat over the back of a chair. She eyed one of the soft, thickly cushioned chairs and then the door to the bedroom. Lying down was very appealing, but the chair was closer.

She collapsed into the chair, toeing off her tennis shoes and wiggling her toes in relief. "Do we have plans tonight?"

"We're going to draw them out. We'll go to a place tonight that is distinctly vampire-oriented." He walked over to the chair and lifted her, sitting back down with her in his lap.

The man obviously intended to make sure that the fanatics had no doubt that she was a vampire or at least a vampire's lady. In the eyes of some of those zealots, that was just as bad as being a vampire. They were every bit as vicious in dispatching companions as they were with the vampires.

"Where are we going to draw them out?" She traced her finger up the side of his neck.

He smiled and captured her fingers, raising them to his lips to kiss them before returning them to his shoulder. "We're going to a club called Red Heat."

She pursed her lips. "And what are we going to do about the men who want to stake me?"

There would be humans among those vampires. Young, curious women seemed to flock to those clubs. Some just wanted to look, others wanted to feel a vampire's fangs. As long as Jessie was there, they'd be in danger.

"I really want to kiss you when you pucker your lips that way." He brushed his lips over her cheek and his hand slid under her top. "Tonight, the place will be blanketed with vampires. The hunters are most likely to make their move while we're entering the building or leaving. They'll probably wait until we're leaving, while we're waiting for our car."

"What about bombs?" The fanatics had been known to use them in places of known vampire activity.

"That place is checked every day. We know the way they operate." He smiled and tugged her closer.

"Are you sure they'll try? All three times, they attacked when I was alone in an isolated place." Jessie tilted her head up at him.

"They will. And we'll be ready for them." He leaned down and nibbled on her neck.

Jessie leaned down and adjusted her stocking, securing it to the garter belt. She smoothed the red dress over her hips. With its half sleeves, plunging neckline and nonexistent back, it was simply gorgeous. And she adored the matching strappy high-heeled shoes.

She took a deep breath. Nodding, she decided that she was as ready as she'd ever be. She felt sexy, but she couldn't get excited about tonight. Facing death didn't make her want to put on a smile and dance the night away.

She left the bathroom. Just a step outside the bathroom, she stopped. One look at the man standing beside the bed and her thoughts immediately turned to sex.

Devon looked fabulous—an erotic fantasy brought to life. She wanted to take that black suit off him and spend hours learning his every taste and smell. She licked her lips and strolled over to him. Sweeping her right hand up his jacket, she flicked at each button as she passed. She was very tempted to slip them free.

Just a taste. She only wanted a taste or two of those lips. He'd been teasing her all afternoon. He'd nibbled on her neck and ears. His hands had cupped her breasts as he hugged her from behind. She leaned into him, rising on her tiptoes as she tugged his head down to her.

Jessie's mouth slanted over his. Hunger and anticipation built. His lips felt firm and warm beneath hers, but remained frustratingly closed. Moaning, she lapped at his lower lip. She wanted him to kiss her back. His mouth opened over hers as his hands came around and cupped her buttocks, lifting and pulling her against him.

Her tongue slid into his mouth and brushed against his. A spicy taste flowed into her. She sank into the kiss, savoring that delicious essence. His fingers tightened on the globes of her buttocks as he moved her hips against the hard ridge of his cock.

He tore his lips away from hers. "Temptress, you know we can't do this now."

She wouldn't mind giving the entire night a miss. She smiled against his cheek. "Just a little more. Something to last until later."

She pulled back and trailed a finger across his cheek. He turned his head and kissed her fingertip. She nuzzled into the curve of his neck. He smelled so good.

"We have to go." He took a deep breath and set her back on her feet. "And when we get back, we'll take this up where we left off."

She laughed and turned to the doorway. He stepped forward and curled an arm around her waist. Shaking his head at her satisfied smirk, he guided her to the door.

A limo waited in front of the hotel. She sat in the sumptuous leather seat staring forward as he sat beside her. She couldn't ever remember being this nervous. A tight knot had formed in her belly the moment she'd slid into the seat.

The car stopped at the curb in front of a large single-floored building with a line formed in front of it. Devon waited for the driver to get the door. Stepping out, he motioned the man away and took her hand, helping her out of the car.

This was no neon-signed club. A single very discreet plaque on the wall with styled lettering announced the club's name. Devon bypassed the long line, going straight to the door. The brawny man at the door nodded and stepped back, letting them into the club.

The club's light pearl-gray walls gleamed in the overhead lights. Glossy black and deep red accented the soft color.

Devon led her to a private booth at the back of the crowded club.

The music throbbed through her body, loosening the tension within her a little. She leaned into him, her voice pitched so that only he could hear her. "So what do we do now?"

"We let them make their move. Come dance with me." He stood as a song with a slow smooth beat began. Holding out his hand, he waited for her to decide.

"I can't do the minuet or the waltz. So don't try any dances from your youth." She slid her hand into his and followed him out among the dancers.

"That hurts, Jessamine." He chuckled and drew her into his arms. "Just for that, I'll have to make sure we dance those two…soon."

She slid into his arms and let the slow liquid beat move through her. "Now that's a threat."

He pulled her against him. They swayed on the crowded dance floor. His fingers rubbed in a circle on her lower back. The heat of his hand seeped into her tense muscles. She leaned her head against his chest and listened to the slow beat of his heart. For a moment, she forgot about the threat and savored the sensation of being held and wanted.

"You're cuddling against me like a satisfied kitten." He tightened his arm at her back.

They were pressed together from chest to thigh. Their bodies brushed with each slow, smooth step. As they moved together, she marveled at how well they fit together. She'd forgotten how nice it was to dance with him.

She tilted her head up and smiled. "This is wonderful."

"Yes it is. We'll do it again when we don't have to worry about assassins." He lowered his head and inhaled.

She blinked. His comment was really no surprise. The man had been talking about a future permanent relationship since he'd burst back into her life. What astonished her was that a vehement rejection didn't automatically spring to her lips.

Moving with him, she swayed her hips. Her stomach brushed against his cock. He stiffened and his hands tightened. His breath hissed between his lips. His body's reaction was immediate and exhilaratingly obvious. His cock hardened, pressing insistently against her.

She felt powerful, desired, knowing that he couldn't do anything here. She swirled her hips, teasingly. She wanted to push him. His hands clamped at her waist. She looked up at him and couldn't keep the smile off her face.

"Keep it up and I'll show you what I do to a too-confident vix." He smiled widely, his lips showing the sharp points of his fangs.

He couldn't do anything here. Holding his gaze, she slid her hands down his back and gripped his buttocks. She squeezed, pulling him against her. For a moment, his hands gripped just a little too tightly at her waist. His pelvis ground against her.

He groaned and held her body away from his. His jaw clenched and she could see the throb of a vein at his temple. "You're pushing my limits."

"I like playing on the edge." She winked.

On every single one of their dates, she'd found it almost impossible to keep her hands to herself, even in public. The only reason she'd held out for the four dates they'd had was that she'd known nothing about him and he'd seemed reluctant to talk about himself. She'd known he had secrets.

The music ended and he drew in a huge breath. With an excessive show of patience, he peeled her hands off his butt. With an arm around her waist, he began guiding her off the dance floor.

She snaked an arm beneath his jacket when he had to concentrate on the crowd around them. With an impatient tug on his shirt, she slid her hand over his warm back. Her fingers trailed along the waistband of his pants and then slipped beneath it. Her nails skimmed over the top of his tight muscled ass.

He stopped and with slow, precise movements pulled her hand out of his pants. His eyes narrowed and his nostrils flared as he drew in a deep breath. The fierce frown on his face hardened.

She chuckled. She couldn't help it. He was looking at her as if he didn't know what she would do next. She liked the thought of knocking the big man back on his heels.

Chapter Four

ꙮ

His hand manacled her wrist. Towing her after him, he passed their table and headed for the bar. He stopped in front of a tall black-haired man. Tossing her a searing glance, he turned and spoke to the man in a tailored tux—probably another vampire. They spoke in low intense tones. She didn't hear much of the conversation, but did notice the significant glances at her.

The man nodded, smiled and drew a set of keys out of his pocket. He dropped them into Devon's hand and pointed to a door at the end of the bar. Devon nodded and towed Jessie away from the bar.

The door at the end of the bar was unlocked. He opened it and waited until she entered the white-walled hallway in front of him. He stalked over to the first door on the right. Unlocking the door, he pushed the thick metal panel inward. Stepping forward, he felt along the wall to the side of the door and flipped the switch.

He pulled her into the room as the dim overhead light flickered on. The room was filled with boxes and racks of liquor. Looking around the room, her eyes collided with his. The fierce glare he shot her drew a bubble of laughter from her.

"You can't take a little discreet public teasing?" She twisted her wrist, freeing it from his hold.

"Sliding your hands into the back of my pants isn't discreet." He took a slow step forward. "Grinding yourself against my cock isn't discreet."

"My dancing wasn't any different than any other woman's." She took a step back and felt the cool metal of the door press against her back.

"Most of them probably wouldn't have courted being taken over a table." His hands pressed against the door just to the sides of her shoulder.

He nipped at her lips. As he sucked the full lower lip between his, his hands cupped her shoulders and then smoothed down her arms. His sharp teeth scraped over her inner lip as he slowly drew back.

She shivered. Her lip tingled and throbbed. Not even a full kiss and her body hummed with need. She wanted everything he could give her, including the sizzling heat of his bite. It didn't matter that they were in the storeroom of a crowded nightclub. She needed to feel his body against hers, coming into hers.

"You drove me insane on that dance floor." He pressed a kiss to her cheek.

"I had fun, too." She slid her hands to his buttocks and pulled his hips tightly to hers. She slowly rocked against him.

He groaned. "You never told me you were a sex fiend."

She chuckled and wriggled her hips. "Afraid that you won't be able to keep up?"

He pulled back and looked down at her, an eyebrow raised. She saw the light of challenge flare in his eyes. His hands slid over the lush curve of her buttocks, lifting her off her feet. He turned and carried her over to a stack of boxes, setting her down on the edge.

Jessie smiled. "Ooh, so romantic. I expected better from a vampire who's lived as long as you have."

"You'll get your romance later. Now, you get what you've practically begged for—a hard fuck." His palms slid over her waist and slipped down her legs, gathering the material of her dress in his fingers.

His hands slid up her thighs, raking the flowing skirt up around her waist. She shivered. Her skin prickled with heat. And that growl in his voice seemed to shoot straight to her pussy.

He slid the zip down and pushed the bodice down to her waist. His tongue slicked over his lips as his eyes locked onto the red lace of her bra. Deft fingers dealt with the clasp at her back. He tugged her bra off and cupped the full globes. His thumbs flicked across the dark nipples.

A fiery tingle sizzled through her. Her nipples hardened, tightening. Anticipation curled through her as he dropped a kiss on her shoulder and then on the slope of her right breast. Warm moist breath feathered over the taut nipple.

She could feel her heart pounding against her chest and thick moisture gathering in her pussy. She arched, angling her nipple a little closer to that hovering mouth. Damn, she ached to feel his mouth on her breast.

His tongue circled her nipple, wetting the dark areola. She gritted her teeth as he continued to lick all around the tight crest. The man was the biggest tease she'd ever met.

His mouth closed over the dark peak. She felt his sharp canines scrape against her areola as his teeth fastened onto her tight nipple. He tugged. She gasped as a sharp sensation slammed into her. Her fingers clenched the fabric of his suit jacket. She felt her entire body tighten.

His fingers closed on the tip of her other breast and began to pull and twist the taut bud. She moaned as her hands slid over his chest and up to his shoulders. His mouth pressed against her breast and he began sucking.

"Now, let's see how much you want me." He knelt in front of her.

His fingers brushed across the red triangle of silk, gliding down between her slightly parted thighs. She felt a gush of liquid and her inner muscles clenched. God, she wanted him.

"We have wet panties." His teeth grazed the dark skin of her inner thigh just above her stocking.

His fingers slipped beneath the straps at her hips and tugged. She leaned back and lifted her hips, eager to assist in this project. His hands smoothed the silky fabric down her thighs and slid them free of her legs. She wriggled and widened her thighs.

He parted the plump folds of her smooth, shaved labia and leaned close, flicking his tongue over her clit. "Now I'm going to make sure you're on fire."

She shivered and groaned. Tearing pleasure pulsed inside her. If he took her any higher, she was going to explode. His tongue swirled, tormenting, flaying the hard, swollen nub. Scalding heat built with each deliberate lash. Her body tensed, tightened.

He lapped at the juices spilling from her. Probing touches along the sensitive rim of her pussy drew a long intense shiver from her.

Her hips bucked upward and her toes curled. "Devon!"

He looked up and two of his fingers replaced his mouth. They stroked into her, slowly fucking her. She felt her inner muscles clench. Her body trembled on the edge of bliss.

"Now you're there. You're as desperate as you made me." His fingers twisted as they thrust into her.

She tangled her hand in his blond hair and jerked—hard.

"Ow, woman!" He grabbed her wrist, but a smile spread across his face.

He rose, unbuckled his black belt. His hands dealt with the single button and zipper in a blink. She licked her lips as he pushed his pants down, revealing his long thick cock.

He pressed his shaft to her slit. With a smooth roll of his hips, he surged into her tight wet sheath. Her legs rose and wrapped around his hips. He slowly pulled out and then rocked forward.

"You call this hard?" Jessie grated. This was too slow, too gentle. Her body throbbed. She needed to feel his body surging against hers.

His eyes locked with hers and she saw his nostrils flare. She knew the exact moment when his control broke. His lips pulled back, flashing those fangs.

He leaned forward, locking his lips with hers in a fierce claiming kiss. She felt the sharp points on his canines as her tongue danced into his mouth, but didn't care. She needed him.

He pulled back and then slammed into her. His lips tore away from hers as his hands gripped her buttocks. His fingers sank into the full globes, pulling her to the very edge of the box. His hips ground against hers with every deep hard thrust.

Her hips rose, meeting every driving stab. Gasping, she clawed at the thick material on his shoulders. Her body bowed and trembled. A scorching climax ripped through her. She tingled from head to toe as if an electric current was pulsing through her.

Just as she was coming down from the peak, she felt his teeth sink into her shoulder. The sharp slash of sensation speared through her. She felt passion reignite.

He continued to drive against her. She moved with him. Her body already screamed on the edge of another climax.

"Devon…" She gasped as he ground his hips into her.

He groaned against her neck and lifted a hand to cup a breast. His fingers closed around the hard tip. He plucked at the tight nipple.

She groaned, straining toward release. Her pussy clenched around his cock as he thrust deeper. He tensed, his large body shuddering as he came. Hot semen spurted into her. The grinding pressure of his pelvis against her clit threw her into climax.

She buried her face against his shoulder and screamed as ecstasy exploded. Her body rippled with pleasure.

She stroked her fingers through the short hair at the back of his neck as she slowly came down. The air felt cool against her sweaty skin. Drawing in deep breaths, she just held on to him.

As the pleasure faded, she couldn't believe they'd actually done this. She'd felt as if she was going to burn the place down at one point. Yes, she'd teased him, but she hadn't thought he'd do anything about it. She closed her eyes. It had been delicious.

Devon's tongue swirled across her shoulder. She shivered as he drew back. He looked up and a wicked smile curled his lips. He dropped a kiss onto her head.

"Don't move. I'll be right back." He smoothed his hands down her still-splayed thighs.

She watched him walk over to a box and pull it open. Reaching inside the carton, he pulled out a handful of red paper napkins. He came back with them and pressed them between her thighs.

Jessie blushed. She reached down and grabbed his wrist, intending to take over the task. His hand wouldn't budge and he just smiled at her.

"I'll do that." She tried to slip her fingers underneath his palm as he cupped her pussy.

"I helped too. The least I can do is help clean you a little so that you don't walk around with soaking panties all night. Just relax." With his free hand, he pulled her hand away from his.

Chapter Five

ℬ

Jessie took a sip of the chilled white wine that had just been brought to their table. She stole a glance at Devon. Lounging beside her in the padded booth, he seemed utterly relaxed. For a few minutes after they'd left the storeroom, she'd felt the same way. Sated, happy. Then her eyes had caught those of a young man across the room. His eyes narrowed and a sneer crossed his face. Pure hate flashed in his eyes. She had no idea if he was a human or vampire or why he'd looked at her so venomously. That clash had forcibly reminded her that this wasn't a normal date. She was here as bait.

Devon's hand covered hers. "You're safe."

She looked up and found his eyes locked on her face. She tensed as the truth suddenly hit her. She did feel safe with him. If she hadn't, she wouldn't have lost track of the real reason they were here for even a second. She'd done more than that. She'd teased him and had hot mind-blowing sex with him all without a thought of who might try to shove a stake through her heart while they were vulnerable.

"You're overconfident." She narrowed her eyes at him.

"Confident, not overconfident." His fingers slipped beneath her palm and he gently squeezed.

She smiled. "I'm supposed to take this on faith. I've never even seen you in action."

"Never? Weren't you in that storeroom with me?" His mouth curved into a predatory grin.

"You can cheer me up later after we're both safe." She frowned.

"Relax. I have very long-term plans for you." His eyes skimmed over her face and then dropped to the full swell of her breasts.

She rolled her eyes. "Long term, you might just drive me to murder. You know I'm not some civilian who's never had any dealings with danger."

"Trust me. The only people in real danger tonight are the men trying to hurt you." His lips brushed against the shell of her ear as he leaned close to her.

Only a short time later, they stood side by side near the coat room. Devon watched as Jessie buttoned her coat. He waited until she stepped up beside him before turning toward the door. She reached out and slipped her palm over his. His fingers tightened and he nodded. He knew she was frightened, but he couldn't reassure her in this crowd.

The plan was working. The vampire hunters would have to try a strike on foot. All of the buildings near the nightclub were manned by vampire guards. He went over the plan again. Even with all of the precautions, so many things could go wrong. He didn't want to lose her.

He felt something loosen inside him at the small smile on her face and the easy way she'd stepped up beside him. She trusted him. He just didn't know if she realized it. He wouldn't fail her.

He pushed the door open. He slipped his hand free of hers and slid his arm around her waist. Even at this hour there were still people milling around outside the club's entrance. He knew that vampires mingled among the humans, watching and waiting. Two people stood near the doors, talking to the large doorman.

Devon had called for the limo, but it wasn't there yet. While he waited, his eyes slowly swept the area. Down the sidewalk, he spotted a couple slowly walking toward the club. Across the street, the opposite sidewalk was heavily shadowed. The bulb of the streetlight had burned out or broken.

He felt Jessie step closer to him as they waited in front of the club for the driver to bring the limo. He knew she was nervous. He felt her heart slamming against her ribs even through the material of his jacket. He looked down and saw her eyes flitting from the people to the shadows across the street. Standing in the open when the threat was very real was enough to make anyone feel anxious.

The sound of high heels striking the concrete seemed loud and staccato. He glanced toward the sound and saw that the couple was getting closer. He had no idea if they were the assassins, but their presence was suspicious. There wasn't a restaurant or store still open in that direction.

The quiet purr of a car coming up the street drew his attention. As it passed under the streetlight, he recognized the limo. It pulled up beside them and the young driver got out of the car and began walking around the car to open the door. Devon waved him back, urging Jessie toward the car.

His tension grew. He wanted this to be over, but he wasn't going to rush things. That would put her in more trouble than already followed her. Hopefully, by morning, she could relax at least a little. He didn't try to fool himself. She was on their hit list now and it would take years to get to all of the people in the organization.

"Weapon!" A deep male voice seemed to echo off the buildings as Brendan, the vampire guard posing as the club's doorman, shouted the warning.

A high-pitched female scream erupted and a group of people ran for cover.

Devon whipped his head around and saw the man and woman who'd been walking toward them raising pistols. He pushed Jessie behind him, sheltering her with his body.

The two assassins' attention was divided between the men near the door and their targets. When Brendan and another man stepped forward, both pistols swung to the advancing men.

They were amateurs or hadn't worked with each other before. If this followed other vampire assassinations, they intended to use the bullets to weaken their prey and then stake and behead them. He knew that those guns likely held silver bullets. The silver wouldn't be a problem for a vampire unless it hit something major, but he'd likely survive if he could get away from them. Jessie wasn't yet a vampire. A bullet through the chest could kill her.

While he was thinking, he tried to get both of them closer to some shelter. Slowly, he took a few steps back until they were almost even with the back of the limo. He felt Jessie's hands on his back just briefly and then heard a thud and a scuffle as she dived behind the protection of the car.

If necessary, he'd use his abilities out here on the street. That was something vampires tried to avoid, but he'd do what he had to do to keep her safe. He wouldn't lose her now.

The man raised the gun and pointed it at the right side of his chest. With Jessie safe behind the car's bulk, Devon dived, rolling across the car's trunk. The bullet slammed through the passenger window and the back windshield. He landed in a crouch on the opposite side of the car.

"Come out, vampires. We're going to dust two of you in full view of the public," the woman's shrill voice rose. "Stay the fuck back or you'll be just as dead as these vampires will soon be."

Devon moved down the side of the car and rose to a knee to glance through the backseat window on the driver's side. The woman was pointing her gun toward the crowd. The man caught sight of Devon and fired. Devon flattened himself to the pavement, just as the window above him exploded.

He glanced over at Jessie. "Stay here and stay down."

Her expression turned distinctly mutinous. He cursed silently. She wasn't the type of woman to step quietly to the side while he walked into danger. Her job as a Protectorate operative was a prime example of her character. He'd have to do this quickly.

Summoning energy, he flung bright flashes of light just over the crowd. He leapt over the car while everyone was still blinded. Grabbing the male assassin, he wrenched the gun out of his hand. He tossed it to a vampire standing at the edge of the crowd, while Brendan took the weapon from the female fanatic and held her by the upper arms.

"Someone call the Protectorate. We have two assassins for them," Devon called. "Jessie, you can come out now."

Jessie rose from behind the limo and walked over to them. She looked at the two people, the gathered crowd and then to Devon.

"You should search them," she said.

Devon looked at the female assassin. She wrenched in Brendan's arms, pulled a silver dagger from a hidden fold and drove it into Brendan's thigh. He growled, but kept his hold on her.

A figure dashed out of the crowd. Devon's eyes widened as he saw a thin young man dressed completely in black running at Jessie, a silver dagger in his hand. Horror washed through him. Even if he tossed the assassin he held to another vampire, he wouldn't get to her before the man reached her.

Time seemed to slow. Jessie stepped forward as the man raised the knife. Her fingers circled the man's wrist and then she glided to the side. Devon watched in stunned amazement as she wrenched the man's arm up behind him and forced him to the ground. She looked wicked, dangerous and sexy as she knelt over the man, holding him in place.

Devon's cock hardened as arousal slammed through him. He wanted nothing more than to strip that dress off her and watch her move over him. Unfortunately, it would probably be hours before they'd be alone.

"I was wondering where you were." Jessie plucked the dagger out of the assassin's hand and pressed her knee into the fanatic's back. A wide smile curved her lips. "Move and I'll break your arm."

She'd known there was another assassin? His eyes widened and he wondered why she hadn't said anything. They'd definitely have to talk about that.

The short loud *whoop* of a siren rang through the street. A burst of red and blue lights occurred almost simultaneously with the bright beam of a spotlight. Risking a glance over the car, Devon saw men moving up behind the assassins.

"Get on the ground, now!"

It was over in moments.

Eventually the three people were taken into custody by uniformed officers of the Protectorate unit. Devon walked over to Jessie, pulling her into his arms. She wrapped her arms around him and just held on to him.

Chapter Six

ꙮ

Jessie sat tensely in the large plush chair. Tossing a glare toward where Devon sprawled on the couch, she clenched her jaw. The man looked just too comfortable. He'd tossed his jacket on the back of a chair and loosened the top buttons of his white shirt. His shirt cuffs hung loose around his wrists and he'd slipped out of his shoes.

She should be tired, but she felt too restless. Gripping the arms of the chair, she resisted the urge to get up and pace again. Walking up and down the room hadn't helped the first four times. She needed to think. He wanted to talk.

She hated feeling out of control and she hadn't been in control since she'd found Devon in her hotel room.

"You knew there was another assassin?" he asked slowly.

"I suspected. He looked at me when we were in the club. I could swear he hated me. There was only one reason for that." She shrugged. Her feet tapped against the carpet.

"You didn't say anything," he said. Strangely, he didn't seem as angry as she would have thought he'd be.

"I didn't know if he was even human. Working with the Protectorate, I've gotten a few young vampires in trouble with your council when they were endangering others, but doing nothing really criminal. He could have been one of them." She crossed and then uncrossed her legs.

"Have you calmed down any?" He raised an eyebrow, lacing his hands behind his head.

"I'm still on their kill list. I can't have any kind of normal life while someone's trying to kill me." She scowled as she leaned forward. Frustration boiled inside her. If anything, this little excursion had just made the situation worse.

"Your life wasn't normal before they decided you were a vampire." He smiled and held out his hand. "Come sit with me."

"You're being nice." She stood and put her hand on her hip. "I'm not in the mood for nice."

"I'm not going to fight with you. Come over here and talk to me." He wiggled his fingers.

She grimaced. Conflicted, she just stood there. She wanted to be held, but she also wanted to hit, scream and cry. She'd hoped to be free of this, but she should have known that this one trap wouldn't get everyone in the group. She'd wanted it to be simple, easy and hadn't thought about it much.

"Come on. Put us both out of our misery. I will come get you if I have to." He sat up straight and his gaze sharpened. The lazy complacency in his gaze vanished. His eyes narrowed and his body tensed.

Misery… She looked up at him. Her eyes ran over his face. Taking a step toward him, she bit her lip. Did he feel as unsure and desperate as she did?

"Do you think it was easy for me to take you out into the open knowing that there was going to be an attempt on your life? I hated it, but it was the only way to get the evidence against the group." He took a deep breath and looked her in the eyes.

"Yeah, now we really know they want to kill me." She shook her head, but did walk over and sat beside him on the couch.

"We'll get them. Don't worry. We'll give Steven and the Protectorate a chance to bring them to human justice, but if that fails, we'll take care of them." His hand cupped the back of her head and smoothed down her hair.

Jessie tried to keep her body stiff, but she couldn't. The heat from his body seemed to seep into her muscles. She couldn't deny that this was where she wanted to be. She found such comfort in his arms, in his presence.

"Tell me what you're thinking." He brushed his lips over her cheek.

"Where do you want me to start? Should I begin with the fact that I'll be a walking bull's-eye for a few more years? Or maybe I should just tell you about the fact that I never acquired the taste for blood." She clenched her fist.

No one would be safe around her. She couldn't go near her friends. Not that she'd ever heard of any vix visiting old friends and relatives after fully transforming.

"Yes, until the Society is destroyed, you will be marked for death, but I'm not about to let you die. If they get too close, we'll go away for a while." He dropped a kiss on her lips.

"Go away… There are cells of fanatics everywhere. If I just disappear, they're likely to send my picture to every one of them." She plucked at the buttons on his shirt.

"Ah, but as a vampire, you can afford to wait fifty or sixty years for their vigor to fade. When you do fully transform, drinking blood will be as natural as breathing. You'll love the taste, but it usually takes a few tries before a vix feels comfortable drinking blood from a human donor." His lips feathered over hers. "Kiss me."

"Umm…" She'd opened her mouth to talk and his tongue had slipped into her mouth, ending any conversation.

She was frustrated, but she couldn't maintain it. She relaxed against him, her arms sliding up around his neck. Her mouth moved against his and she stroked her tongue against his. All thought of the future was pushed away by his kiss and the feel of his body against hers.

"Make love to me, Jessie." His mouth moved over her jaw and down her neck.

She looked up at him, her eyes moving over his face. Her mind immediately went to the mind-blowing pleasure he'd given her this morning and in the storeroom. Oh, yeah, she wanted that. Her body responded to the sensual images in her head with an immediate rush of slick juices between her thighs.

Rising to her feet, she took his hand and led him to the bedroom. Stopping at the side of the bed, she slowly unbuttoned his shirt. She slid the fine cloth over his shoulders. Her hands slipped down his taut abdomen even as the shirt dropped to the floor. She unfastened his pants and eased the zipper down.

She looked up at him. She couldn't help wondering what he was doing. It wasn't like him to be so passive.

She slipped her hands into the waistband of his pants as she stood on her tiptoes. Brushing her lips across his jaw, she pushed his pants down his hips until gravity took hold and they dropped to the ground.

"I want it slow tonight, Devon." Her lips brushed against his.

He nodded as he moved onto the bed. "Show me how you want it, Jessie."

It took her only a moment to shimmy out of her dress and she almost ruined those stockings. As she slipped out of her panties, she didn't give a flip about the expensive clothes lying on the floor. She crawled onto the bed and moved to straddle his hips.

Her lips slanted across his. Her tongue tangled with his in an increasingly passionate kiss. She felt his hand slip down her rib cage and between their bodies. His fingers glided across her clit. That tormenting graze sent a spike of desire straight through her. Her inner muscles clenched and the ache only seemed to intensify.

He tore his lips away from hers. "Let's see if you're ready for me."

She felt his fingers circle her slit, probe and then two of them slowly slid inside her. He positioned the head of his cock at her entrance. As she slowly lowered onto his thick shaft, both of his hands slid up her thighs. His large palms smoothed over her belly and up to her breasts. His hands cupped the full mounds, before his fingers began tormenting her nipples.

Her hips rocked against his, wanting a long, slow ride to bliss. She wanted it, but she didn't know if she'd be able to hold out for it. Sharp sensations sizzled through her as he gave undivided attention to her breasts. One of his hands curled around her arm and urged her to lean down. His mouth closed around the hardened tip of one breast between his lips. His teeth scraped over the breast and then he gripped the hard tip and tugged.

Jessie jerked, grinding her cunt against him. Her inner muscles clenched repeatedly around his cock. She threw her head back and sucked in a gasping breath between her teeth. She desperately searched for control as he drew her nipple deep into his mouth.

"Slow." She fisted her hands into the covers as she moved on him.

His mouth left her breast and he smiled up at her. Blatant challenge shone in his brown eyes. He leaned up and scraped his teeth across her neck.

"How do you want it, Jessie?" He sucked lightly on her neck.

Her eyes fluttered closed and she shuddered as the pleasure built. Slow, fast, she didn't care anymore. She just wanted release.

Her hips rose over his then descended. She took him deep and rose again. His fingers tugged at her nipples. Heat sizzled through her. Her inner muscles clenched around his cock. She screamed as she came. Scalding satisfaction pulsed through her.

Devon's teeth sank into her neck. His hips pumped against her as he sucked at her neck. He stiffened, groaning against her neck. Semen spurted deep into her womb.

It was much later when she lay beside him on the bed that her mind began turning everything that had happened and what she'd learned. There was no going back to her human life. The fanatics nixed that idea. If she wasn't transforming into a vix, she'd probably be shuffled into a protection program.

She could feel the changes in her body now. The transformation had been accelerated by his bite and the enzymes it pumped into her body. She was probably already well over fifty percent changed. Somehow, the thought of becoming a vix wasn't as scary as it would have been only a week ago. A lot of it had to do with the man beside her.

She rested her head on his arm and looked up at him. "So what are you doing for the next four months or forty years?"

He tilted his head a smile curved his lips. "Why?"

"I wondered if you wanted to see if we could make this thing between us work—without one of us murdering the other." She bit her lip to hide a smile.

"I've always intended for this 'thing' to work. I think you'd better plan for longer than forty years." He turned onto his side and dropped a kiss on her lips.

She thought for a minute about forty years of fighting and loving with him. She wanted that and more, but she wasn't about to tell him. His smirk was just too smug and he was already much too arrogant. The man needed someone to keep him in line. She'd certainly give it a try.

"We'll see." She patted his chest and snuggled down as if to go to sleep. She waited for the explosion.

His body tensed and she saw his face harden. He leaned down until they were nose to nose. "Yes, we will."

Also by Rebecca Airies

ഗ

Primal Quest

Second Chance

About the Author

ഗ

Rebecca Airies has always loved to read. Futuristic, the classics, mystery or horror, the genre doesn't matter as long as the stories capture her interest and take her on an adventure. She soon discovered a love for writing and characters ust waiting to tell their stories. Since that time, writing has become an obsession.

Rebecca lives in the heart of Texas. She loves the outdoors, growing things, and working on crafts when she's not lost in the worlds of her characters. Please feel free to write and tell her what you think; she'd love to hear from you.

Rebecca welcomes comments from readers. You can find her website and email address on her author bio page at www.ellorascave.com.

Tell Us What You Think

We appreciate hearing reader opinions about our books. You can email us at Comments@EllorasCave.com.

WENDY'S SUMMER JOB

By Charlotte Boyett-Compo

Trademarks Acknowledgement

ꕥ

The author acknowledges the trademarked status and trademark owners of the following wordmarks mentioned in this work of fiction:

Cadillac: General Motors Corporation

Chevrolet: General Motors Corporation

Lamborghini: Same Deutz-Fahr S.p.A

Porsche: Dr. Ing. h. c. f. Porsche Aktiengesellschaft Corporation

Stetson: John B. Stetson Company

UCLA: Regents of the University of California, The

Author's Note

ꙮ

Dear Sweet Reader:

Once upon a time there was a spoiled little rich girl who'd had everything she'd ever wanted handed to her on a silver platter. Mommy and Daddy had never learned to say no to the darling child. Everything had been done for this poor little lamb who'd never been forced to worry about money or wonder where she'd lay her perfectly coiffed head each night.

But—as we who live in the real world know all too well—all good things tend to come to an end. Life can be a hard lesson to learn for those not equipped with the right school supplies.

Case in point is poor little Wendy. Wendy isn't just having a bad hair day, Dear Reader, she'd having the summer from hell until…

Well, step with us now into her make-believe world where she's going to learn all about the very hard things in life such as hard men are good to find.

But please don't expect this to be your grandmama's sweet little romantic tale or even your mama's hotter kind, Dear Reader. Oh, no. Wendy's romp through man-land could never be your run-of-the-mill erotic storyline. Please read little Wendy's story with your tongue firmly tucked in your sweet little cheek and expect the words to be a pretty shade of purple. ;)

Yours truly,

The WyndWryter

Chapter One

ꟹ

For Wendy Cole, life that summer sucked. Her regular hairdresser was out for carpal tunnel releases and the stand-in gave her a chop job that made her look like a dandelion on steroids. Her car needed brakes. She needed a new summer wardrobe. A heated argument with her stepmother Joyce, who had cut off both her college tuition and dorm living at UCLA, plus three maxed-out credit cards, was incentive enough to start looking for alternate means of existence. Wendy was in desperate need of a summer job.

"Bitch," Wendy labeled her stepmother. They'd never gotten along but since Wendy's father had died, the situation between them had only gotten worse. Joyce expected Wendy to come into the family catering business Nathan Cole had founded, to take part in the charity events that kept Joyce's name in the news and to behave as Joyce believed she should.

"You are a disgrace to the Cole name!" Joyce had thrown at Wendy. "It's bad enough wanting to be a cheap, tawdry actress but quite another to spend good money learning such silliness in college. I'll not pay another dime to further this insane quest of yours!"

"It is not a tawdry occupation!" Wendy had thrown at her stepmother.

"It is a profession only fit for whores and prostitutes," her stepmother had said with a sneer. "Which are you?"

That snide, hateful question had been the straw that had broken the camel's back. Not only had Joyce insulted her, she had pissed on the only dream Wendy had ever had—to act.

To add insult to injury, Joyce had cut off all financial support to her stepdaughter so Wendy's dream might die a quick and painful death.

"I don't want to be a star," she mumbled to herself. "I just want to be a character actress who can do any role I am given! I *am* an actress and I am damned good at it!"

But little theater, off-off-off Broadway roles and dinner theater did not a true actress make. She had a craft to learn and college had been the easiest way she'd known to make that happen. But without money, she couldn't take the classes she needed and that hurt so badly Wendy would have cried if she'd had any tears left to shed.

Schlepping from one employment agency to another all day had given Wendy a headache and a sour stomach. She'd broken a heel off her right pump, her blouse had a coffee stain and her hair had started to frizz with the unusual dampness of the California weather. On top of all that, there just didn't appear to be any positions for which she was qualified.

At least none that paid a decent wage.

Flopping down on a bench, Wendy heaved a deep sigh. She leaned forward, propped her chin in her hand and stared at the passing traffic. There had to be a job out there somewhere for her. Burger joints were even starting to look promising.

Had the living god with an ass just dying to be groped not come out of the doorway across the street at that exact moment, Wendy wouldn't have seen the *Extraordinary Receptionist Wanted* sign. As he'd walked past the sign, it had been his luscious butt that grabbed her attention first but her eyes had reluctantly snapped back from that delectable tush lovingly molded in black leather to the white sign with the red letters. Perking up, she looked down the street to watch him until he disappeared, then scrambled off the bench.

Paying no heed to what kind of business was seeking a receptionist she squeezed between two parked cars at the curb.

With a couple of cars blasting their horns at her as she sprinted across the street—rolling like a ship under full sail with only one heel stabilizing her dash—she entered the establishment, chest heaving.

The man behind the counter looked up from the cash register, looked down at the drawer and then did a double take as she closed the door behind her. A slow grin stretched across his handsome face. "Can I help you?" he asked.

Wendy stared at him. He was absolutely mouthwatering—dark brown hair with a wayward curl dipping over his brow, green eyes, white teeth, dimples and a nicely muscled chest stretching his shirt.

"Ma'am?" he asked, one dark brow elevated.

She had to swallow before she could squeak out the one word, "Work."

His long-lashed eyes swept down her from head to waist—since the rest of her was blocked by the counter—and he shut the cash register drawer. "Looking for or wanting?" he inquired.

Without realizing she was doing it, Wendy put out her tongue and licked her lips. "Wanting," she said, her voice husky and inviting. "Boy, am I wanting."

Folding his arms over his brawny chest, he gave her a look that set her loins to throbbing. "What I meant was, do you want to work for us or do you want us to work for you?"

Thinking of all the things he could do for her, Wendy had to bite her lower lip, tucking it between her teeth, watching his eyes flare with interest. "Me working for you," she answered, and could feel her heart pounding, her blood rushing through her veins.

"Well, let's go into the office and talk about it," he said.

Wendy watched him skirt the counter. In his dark blue mechanic's pants, his ass was as luscious as the man she'd seen leaving earlier and looked hard enough to bounce a quarter off.

Wendy blinked. "Mechanic?" she heard herself say.

"To the stars," he quipped as he headed for the front door. When he twisted the lock, she felt a stab of pure lust drive right through her belly. He turned to face her. "The receptionist job pays five hundred a week plus benefits," he said, sweeping a hand toward a door off to her right.

At the moment, that was a princely sum to Wendy. Having to move back in with her stepmother would be sheer hell but it would be doable until she could save up enough money to get her own place.

The office into which he showed her wasn't what she expected a mechanic's office to look like. It was large, clean, neat and smelled pleasantly of perked coffee even if the desk was a jumble of papers, invoices and ledgers. A long couch with two chairs to either side of it sat at the far end of the room along with a coffee table and two end tables. An entertainment center complete with a small bar graced the opposite wall. In between were three four-drawer file cabinets.

"Can you type?" he asked, motioning her to the chair in front of the desk.

"Yes," she said. "I can—"

"Count to ten while chewing gum?" he queried as he pushed aside a pile of papers on the edge of the desk and perched on it, his arms folded.

Wendy smiled, giving him her best toothy grin. "If push comes to shove," she answered.

He put out a hand. "Drake Quinlan," he said. "Co-owner and chief diagnostician."

She slipped her hand into his and was impressed with the strength and the calluses. His nails didn't have the grimy, packed-grease look of a mechanic. "Wendy Cole, out-of-work damsel in distress."

"Chief diagnostician," he stressed when he saw her looking at his short-clipped nails. "I can swing a wrench with the best of them but why should I when I have guys in the back who can do it for me?"

Wendy was all too aware he hadn't let go of her hand. He was caressing her fingers.

"Did you pass my brother Kyle on the way in?" he asked. He had put his free hand atop hers and was running the pads of his fingers along the back of her hand.

"Tall guy in black leather?" she asked, losing herself in the verdant depths of his mesmerizing eyes.

"That would have been him."

"I saw him."

"Most women do," he said with a sigh.

She swallowed. "I'm surprised you two don't have women lining up for the job." She risked a glance at his left hand. "Or that your wives aren't here keeping an eye on you."

He shrugged carelessly. "No wives to worry about and—at the moment—no girlfriends either." He was swirling a pattern on her hand. "And we're particular who we hire to work for us."

Her smile slipped a notch. "Oh, I don't suppose you..."

He bent toward her. "We were big into Dungeons & Dragons when we were kids and we still like to role-play." His grin was cocky. "And we like our employees to play along too."

Wendy felt a jolt of pure yearning drive through her lower body. He was incredibly handsome and the look he was giving her could have melted stone. "What kind of role-playing?" she asked.

His slow, sensual grin sent shivers down her spine. "Oh, the usual kind. Poor, down-on-her-luck damsel in distress looking for a job. Dastardly brothers offering her one for the exclusive use of her..." He slid his hot gaze down her. "Bod," he finished with a quirk of his brow.

She drew in a breath. "I beg your pardon?"

"You can do that as well," he said. "Never hurts to add a little begging to the mix to get a man hard and primed."

Wendy was never one to look a gift horse in the mouth. Drawing on her experience in several high school and college plays, she lowered her eyes and eased her hand from his, threading her fingers together in her lap. "I…" she said, letting her voice become meek and hesitant. "I really need a job."

Drake rested the underside of his forearm on his crooked knee and gave her a steady look. "And what would you be willing to do to get that job, Miss Cole?"

Her voice trembling, she lifted her eyes to his. "Anything, Mr. Quinlan," she said, her lips quivering.

"Anything?" he echoed.

Wendy heard the front door opening and her heartbeat accelerated. She could do no more than nod. The blood was roaring in her ears for she'd never done anything like this before but she had good instincts and her instincts were yelling at her that here was an opportunity that didn't come along just any day. She saw Drake look up over her head.

"I believe we have a viable candidate for the position, Kyle," he said.

Realizing the man in the tight leather pants was behind her, Wendy ached to turn around and look up at him, but she didn't get a chance. She tensed as strong, powerful hands suddenly bracketed her shoulders.

"Is that so?" a deep, sexy voice asked.

"And she's willing to do anything for us to hire her."

"Well, now," Kyle Quinlan said. "That's good to know."

Wendy felt those strong hands slide down to her breasts. Beneath the silk of her blouse, she could feel the heat of his palms as he kneaded her gently.

"Nice," the newcomer pronounced. He swirled his palm over her hardening nipple. "Very nice. What's her story, bro?"

"She's a down-on-her-luck lady with a small child she needs to feed. She'll do whatever it takes to keep a roof over the poor tyke's head," Drake said, spinning a tale that brought heat to Wendy's cheeks. "Won't you, baby?"

Wendy nodded, beginning to pant as those expert fingers plied her breasts.

Through the material of her blouse and bra, she could feel Kyle rolling her nipples between his fingers.

"Then why don't we try her out for size?" Kyle suggested.

Drake stood. "Did you lock the front door?"

"Is the Pope Catholic?" his brother countered. He was running his hands up and down Wendy's chest, standing so close behind her chair she could feel his body warmth.

Before she could react, Kyle Quinlan moved his hands from her chest to the arms of the chair and lifted it with her in it, taking it back about three feet from the desk. When she would have gotten up, he clamped his hands on her shoulders.

"Sit right where you are, baby," he ordered.

Drake hunkered down before her and reached up to take her chin in his hand. "Here's the scenario," he said. "If you really want the job, you get up and go out the office door, close it behind you then knock. When you come in, you do everything we tell you and the job is yours." He caressed her jaw. "Understand?"

"Yes," she said breathlessly. She was aching between her legs already.

Kyle was once more massaging her breasts. "We're both clean and I assume you are but we'll be using protection, so don't worry. We can provide health certificates and if you agree, we'll set you up an appointment with our sawbones to look you over so we can do all the really delicious things the four of us will want to do."

"F-Four?" Wendy questioned, twisting her head around to look up at him.

"We have a younger brother but he's not here today."

"His name is Lance and he'll be kicking his own ass for taking the day off," Drake said with a chuckle.

"So if you don't mind having three men taking good care of you," Kyle said, "and I mean *really* good care of you, the job is most likely yours."

"Most likely?" she questioned.

His hand tightened on her breast "Well, let's see what you got first before we decide." He removed his hand.

For one wild moment she thought of running away but the handsome men gazing at her as though she were a scrumptious side dish made her own mouth water. On legs that threatened to buckle beneath her, she hobbled over to the door.

"Poor little thing," she heard Drake say. "She can't even afford a decent pair of shoes."

"That's all right," Kyle returned. "She'll earn some new ones, won't you, babe?"

Heat rushed through Wendy and pooled between her legs. She could barely nod as she moved toward the door. It took every ounce of her courage to open the door, go out, close it behind her and then turn to stare at the portal. She took a deep breath then lifted her hand to knock timidly.

"Yeah?" came a rough voice from behind the door.

Screwing up her nerve, she wrapped her hand around the door handle and opened it.

Both men were seated—Kyle behind the desk and Drake in the chair she'd vacated. Kyle's feet were up on the desktop and his brother was sitting with his ankle crossed over the knee of his other leg.

"What can we do for you, lady?" Kyle inquired.

Wendy came into the room and closed the door behind her. She came over to the desk, wringing her hands in front of her. "I'm l-looking for work," she said. "Just a summer job."

"Is that so?" Kyle asked. He leaned back in the chair with his hands clasped behind his neck. "How badly do you need the job?"

She risked a glance at Drake but he wasn't looking at her. He was staring at his brother. "Real bad, Mr. Quinlan," she said.

"How bad?" Kyle repeated.

"Very bad," she said, lowering her eyes and pretending to tremble.

"And how bad will you be to get the job?" Drake asked.

Wendy put a hand to her lower tummy where a spike of desire had shot through her. "As bad as you want me to be."

The two men were silent for so long, Wendy was beginning to feel nervous. She lifted her head just enough to look at the man behind the desk and found him gazing at her with such a heated stare it made her knees weak.

"Come here, baby," he said.

She walked around the corner of his desk and came to stand beside his chair. The sleek black leather covering his long legs made her want to trail her hand along his thigh.

"You sure you're desperate enough to do what it takes to get this job, now?" Kyle queried.

Wendy met his dark green eyes—a shade darker than his brother's—and was fascinated by the tiny glints of gold striations running through the iris. She licked her lips. "Yes, sir. I am more than desperate for this job."

"Then put your hand between my legs," he ordered.

Her hand trembling—and it wasn't pretense now—Wendy reached out to lay her palm over the bulge at the junction of his hips. Rock-hard, it was the most erotic thing she'd ever touched and it leapt with promise.

"Like that?" Kyle asked.

"I believe I will," she said breathlessly.

"No believing about it, babe," Kyle said, covering her hand with his and pressing her palm tightly to his growing erection. "I can personally guarantee you'll get your money's worth with that rod."

"I'm rather enjoying her rack and I can't wait to pinion her," came an amused voice from the doorway.

Wendy turned to see a tall, even more handsome version of the two men sitting in the office standing behind her. He was leaning against the doorframe with his arms crossed over a muscular chest that stretched a white T-shirt to absolute perfection.

"Thought you took the day off, baby bro," Drake drawled.

"And let you two have all the fun?" Lance Quinlan inquired. "Everybody knows when the window shade's down, you two horn dogs are at play."

Her face bright red, Wendy's eyes widened and she snatched her hand back from Kyle's crotch. The last thing she wanted to do was have everyone on the street know she was the men's whore.

"He's joking, baby," Drake said as he lowered his foot to the floor and stood. "It's lunchtime and he's the one who lowered the shade." He came over to her and backed her up against the wall. "You want something to touch, touch this."

Wendy let him take her hand and place it over the hardness at his groin. She groaned for the bulge she felt against her palm was like steel through the mechanic's pants. He was leaning into her, pressing her back against the wall. Lowering his head, he flicked his tongue along the column of her neck even as he rubbed her palm over his taut erection.

"The little lady needs a job, Lance," Kyle told his younger brother, "and we're willing to give her a try."

"Needs a job, eh?" Lance repeated. "How bad?"

"Real bad," Kyle stated.

"Then let's see what she's got," Lance said. He sauntered over to Wendy and nudged his brother aside, moving into place in front of her. His eyes—a paler green than either of his brothers'—swept down her, up again and then settled on her bosom. Holding her gaze, he put his fingers to the buttons of her blouse and began to undo them.

Wendy groaned, her breath coming in tiny little gasps as the backs of his fingers grazed the flesh of her chest.

"Tell me what you'll do for us, baby," Lance ordered as he flicked open the last button and slid his hands along her rib cage, reaching behind her for the closure of her bra.

"L-Like what?" she asked, feeling lightheaded.

"Like are you going to fuck us or are you just going to lie there and let us do all the work?" he inquired.

"We're equal opportunity employers but we expect equal opportunity from our employees too," Drake said, stroking the side of her waist.

She felt the hook of her bra give way and swallowed nervously. His hands moved up to peel the blouse from her and before she could say anything, he had plucked the bra from her as well.

"Nice tits," Drake commented.

"Just begging for a man's lips to suckle them," Kyle agreed.

Heavy heat throbbed between her legs as the brothers converged on her, crowding her against the wall with one on each side of her and Lance in front, his fingers on the waistband of her navy skirt.

"Please," she whispered.

"Oh, we aim to please, baby," Kyle assured her. "Just like you're going to please us."

Moving in tandem, Kyle and Drake leaned toward her and each took a nipple in his mouth. Hissing with pleasure, Wendy closed her eyes as those hot tongues laved her puckered flesh and Lance slid her skirt down to the floor, tugging her half-slip along with it.

"Garter belt and hose," Lance said in a soft voice. "My kinda woman." He went to his knees before her, one hand wrapped around her calf as he removed her broken shoe and then the other one. With infinite care he unhooked her stockings from the garter belt, rolled them down and off her legs then slid his hands up her thighs to pluck at the waistband of her thong.

With Kyle and Drake suckling her, Wendy was in seventh heaven. The brothers were holding each of her hands as they flicked their tongues over her taut flesh and lightly nibbled her nipples. As though that wasn't enough pure, intense joy, she felt Lance stroking her between the legs, his middle finger dragging deliciously across her slit.

"She smells like lavender," the youngest Quinlan brother proclaimed, and he slipped his finger inside her.

"Ah!" Wendy said with a gasp, and would have sagged to the floor had not Kyle and Drake put up hands to cup her beneath the arms.

The one thought that kept spinning through Wendy's mind was that these men knew what they were about. They had pleasure down to a science. It felt as though the two suckling at her breast were doing so alternately, drawing the maximum amount of chills from her body, and Lance's finger was slipping into and out of her with the same delectable rhythm.

"She's slick for us, guys," the youngest brother said. "Good and primed." He withdrew his finger and stepped away.

"No," Wendy whined, wanting that heated digit plying her still.

"He's just getting things ready for us, doll," Kyle said. "Not to worry."

Looking across the room, Wendy watched Lance pick up the coffee table and set it to one side. With a wink at her, he went to the sofa and took off the black leather cushions. As he pulled out the king-sized sofa bed, she saw red silk sheets stretched over the mattress.

"Yummy," she said, and met Drake's smiling gaze.

"Only the best for our ladies," he said, and scooped her up in his arms to take her to the sofa bed.

"I've got dibs on her toes," Lance said.

"He has a foot fetish," Drake laughed.

"And a finger fetish," Kyle put in. "We nicknamed him Widget."

Drake lay her down gently and she felt as though she were a new car the men were inspecting as they stood beside the bed. Their comments made her blush.

"Nice chassis," Kyle commented.

"Streamlined and elegant," Drake agreed.

"A racy model if I ever saw one," Lance added.

Flicking her tongue over her lips, she watched the men undress. Lance was quick to cross his arms over his chest and peel the white T-shirt from his broad chest, slower to unbutton his faded jeans and kick off his tennis shoes. Kyle tugged the black polo from his leather pants and bent his arms over his shoulders to pull the shirt off. Drake unbuttoned his blue uniform shirt slowly—and with as much grace as a male dancer would. He slipped the leather belt from his pants then flicked open the button at his waist. He kicked off his shoes with a cocky grin.

"You like watching us strip, huh?" Drake asked as he stepped out of his pants to reveal he wore no underwear.

"Oh yeah," she replied. Her eyes were on the steely erection jutting from the nest of crisp dark curls at his thighs. "What's not to like?"

Kyle pulled off his boots and wiggled out of his tight black pants. Like his brother, he wasn't wearing underwear. He was the first to stretch out beside her on the left side of the sofa bed.

Lance was next as he peeled off his socks and hunkered down at the foot of the sofa bed, reaching out to lift Wendy's foot from the mattress. "Beautiful," he pronounced, massaging her toes. "Absolutely beautiful." He brought her foot to his chest and braced the sole against him as he kneaded her calf.

Drake joined his brothers on the bed, lying on his side to Wendy's right. He reached out to trace a lazy pattern on her flat belly. "You have such soft skin, baby," he said. "I want to lick you all over." He lowered his head to her stomach and lapped at her belly button.

It was Kyle who leaned over her to capture her lips with his. He nibbled on her lower lip until she opened her mouth and he could slip his tongue sensually inside. His hand was on her breast—lightly squeezing, plucking at her nipple—as he kissed her.

Lance had the toes of her right foot in his mouth, sucking each one in turn, licking the valleys in between as his hand moved up and down her calf.

Drake licked his way up her chest, circled each nipple and then trailed kisses to her ear, spiraling his tongue inside to send shivers up her spine.

"Who's gonna be first?" Kyle asked.

"Hold her for me, boys, and I'll take the lead this time," Lance said, slipping on a condom he'd taken from the drawer of the stand beside the sofa bed. He took her ankles in his hand and splayed her legs wide, scooting up between them until his rigid cock was poised at her cleft.

Drake and Kyle lifted Wendy's arms over her head and held them down as their baby brother positioned himself between her legs and slid his hands beneath her hips to bring her up to meet his thrust.

Reveling in the delight of the hard male hands holding her, the brawny chest pressing down on her, the thick rod sliding possessively inside her, Wendy arched her head back and groaned with the intense pleasure of it. This was not her first time partying with more than one man but it was the first time she'd ever had such penetrating delight coursing through her.

Lance moved in and out of her slowly, going deep, holding himself still for a moment before rolling his hips so his cock touched every inch of her clit with each pass. He would almost withdraw then pound into her with a fierceness that moved her up on the mattress every time he thrust.

"Take her, bro," Kyle whispered as he leaned over to probe the sensitive flesh of her ear. "Take her hard."

The momentum of Lance's thrusts came faster, harder, deeper. He was pistoning in and out of her with enough strength to make her grunt with each upward movement. Just as her quivers began, he pushed hard into her and let the pulses milk him before he spilled himself deep inside her.

Wendy moaned as the last vibration faded away. She was breathing hard, her body feeling every touch on it as though that touch had been magnified a hundred times over. She could hear her blood pounding in her ears and as Kyle flicked his tongue along her cheekbone, Lance pulled out to be replaced by Drake.

"Let's see what you got, babe," Drake said, his condom-clad penis driving into her with precision timing.

Thicker than his brother—longer—Drake pummeled her with rapid thrusts that fired every nerve ending in her body. His pulsing rod went deep and filled her with such heady delight, she dug her heels into the mattress, arching up to meet him thrust for thrust.

"That's it, baby," Drake said, digging his hands into her soft buttocks. "Give me everything you've got!"

When she came, she came hard, crying out her release. Drake's cock was hitting her G-spot just right and the orgasm that rocked her made her see stars behind her tightly closed eyelids. She barely had a chance to take a breath before Kyle was stretched out atop her, dragging her legs up over his shoulders as he slid his latex-covered rod inside her.

"Let a real man show you how it's done, boys," Kyle said through clenched teeth.

Drake and Lance chuckled as their older brother slapped his lower body vigorously between Wendy's thighs. Lance was nibbling the fingers of her left hand as Drake kissed his way down her right arm, lapping at the light sweat that had popped up on her flesh.

Kyle's cock was the biggest of the three and it filled Wendy beautifully. He was a robust lover with broad shoulders and a thick mat of hair on his chest that sweetly abraded her taut nipples. She could hear his flesh pounding against hers and the sound sent tremors of lust rippling down her sides. When he shot into her, he threw back his head and bellowed like a sated bull, holding her to him tightly as the last of his seed spilled into her. He collapsed atop her, his breathing heavy, fanning across the soft pillow of her breath.

"Don't squash her, bro," Drake warned, shoving Kyle.

Reluctantly Kyle slid off her to lie on his back at her side, one arm flung over his eyes. "Man, that was intense," he said, dragging in loud breaths.

Lance was sitting Indian-fashion at the foot of the sofa bed, once more toying with her right foot. Drake was lying at her other side, his hand gently on her waist.

"Do I have the job?" Wendy asked.

"Is the Pope Catholic?" the brothers asked in unison.

Chapter Two

ᢀ

Wendy arrived early to work the next morning. She looked around her as she put the key Drake had given her in the lock. No one seemed to be paying her any attention and she was relieved. She'd asked the men how many receptionists they'd had since starting up their car repair shop.

"Just two," Kyle had replied. "One quit because she didn't like our off-color remarks."

"The other one lasted a few weeks but when Lance hit on her, she up and took off," Drake explained.

"Didn't really want her anyway," Lance complained. "We've been looking for just the right lady ever since."

"And how long has that been?" she'd queried.

"A year," Drake had answered with a deep sigh. "Good women are hard to find."

"Hard men are good to find," Wendy countered.

"We're that if nothing else," Kyle had laughed.

Entering the office, she could hear the unmistakable sound of a power wrench revving up in the garage out back. She knew there would be a couple of mechanics already on duty, awaiting Drake's arrival in a few minutes.

She was just putting on a pot of coffee out in the reception area when Kyle strolled in. He gave her a once-over look that made the hairs on the back of her arms stir.

"Good morning, Mr. Quinlan," she said shyly.

"It will be," he said with a wink.

"Is there anything I should be doing?" she asked, and let her voice sound unsure.

"Yeah, when you get through with the coffee, get your ass in my office," he said as he continued on toward his office. "I've got some dictation for you, baby." He stopped and looked back at her. "Remember your place and act accordingly."

She nodded, understanding his warning. He was in mischievous mode and she would be expected to play along.

Expectation trilled through Wendy as she finished with the coffee. She had dressed for work just as the brothers had instructed and already she was beginning to throb between her legs. She could almost feel the juices gathering. Smoothing down the skirt of her loosely fitting dress, she went to the office door and knocked.

"Come in."

Kyle was perched on the corner of the desk, his arms folded as she entered and shut the door behind her.

"Lock it," he said in a gruff tone, "then get over here."

Meekly, she twisted the lock into place. With her head down, she shuffled over to him, her hands clasped together in front of her.

"Did you lose the panties?" he asked.

"Yes, Mr. Quinlan," she said, keeping her eyes on the polished toes of his black boots.

"And the bra?"

"Yes, sir."

She could feel his gaze crawling down her.

"Come closer."

His voice was rough, demanding, and it sent shivers of anticipation along her spine. She moved closer and gasped as he grabbed her and pulled her between his legs.

"Let's see what you've got," he growled.

The dress she'd been instructed to wear had an elasticized neckline that could be worn off-shoulder. Its design made it easy for Kyle to tug it down below her full breasts to expose her to his avid view.

"Not bad," he said. "Lift them up for me to get a better look."

Pretending she was trembling, she put her hands beneath her breasts and lifted them for his inspection. As she held them, he ran his thumb back and forth over her left nipple until the nub was hard and aching.

"It'll do," he pronounced. "Let's see what you have between your legs."

She hesitantly looked up at him and when he arched an impatient brow, she grabbed handfuls of her skirt and lifted it until she was open to his scrutiny. When he slid a rough, calloused palm between her legs, she felt her knees growing weak with desire. As he continued to rub her, she could not keep from groaning.

"Like that, do you?" he asked.

"Yes, sir," she said, and forced a blush to her cheeks.

"You're a little whore, aren't you?" he said, cocking his head to one side.

She shook her head. "No, sir. I'm a good little—"

"On your knees, slut," he ordered. When she hesitated, he reached up to grab her chin between his fingers. "If you don't want the job, Miss Cole, I know a lot of women who do."

"Please, sir," she said. "I do want the job."

"Then get on your knees," he snapped.

Wendy sank to the floor between his legs. He was wearing jeans that were molded to his muscled thighs and when he shifted his thighs apart in invitation, she knew what he expected and put her hands on his fly.

Behind her, the door rattled and she stilled, her head snapping up as her eyes widened.

"Yes?" Kyle called out, holding Wendy's stare.

"Are you busy?" It was Drake's voice.

"I'm in the middle of something."

"I'll come back."

Kyle nodded at her.

He was already hard and oozing as she unzipped his jeans and gently extracted him from the confines of the material. The day before each of the brothers had provided an up-to-date health certificate so she had no qualms about giving him a blowjob. She licked clean the broad tip then took him into her mouth, her jaws aching at the size of his tool. He was so large it was almost painful for her to blow him. She would much rather have had that throbbing rod between her legs for she was aching for him.

Kyle threaded his hands through her hair to anchor her head as she did him. His head was thrown back, his eyes closed as he enjoyed what she was doing. When he came, he tensed all over, his cum coursing down her willing throat as she relaxed it to accommodate the spill. With his cock still pressed between her sweet lips, he lowered his head and looked down into her eyes.

"That was unbelievable, Wendy," he said, stroking her hair. "Thank you and good morning."

She eased back and smiled at him. "You are welcome and good morning to you, Mr. Quinlan."

"Kyle," he corrected. He tucked himself back into his pants and zipped up before holding out a hand to help her from the floor. "Ready to do some work?"

"I'm all yours," she said, straightening the skirt of her dress.

He was all business as he showed her what needed doing. There was filing, a bit of data entry, some invoices that needed to go out, deposits that needed to be made. Nothing that was beyond her ability to do.

"Of course when one of us needs you," he said, meeting her eye, "you're to drop whatever you're doing to accommodate us."

"Of course, sir," she said. Her cleft was throbbing with need and she hoped the next accommodation would accommodate her as well.

"That'll do it for now," he said, dismissing her as he moved around behind the desk.

Wendy unlocked the door and left his office. She'd only taken a few steps before she felt someone pressing up against her back, firm hands sliding up and down her arms.

"I've a slight problem with my laptop, Miss Cole," she heard Drake say. "Would you step into my office and take a look."

Chapter Three

ꟿ

The three mechanics who worked on the sleek sports cars and expensive SUVs rarely came in to the main part of the shop but when they did, they gave Wendy a look that said they were aware of what went on in the private offices. Handsome in a rough, blue-collar way, the men were respectful but their heated gazes filled her with a sense of power that—had she encouraged them—would have added another trio of admirers to her thrall. In her more fanciful moments, she imagined walking back to their brightly lit, oil-scented haven and offering herself to their eager, grimy hands. Such thoughts sent shivers through her lower body.

"Penny for your thoughts," Drake said.

Wendy glanced at him as he leaned on the receptionist counter.

"It wouldn't do to reveal them," she said.

He glanced past her to the door leading into the garage. "Hankering for greasy fingers slithering around on those pearly globes, are you?" Her blush must have given her away for he shook his head. "We don't share, darling."

"So noted," she said, and extended an invoice for him to sign. "Mr. Wilson isn't going to be happy with that estimate."

Drake nodded. "I don't imagine so." He scrawled his signature on the invoice and slid it back to her. "What you got planned for supper tonight?"

She'd been working there for four months and not once had any of the brothers invited her out after work. Her heart did a rapid little tattoo for of the three men, she found Drake the most attractive and flirted outrageously with him every chance she got.

"Just warmed-over whatever my stepmom's maid is preparing for her," she answered.

"Ugh," Drake commented. He put his elbow on the counter and braced his chin in his palm. "How 'bout steak fajitas and a pitcher of margaritas instead?"

"Sounds good to me," she said.

"Then south of the border it is," he said, straightening up and rapping the counter with his palm.

She watched him walk off—admiring the way his ass looked in the dark blue of his uniform pants. Realizing she'd never once seen a grease or oil stain on either his shirt or pants, she wondered how much actual work he did in the garage area of the shop. Kyle hardly ever stepped foot out of his office unless it was to come to Drake's to partake of a little bit of her.

That thought made Wendy sigh. Each brother had his own special place in her heart. They were good men who liked to play but they were always careful of her, gentle and never out of line at any time other than during their playful sessions when playing lord and master over her was at the top of the agenda. At those times, anything could—and usually did—happen and she enjoyed it as much as they did.

* * * * *

Supper was delicious and when Drake whipped his sleek gunmetal gray Porsche up into Beverly Hills, Wendy was impressed.

"You live up here?" she inquired as they passed gated homes she'd often read about but had never seen in person.

"We have a little place our dad left us," he said.

"You and your brothers?" she inquired.

He nodded. "There is an art studio out back our dad built for our mother and Kyle claimed that as his as present patriarch. Lance and I share the main house but we're on opposite ends of it so we can go days without seeing one another."

"Are they there tonight?" she asked, disappointed she might not be spending some quality time with just him.

"Lance may be but Kyle drove up to Sacramento to spend the weekend with his son."

Wendy's eyebrows shot up. "Kyle has a son?"

"And a daughter," Drake replied. "Jory, his daughter, lives with her mom in Laguna Beach. He sees her every other weekend and Dallas, his-two-year-old son, one weekend a month." He expertly passed a slow-moving Cadillac. "Jory's mother is a lot more lenient with visitations than Dallas' mom is."

"I didn't realize any of you had been married."

"We haven't," Drake said, casting her a look. "Mistakes—or in the case of the two rug rats, deliberate mistakes—happen."

Wendy thought about that for a moment. "Did either of those ladies work for you?"

Drake laughed. "No," he stated emphatically. "Neither is the type to have fun. Nina, Jory's mom, knew Kyle in college and Lynda, Dallas' mom, was Kyle's steady for about a year before she got in the family way." He zipped around another car. "He loves his kids and supports them and their moms, although for my money he could hire a hit man to take out Lynda."

"Not one of your favorites, huh?"

"Not by a long shot," he replied.

"What about you and Lance? Any rug rats of yours around?"

He shook his head. "Nope. We've both been very careful, but I'd like to have a couple of each gender one day."

"I've always wanted kids," she said with a wistful sigh. "When I'm older."

He gave her a look that just about melted the heels off her pumps. "That could be arranged, I'm sure," he said in a husky tone.

Wendy clenched her hands in her lap and turned to look out the windshield instead of at his delectable face. "Would it bother you to have shared a woman with your brothers?"

He was quiet for a long time and when he answered, there was no playfulness in his tone. "No, I don't think it would if it was understood that from the wedding day on she'd be exclusively mine."

"That's good to know," she said.

Chapter Four

"You live there?" she whispered, completely awed by the house as Drake turned in to the huge circular driveway.

"Yep, that's home," he said.

Wendy whistled, her eyes as wide as saucers as the gate slid to one side and Drake drove onto the serpentine driveway and up toward the magnificent home. "What did your father do for a living?" she asked.

Drake shrugged. "He was into producing movies," he replied. "Our mom starred in most of them."

"And your mom is…?"

"Was," he said, sadness shadowing his eyes. "Beverly Delaney."

Wendy nearly choked as she drew in a gasp. Her mouth dropped open. "*The* Beverly Delaney?" she asked. "From the Gizelle movies?" She reached out and grabbed Drake's arm. "Oh my God! Your father was John Quinlan?"

He nodded. "That he was."

"I *loved* the Gizelle movies!" she said, sitting up straight in her seat. "I saw every one of them at least five times." She ticked off the titles on her fingers. "*Gizelle in Hawaii. Gizelle and the Veterinarian. Gizelle Goes To Paris. Gizelle and the—*"

"Okay, okay! Enough already!" he said, laughing and holding up his hand. "I'm fairly familiar with the flicks!"

"Oh my God," she said again. She jerked on his arm and it was good thing he'd braked to a stop or she might have caused him to wreck the car. "Kyle was the name of the character in the Hawaii movie. Drake was the name of the veterinarian and Lance was her boyfriend in the Paris movie!"

"Brennan was the leprechaun for the *Gizelle and the Wee Folk* flick," he said.

"You have another brother?"

"He died in the plane crash that killed Mom," he said, sobering. "He was only two at the time and they were flying back from Acapulco where she'd done her last movie."

"Oh Drake," she said, rubbing his arm. "I'm sorry."

"Not your fault," he said, and turned to look at her. "Let's go in, okay?"

The house was stunning with a wide vista of dark copper-colored Moroccan tile sweeping from the foyer all the way through to the great room at the back of the imposing structure. A wide expanse of windows overlooked a sumptuous outdoor pool and three patios—one enclosed, one covered and one open.

"This is unbelievable," she said, thinking of the house in Brentwood her dad had left her stepmother when he passed away. In comparison, her family home was a paltry shack compared to the Quinlan mansion.

With her hand in his, Drake led her up a truly magnificent curving staircase and to his room on the third floor. Beneath their feet, the carpet was so plush she felt as though her shoes were sinking into it. He opened a beautifully carved oaken door to give her a view that brought a gasp of shock from her lips and complete immobility.

Walking into Drake Quinlan's bedroom was like taking a stroll back in time. The walls were done in fieldstone with large exposed wooden beams overhead and cobblestones on the floor. Tapestries depicting jousts and Renaissance fairs adorned the walls alongside swords and battle-axes and crossbows. Torches hung in brackets along the walls and the windows were mullioned with heavy damask drapes hanging to one side and deep cushioned window seats beneath. The entire expanse of the bedchamber looked like a room from a medieval donjon. A magnificent brass bed with intricate scrolls, swirls and curves sat on the longest wall with soft hangings in black velvet fastened to the four posts. Thick, black fur sewn into a coverlet stretched across the mattress and vied with oversized pillows covered in zebra, black leopard and white ocelot patterns to draw the eye.

"The fur is fake," he said. "I was named after the vet, remember?"

Huge armoires flanked an ornate desk and leather-upholstered lyre chair. Two full sets of armor stood side by side wearing surcoats bearing the Quinlan and Delaney coats of arms. Banners rippled along a wall containing row after row of hardbound books.

"If ye look behind yon screen, wench, ye'll find a gift," he said in an accent that made tingles spread up and down her arms.

"Will I, now, milord?" she said.

"Be quick about it lest I find the need to take a hand to yer backside," he warned, one eyebrow arched.

Wendy hurried to the opulent carved screen inlaid with mother of pearl and complex marquetry that took her breath away. Behind it, she found a snowy-white chemise with drawstring top and sleeves and a brocade kirtle in a pale green color.

She smiled, stroking the softness of the kirtle and quickly began undressing, kicking her shoes as her fingers flew through the buttons of her blouse.

"What takes ye so long, wench?" Drake called out.

"I am hurrying, milord," she said, stripping down to her bare skin before pulling the chemise over her head.

"Best ye make haste for my sword needs sheathing," he said.

Her lord and master was lying on his side on his sumptuous bed. The tawny bare skin of his broad chest with the thick mat of dark curls that stretched from well-turned shoulder to the tiger line that disappeared beneath his navel, beckoned to her. With one leg bent, his muscular arm concealing the brazen treasure at his thighs, he looked every inch the laird of his domain.

"What are your wishes, milord?" she asked, drawing near on her bare feet, her eyes cast down.

"Fetch me a flagon of yon ale," he ordered, nudging his chin toward a table across the room.

Padding over to the table, she was surprised at the coldness of the metal vessel as she lifted the handle and poured him a tankard of the brew. She brought it to the bed and held it out to him.

He swiped the tankard from her—sloshing the amber beverage on his naked chest—and took a healthy drink. Handing it back to her, he looked down at the trickle of ale running through his chest hairs then gave her an arch look.

Setting the tankard on his bedside table, she hiked up the skirt of her chemise and climbed onto his bed. Without hesitation, she leaned down to flick her tongue along the spilled brew.

"Make sure ye get it all, wench," Drake said, threading his fingers through her hair.

"Aye, milord," she whispered against his belly button. Dipping her tongue into the deep indention, she heard him draw in a wavering breath and slid her hand between his legs to cup him.

"Did it run down there as well?" he asked.

"Aye, it did, milord," she said, using her elbow to push his leg aside so he would lie flat on his back.

"Well, we can't have that now, can we?"

"Nay, milord," she agreed, and flicked her tongue along his burgeoning length, lapping at the head and underside of his stiff cock.

One moment she was about to take him into her mouth and the next his hands were on her shoulders and he was flipping her so she was lying on her back, his hard body pressed halfway across hers, one muscular leg prying hers apart.

"I've never cared for such folderol," he said, and ripped at the brocade bodice, tearing at the laces until he had it open. Dragging the chemise down below her breasts, he took her nipple between his lips and suckled her.

"Aye, milord," she said, burying her hands in his thick dark hair. "Take what you wish from me."

His hands were all over her—ripping fabric, tossing it aside, plucking at her straining flesh, entering her hot crevice to explore with strong, sure fingers. He claimed her mouth and dueled with her tongue, tasting the honey of her lips before trailing kisses to each breast to lap at her nipples. Traveling farther down her lush curves, he placed gentle kisses on her flesh, flicked the tip of his tongue into her navel and scooted down until he could grab her hips and lift her up for his greedy mouth to devour.

"Milord!" she cried out as his tongue slid into her warm channel. His hands were holding her folds apart as he lapped at her, suckled, licked and nibbled his way beneath the crisp triangle at the junction of her thighs.

He pulled her legs up over his shoulders and made a feast of the warm juices that flowed freely from her folds. When he had the full taste of her on his lips, in his mouth, he moved up the bed—pushing her thighs tight to her breasts—and slanted a heady kiss upon her that made her toes curl.

Open to him, she could feel the stab of his heavy shaft pressing against her ass and she wriggled beneath him in invitation, seeking to place her aching channel at the prow of his fleshy vessel.

Drake lifted his head and looked down into her lust-glazed eyes. "Ye want me, wench?" he asked, moving his hips so his cock slid back and forth along the cleft of her ass.

"Aye, milord. I want you bad!" she replied.

"Tell me how you want it then," he demanded.

"In me, milord," she said through clenched teeth. "In me hard and wet and deep!"

He laughed and moved so he could unerringly thrust that hot rod deep inside her, making her cry out with the sheer pleasure of it entering her to the hilt. He held it there—in as far as her wet channel would allow—as it throbbed and oozed salty juices into her.

"Are ye mine, wench?" he asked, his eyes holding hers.

"For as long as you want me," she said.

Drake Quinlan tilted his head slightly to one side. "And if I say I want you for as long as we both shall live?" he questioned. "As mine and mine alone?"

She tucked her lower lip between her teeth, staring up at him with her heart in her blue eyes. "What are you asking?"

"I am asking you..." He stopped and shook his head. "No, I want to have you telling our children their father proposed while he was fucking their mother."

Wendy gasped. Surely he didn't mean what he was implying. She opened her mouth to question him but he began moving so purposefully, so strongly inside her, every thought fled her head.

"Love me, Wendy," he said as he thrust hard into her. "Love me as I have come to love you. I want you to be my wife."

It had to be said and though it put a damper on the tenderness they were sharing at that moment, she had to get it out in the open.

"What about Kyle and Lance?" she asked. "A few years from now..."

"They'll have to find playmates of their own," he said firmly.

"But..."

"But nothing. My brothers know how I feel about you—they've known for a while now—and they'll support us. Don't worry about it, sweetie."

She toyed with the hair on his chest. "Are you sure?"

"As sure as I am lying here," he said.

"I told you I know everything about you, Wendyline Lenore Cole," he stated. "And I know more than anything you've always wanted to act." He ran his thumb over her lower lip. "We've still got contacts in Hollywood and if you wouldn't mind starting at the bottom in Ray Nixon's acting class—"

"Ray Nixon? The Ray Nixon of the Actor's Emporium?" she gasped, her eyes widening. "Drake! You can't be serious! Do you realize what it takes to get into one of his classes?"

Drake grinned. "I know he's my godfather and that I'm holding his prized Lamborghini hostage until he agrees to enroll you in his school."

"You can't do that!" she said, sitting up and twisting around to stare at him with shock. "He'll hate me right off the bat and—"

"He has seen your transcripts from UCLA and he was suitably impressed. I'm sure Lance has talked you up to him every day since you've been at the shop."

"That's where Lance goes to class?"

He nodded. "And I hear he's fairly good."

Wendy was so excited, she was trembling. She put her hands over her face. "Oh Drake, this isn't happening."

"Aye, it is, wench," he said, pulling her down beside him again. He snuggled her against his side. "Dreams really do come true, you know."

"Not mine," she said as tears filled her eyes. "Mine never have."

"Well, it's time they did," he said. He stroked her hair back from her forehead. "Did I ever tell you how Kyle and I came to own the shop?"

She shook her head, afraid she'd cry if she spoke.

"When we were kids, we used to take things apart just to see how they worked and to see if we could put them back together again," he said, and laughed. "I don't remember how many times we got our asses whipped for tearing something up and then not being able to make it work afterward. When we screwed up his dune buggy, Dad got so disgusted with us he finally went out and bought an old '56 Chevy Bel-Air. He had a little garage built at the back of the property and equipped it with everything budding mechanics would need. We spent hour after hour out there just reveling in taking the engine apart."

He sighed.

"The trouble was, we couldn't put everything back in that had come out so Dad hired a master mechanic to come out and teach us. We were in our glory. Mom hated every minute of it because we'd come in covered in grease and grime and smelling of oil."

"Where was Lance?" she asked, getting into the story.

"He was about nine, I think, and we would have to lock him up in the closet to keep him from annoying us. All he was interested in was playing pirate. Since Kyle had gone through his cowboy years and I'd gone through my medieval knight period, we knew he'd eventually settle down and come out to learn what we were learning. He's never taken to it as Kyle and I have but he can wield a pretty mean ratchet if push comes to shove."

"Did your father buy you the shop?"

"God, no!" he laughed. "Whatever we wanted, we had to earn for ourselves. Our parents were strict about that. Both of them had grown up poor and they valued three things—honesty, loyalty and hard work. None of us ever got one dime of allowance we didn't earn. We had paper routes and worked at supermarkets or fast-food places, raked yards, washed cars, did odd jobs. We had to maintain an A average in school. For Kyle that was easy but Lance and I had to work at it. Nevertheless, we all earned scholarships to college but we worked our way through doing automotive work for our fellow students in that little garage out back. Every penny we could spare went into savings. Dad had said he'd match us dollar for dollar for every one we saved if we were serious about having our own automotive shop." He shook his head. "I don't think either he or Mom thought we'd stick to it and see the dream to fruition. The day we opened that shop, we had customers waiting in line thanks to Dad."

"Did you graduate from college?" she asked.

"I have a master's in mechanical engineering and Kyle has his in business admin. Lance is working on his BA."

"The shop is certainly operating in the black," she said.

"Mom and Dad sent customers to us when we opened, but if we hadn't been good at what we do, they wouldn't have kept coming back and we wouldn't have the elite clientele we have today."

Elite, Wendy thought, was an understatement. Their list of customers read like a Who's Who in Hollywood and they had many stellar clients from overseas who came in when they were in the States to have their cars worked on by Quinlan Automotive.

"That is a wonderful story, Drake, but what if people find out about our little games? Won't someone…?"

"Sweetie," he said, laying a finger over her lips. "This is Hollywood. Do you have any idea how many games are being played at this very moment and just how bizarre and truly pornographic some of those games are?" He grinned. "And no one is going to find out."

"The guys in the back know," she said, blushing.

"Steve has been with us since the first week we opened. Todd and Kurt each have five years invested in Quinlan Automotive. Do you think they'd risk losing such cushy jobs where they meet hot-pantied ingénues and horny fading actresses to tell someone what their bosses do in their spare time?"

"Well, maybe not but—"

"Enough, wench!" he said, his eyebrows drawing together. "Ye do not want to irritate the laird lest he punish ye."

Wendy lifted her chin. "If the laird wishes to join with his lady, he had best be putting knee to carpet and asking her in a right and proper way, I'm thinking!"

Drake's eyebrows shot up. "Then you'll marry me?"

She shook her head, folded her arms over her naked breasts and turned her head to one side with a sniff. "Not without the proper asking, I won't."

A slow smile lit the handsome features of Drake Quinlan and he slid off the bed, going to one knee, reaching out to take her hand in his. "Milady," he said, his free hand to his heart. "Would ye do me the honor of becoming my bride?"

Wendy put a finger to her chin. "Well, now. I will have to think on that one, milord."

"Milady, please," he whined. "I shan't live another day if ye refuse me."

She pretended to think. "But ye've no ring to do the binding," she said. "How can ye expect…?"

Drake leaned over and opened the drawer of his nightstand, bringing out a small black velvet box. He let go of her hand just long enough to open the box to reveal a beautiful emerald-cut three-carat yellow diamond.

Her eyes misting, she looked into his devastatingly handsome face. "You had this planned," she accused with a breaking voice.

"For weeks now," he said. "Wendy, will you marry me?"

Epilogue

ꙮ

They were running across the meadow with their skirts hiked up to allow them to sprint faster. Though they weren't laughing, their eyes were bright and happy and filled with expectation.

"Hurry, Penelope," Darcy Quinlan encouraged the tiny blonde woman who was lagging behind. "They are gaining on us!"

"I'm moving as fast as I can, Prudence," Gayle Quinlan grumbled. "My slipper has broken its lace."

In the lead, Wendy glanced back up the hill and saw the three imposing men standing with their legs spread, arms akimbo, watching them. She bent forward with her hands on her knees, panting. "If you two don't wish to be ravished, you'd best get a move on, ladies."

"But I like being ravished, Patience," Gayle exclaimed with a toss of her honey blonde curls. She adjusted her crimson velvet gown.

"You're not supposed to enjoy it," Darcy snapped. She tugged at the skirt of muslin dress. "You are supposed to fight them tooth and nail or they'll pout for the rest of the afternoon."

"And there is nothing worse than a pouting black knight," Wendy complained. She frowned at a tear in her chemise that had become tangled in a bramble.

"Or a moping cowboy," Darcy added.

"Ah, but a glowering pirate is just so appealing," Gayle said. She looked up at the hill where the men were still standing. "Just look at him in that black shirt and those leather pants. He is so sexy and with that black eye patch and black bandana tied around his head..."

"Uh-oh," Darcy said. "Here they come!"

Wendy straightened up and watched her beloved husband skidding down the hill in his black chausses and elegant black tabard with his family's coat of arms emblazoned on the front. Beside him, the eldest Quinlan brother was also in black but the six-shooter on his hip and the Stetson on his head called attention to his cherished fantasy.

"Run, sisters!" Darcy said, laughing.

Taking out across the meadow the three women—each in the costume of their era—separated, leading their husbands on different paths to the little cottages that had become their homes away from home when they vacationed together. It was toward the thatched hut Wendy—or Patience as Sir Drake called her—ran. The little stone cottage was Penelope-Gayle's destination and the log cabin with its whitewashed corral beckoned to Darcy—or Prudence, gunslinger Kyle's schoolmarm.

As they ran inside the thatched hut with its goose-down bed covered in soft brown fur, Wendy shut the door and stood waiting for her knight to kick his way in to her. She tugged at the neckline of her chemise until it was down over her shoulders and flicked out her tongue to lick her lips. She was trembling with excitement, alive with longing for her husband of four years, as happy as her two sisters-in-law who had each come in turn to replace her as the Extraordinary Receptionist at Quinlan Automotive.

"Ho, wench! Where be ye?"

The sound of his voice never failed to send tremors of sheer lust through Wendy. As soon as his booted foot hit the poor door dead center and it flew open, she could feel her juices begin to flow.

"Thought you could escape me, did ye?" he asked as he came into the room and slammed the door shut behind him.

"Milord, I beseech ye!" she said, clasping her hands together. "Be mindful of me poor body. I've a casting call on morrow."

The black knight put his hands on his hips. "Think ye such will tame this beast, wench?"

"It had best, milord," she said, one eyebrow crooked. "We're talking Spielberg here."

Her knight threw back his hood to reveal his dark hair. "Then best ye be satisfying this laird's beastly needs lest he do harm to yon soft white flesh."

Swishing her skirts as she came to him, she thrust out her soft pink lips. "What say ye, milord? Ye wish this naïve damsel to be sinning with ye?"

He lifted his foot. "Remove me boots, wench, and we'll discuss the matter."

Sinking to her knees, Wendy tugged off his soft leather boots and knelt there looking up at him, her heart in her eyes.

The hooded tabard was pulled over his head and the chausses were unlaced to fall at his feet. Linen braes were the only thing between the knight and his intended target. He stepped out of the chausses and kicked them to one side before putting his hand to the laces of his braes.

"Milord," she gasped upon seeing the jutting evidence of his hard arousal. "What a big weapon you have."

One eyebrow lifted. "Aye, wench. The better to pierce your maidenhead," he said in an evil voice.

Putting the back of her hand to her forehead, Wendy said, "Woe is me. I am about to be ruined."

"Aye, that ye are," he said, and reached down to take her shoulders and drag her up against him. "And with much deep thrusting, I'll warrant."

Slashing his mouth across hers, he took her lips with heated fierceness, his tongue flicking across hers as he flattened her breasts to his hard chest. His lips left hers to trail kisses over her cheek and down the column of her neck, one strong leg planted firmly between her chemise-clad thighs.

"Ah, wench, but ye be a handful," he said as he lowered her chemise and molded his mouth around her nipple.

"And ye be a randy warrior, I'm thinking," she said, threaded her fingers through his dark hair.

He backed her up to the bed—not once relinquishing his attachment to her lush breast—then put his hands to her waist and lifted her onto the mattress. Shoving up the skirt of her chemise, he pressed his hand to her bare cleft.

"Nay, milord! 'Tis a virgin I am!" she said, batting at his hand.

"'Twill not be so much longer," he said, and used his knees to spread her legs wide for his invasion.

"Poor lass!" she said, her hand once more to her forehead.

Her knight laughed evilly and with one well-timed and manly thrust, he was inside her to the hilt, his weapon throbbing in her soft, moist sheath.

"I am ruined!" she said, wrapping her long legs around his waist. "Woe is me."

Drake chuckled. "Ham," he labeled her as he lifted himself up to look into her beautiful eyes.

"I think of myself more as a tart," she said, and gave him a saucy wink.

"Aye, that ye be," he said. "Quinlan's insatiable little tart."

His strokes were long and deep as he filled her. The deep affection they had found and that had continued to grow over the years made their love play so much more wondrous. When they came, it was to an echo of her quivering and his pulsing and it brought hisses of sweet pleasure from them both.

Spent, he collapsed atop her with his lips at the center of her chest.

"I love you," he whispered.

"No more than I love you," she returned.

He fell asleep for just a while and when he woke, his lady wife was sitting astride him, her pert breasts in both hands.

"Be ye thirsty, milord?" she inquired sweetly.

"Aye, wench," he said with a yawn. "What have ye for your laird to drink?"

She bent over him. "Mother's milk," she teased. "Take a taste of me wares, milord."

His lips closed over her nipple and he drew upon the puckered flesh even as he slid his hand down between them to finger the pearl of her clit.

"Och, ain't that a delicious feeling," she proclaimed, wriggling against him.

He withdrew his hand, took hold of her hips and flipped her over so he was poised above her. "I've created a harlot," he said on a long sigh.

"That you have, milord," she said, arching her hips up to meet him.

* * * * *

Back at the mansion these gamers called their vacation home, a brace of little boys—one belonging to Kyle and the other to Drake—looked at one another and frowned. The DVD player lay in pieces at their little feet.

"I can't put it back together," six-year-old Dallas complained.

"That's okay," three-year-old Kiernan said. "Daddy can fix anything. Won't he, Letty?"

Letty Cavanaugh, the boy's nanny, smiled as she diapered Lance and Gayle's newborn baby boy Brent. "That he will when he comes in from playing," she said, a knowing twinkle gleaming in her cornflower blue eyes since Gayle was her sister and the two had no secrets.

"I don't know why we can't play with Mommy and Daddy and our aunts and uncles," Dallas complained.

Kyle's eight-year-old daughter Jory rolled her eyes as she looked up from her coloring book. "Because grownups play games we can't," she declared.

"Like what?" Kiernan asked.

Jory returned to coloring. "I don't know but it takes them all day to play their silly game."

Letty bit her lip to keep from laughing and picked baby Brent up to feed him his bottle.

"But what do they play, Jory?" Kiernan insisted.

"Do you know, Letty?" Jory asked the nanny.

"Tennis," Letty said, spying a racket across the room. "Grownups play tennis."

"Eeewww," the children said in unison.

"You'll like playing tennis when you're grown up," Letty said. Brent was in her lap, sucking his bottle and she reached for her glass of soda.

"Not if I have to play with girls," Kiernan pronounced.

"They're not so bad," Dallas told his cousin.

Hero-worship had already set in for Kiernan and if his older cousin said girls weren't so bad, he'd take his word for it. "Well," he said, "I guess if they'll do just what we tell them to while we're playing, it'll be okay."

Letty nearly choked on her soda.

* * * * *

Twenty years later, Maria Sanchez walked into the Quinlan Automotive shop to apply for the *Extraordinary Receptionist Wanted* job on the sign. Her dark eyes met those of the shop's owner and she smiled saucily. "I'd like to apply for the job," she said.

Dallas Quinlan grinned. "Let's go into the office and talk about it."

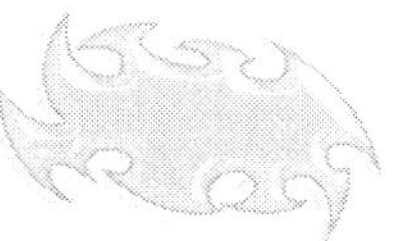

Also by Charlotte Boyett-Compo

Ellora's Cavemen: Dreams of the Oasis IV (*anthology*)

Ellora's Cavemen: Legendary Tails I (*anthology*)

Fated Mates (*anthology*)

Ghost Wind

HardWind

Passion's Mistral

Shades of the Wind

WesternWind: Prime Reaper

WesternWind: Reaper's Revenge

WesternWind: Tears of the Reaper

WesternWind: WyndRiver Sinner

WindVerse: Ardor's Leveche

WindVerse: Hunger's Harmattan

WindVerse: Phantom of the Wind

WindVerse: Pleasure's Foehn

WindVerse: Prisoners of the Wind

WindWorld: Desire's Sirocco

WindWorld: Longing's Levant

WindWorld: Lucien's Khamsin

WindWorld: Rapture's Etesian

About the Author

ꟷ

Charlee is the author of over thirty books. Married 40 years to her high school sweetheart, Tom, she is the mother of two grown sons, Pete and Mike, and the proud grandmother of Preston Alexander and Victoria Ashley. She is the willing house slave to five demanding felines who are holding her hostage in her home and only allowing her to leave in order to purchase food for them. A native of Sarasota, Florida, she grew up in Colquitt and Albany, Georgia, and now lives in the Midwest.

Charlotte welcomes comments from readers. You can find her website and email address on her author bio page at www.ellorascave.com.

Tell Us What You Think

We appreciate hearing reader opinions about our books. You can email us at Comments@EllorasCave.com.

CHASING THE DRAGON

By Megan Kerans

Chapter One

ജ

Cad slammed his foot into his attacker's stomach, launching the man into a hovercart. Contraband silks and sugar candies rained over the broken asphalt. Fire seared through his veins.

His two remaining opponents drew their power swords and charged.

Their blades screeched as the electrified metal clashed against his weapon. The force of the double blow knocked Cad to one knee, but he maintained his defensive position.

"We don't want you, just your fingerprint and your money." The squat, genetically muscled man on his right grunted.

"Try and I'll cut off your hands," Cad growled. Every Solar Credit to his name he'd earned with his blood. If the thieves wanted his wealth, they'd pay the same price.

Twin diamond-encrusted blades screeched as they crossed. Their edges loomed inches from Cad's nose. Pain shot through his arms. Still he held. A dragon's will did not falter. He wouldn't die in one of Shangcau's filthy back alleys. He focused his strength and surged upward with a roar.

The force knocked his enemies backward.

"Forgive the intrusion, Raj Cad." Yinlo's tall form breached the city hologram.

Before he could ask why, his assailants launched another offensive. "*Cao*!" He cursed his lapse in focus and dodged a slash aimed at his chest.

Enough.

He brought his left hand to the hilt of his sword, tightened his grip and swung. The blade arced through the air and severed his opponents' heads.

Immediately, the virtual star-toucher buildings vanished. The uneven, gray cave walls of Cad's training room reappeared. He powered off his weapon. Two hours of intense combat simulation and still his blood blazed. "Do I pay you well, Yinlo?"

"Yes, very." The narrow-faced man nodded.

"Loyal 'til my last Solar Credit." *Like all my employees.* "What is my one rule?"

Yinlo's neck sank into the mandarin collar of his red shirt. "Never disturb you when you're training."

Cad glared. As he scooped his black silk robe off the floor, sweat dripped from the ends of his long dark hair. The drops fell and plopped onto the bamboo planks.

Yinlo swallowed. "A United Planetary Federation ship requests permission to dock."

The fury of past wrongs ignited in his stomach. He'd fought and killed for the UPF. In return, they massacred his fellow Rajs. He'd been damn lucky he and his crop of Dragon's Eyes flowers had survived. His fingers squeezed his sword's grip. Metal dug into his flesh. "Request denied," he ground out and headed toward his personal quarters.

"Captain Ahnat demands an audience with The Dragon."

Cad burst into laughter as he slid open the paper screen leading to his private quarters. "Did he threaten to end my worthless life and destroy my miserable little rock?"

"No."

At least this one had a brain. The firepower of an entire starfleet couldn't penetrate ten thousand meters of Shilin rock. "Warn the captain, then fire a shot across the ship's nose."

"I told her you would not see her."

"Her?" Cad glanced back over his shoulder. So, the UPF had sent a female officer this time. "When you cannot dig with a shovel, use your hands," he murmured. Dangerous curiosity around the type of woman who'd dare enter a dragon's lair and her reasons wove through his thoughts. Whatever she wanted, it wasn't him.

Memories of the Shepard's Temple Orphanage rose. He'd buried his past and all the acrid seed had borne was bitter fruit. He gripped the screen's frame until his knuckles turned the same pale shade as the wood. The opportunity to teach the UPF humility at the feet of a dragon had arrived. "Authorize the landing. I will meet with the captain—*alone*."

Yinlo bowed and backed out the black carved doors.

"Warn her any man who leaves her ship without my permission will be shot." He blew a hot breath from his lungs.

In his chambers, a thick veil of steam from his sunken stone bath greeted him.

Saree bowed and closed the vent to the underground hot spring. "Would you like assistance, Raj Cad?" The auburn-haired girl reached for the tie on her amber robe.

"No. You know the rules." *And are far too young.*

"You pay other women to come to your bed."

He leveled a hard stare to frighten the girl for good. "If you want to leave Shilin, join me," he growled.

"No, you pay too well." She scurried out of the room.

Alone, Cad shed his pants. He stepped into the hot water and hissed. Little fool. Another man would take her regardless of an offer, but he couldn't. The Raj code forbade acceptance of anything not deserved. Not once had Cad ever been deemed worthy of trust or love.

He scoured his skin. The UPF had taught him to battle like a merciless dragon. Today, he'd give them a taste of their own lesson.

* * * * *

Captain Jade Ahnat sat naked behind the desk in her cabin. Columns of blue code scrolled across her work surface's embedded computer screen. The cool sterilized air prickled her skin as she gazed upon her virtual painting gallery. Vivid purple flower petals and warm yellow sunrays popped from the sea of white walls and fixtures.

How did ridges of built-up paint feel? She rubbed her fingertips on the cold desktop.

Pppppffffffffftttttt. Pppppffffffffftttttt.

Jade yanked her hand back. The furniture's built-in anti-contamination system sprayed disinfectant over the area she'd touched. If UPF scientists could eliminate all germs down to the common cold, why couldn't they prevent canvas from deteriorating and breeding bacteria?

"Five minutes until landing, ma'am." Her pilot's voice rumbled over the comm system.

Damn. "I'll be there in three, Mr. Rivers."

She jumped up and grabbed a new antibacterial suit. It never failed, just when her skin began to breathe. She donned the stiff, white garment and closed the portrait gallery.

No time for art. She had a dragon to chase. Thousands of lives, including her sister Dr. Ivory Ahnat's, depended on her. She blinked back her tears. Only Dragon's Eyes seeds could cure the Dark Sickness.

Her superiors called for her to stop a pandemic. Her family expected her to secure a general's promotion and continue the Ahnat military tradition. No one had ever asked what she wanted. She snapped her titanium boot heels against the metal floor as she strode toward the steering bridge.

"Set her down, Mr. Rivers," she ordered and took her place in the captain's chair.

Her young four-member control crew hunched over their blue instrument screens and went to work. The *Galleyhawk* swung a path between Shilin's jagged, gray snow-capped peaks. She held her breath until the runners touched down on the landing platform. The ground descended between the ominous spires like a slow slide through a dragon's teeth and into its belly. She swallowed her apprehension.

"Attention on deck." She rose as the exterior pressure locks popped. "Everyone will remain on board. Anyone in violation who survives Raj Cad's men, I'll shoot myself." She didn't wait for a response before exiting the steering bridge with Dalton Rivers at her stern.

"You should be captain," she said to the tall, handsome man over the hiss of the hatch release.

"Not without a miracle." Dalton shrugged. "Jade."

She paused on the gangramp. Concern darkened her long-time friend's brown eyes.

"Rajs are masters of the mental as well as physical."

"Don't worry, I'm prepared to speak his language." She slipped a thin, silver Solar Credit transfer manager from her pocket and forced a smile.

* * * * *

A tall man in red pants and a tunic appeared on the dock. "I am Yinlo. Follow me, Captain."

With no alternative, she fell in step. The air in the long, gray tunnels thickened with each turn. She ran her tongue along the suddenly moist roof of her mouth. The knowledge a thousand forms of bacteria had entered her lungs didn't diminish the pleasant sensation.

Yinlo rounded a corner and pointed to a pair of enormous, black double doors carved with savage serpentine dragons. "If you harm Raj Cad, you will not leave Shilin alive." Promise burned in his hard, dark eyes.

Jade caught herself before she stepped back. Absolute devotion from employees was unknown. What did a man do to inspire such loyalty? She forced herself to relax. "I only wish to bargain."

Yinlo nodded. "The Dragon is waiting."

She flexed her fingers around the door's heavy metal ring and pushed. The bottom edge squealed as wood scraped over stone.

She stepped inside the dark chamber. A trickle of sweat ran down her spine before her flightsuit vaporized the moisture. Sharp spicy smoke tinged with sweetness assaulted her nose. Had The Dragon been sampling his own crop?

As her eyes adjusted, the lengthy room came into focus. A long red-and-black floor pad led to a dais at the far end. Rounded lanterns threw small pools of golden light on colorful pillows in every shape and size. In their midst sat shiny, ornate urns, with eight thin hoses connected to a narrow pipe lying in the sculpted stone basin below.

"Curious."

She whirled at the deep, masculine voice from the opposite end of the chamber.

"Did you come for *chui lung*?"

"The only Dragon I'm *chasing* is you." She strained to see the man, but the soft light from behind the throne made him invisible.

The slide of a metal blade echoed in the dark.

Jade's pulse quickened. "I'm here to talk. I mean you or your crops no harm."

A hard chuckle sent goose bumps over her skin.

"You wouldn't succeed if you tried."

His arrogance reflected in his voice. Although he was right, she bristled. She strode down the aisle and stood at the smooth steps of the dais.

"While nothing would please me more than proving you wrong, it's not why I've come."

"Are you certain *nothing* else would satisfy you?"

His delicious rough voice carried erotic promises that curled around her like smoke. Warmth bathed her skin. Her flightsuit adjusted its temperature. But instead of cooling, her body heat increased. Her suit must have a malfunction. "I've come to purchase a sizeable amount of Dragon's Eyes seeds." She squinted into the darkness.

"No." The single word packed anger hotter than the blue flame of a comet's tail.

"I haven't made an offer." She struggled to keep her temper from her voice.

"You don't have the funds."

Jade's boots rapped against the marble steps. The hell if he'd dismissed her when thousands of lives were at stake. "How do you know?"

"Money can't buy everything." Bitterness replaced his sexy tone.

"I'm not leaving." She no sooner took a second step forward than an enormous, fierce shadow shot toward her. She jumped backed.

"Men have died for annoying a warprince."

Over a head taller and twice as wide as her own soldiers, Raj Cad made an awe-inspiring sight. Shiny black fabric, the same shade as his long hair, covered his muscular body. Her breath caught. Power and virility surrounded him and neither was related to the wicked blade in his right hand.

"I am not a man," she said.

The flicker deep in his ice blue eyes told her he'd noticed.

Her nerve endings tingled. "Nor do I have the luxury of cowardice."

As his gaze raked over her, his sensuous mouth pulled tight.

Her pulse quickened. Dark stubble peppered his tight jaw and sculpted cheeks. Despite his anger, she had the urge to touch his face. His raw untamed strength beckoned her long-suppressed curiosity. He was so different from UPF males who removed facial hair for hygiene.

"Make your offer." The edge of the sword gleamed.

"Eight million Solar Credits for five thousand units of Dragon's Eyes seeds."

"The going rate is two thousand credits per unit." He stepped closer. Black leather pants hung low on his narrow hips and clung to his muscular thighs.

"You're the only grower, you can adjust the rate." She willed herself to remain calm.

He leaned closer and dark hair fell against his cheek. "No."

Jade refused to give up. "I can give you eight million now and the promise to transfer an additional two million."

"You'll forgive me if I don't trust UPF promises." A smile curved his lips, but his blue eyes remained colder than space ice. "I warned you, Captain, I don't make deals with the UPF."

He turned toward the door behind the throne.

She couldn't let him leave. Ivory would die without Dragon's Eyes seeds. "Make a deal with me." She blurted out.

The Raj stopped and pivoted with slow lethal grace.

"Personally." She licked her lower lip.

"What can you offer I don't already have?"

Her mind raced. He had money and power. All she knew about Rajs were their extreme fighting skills and their demand for enemies' total submission. She swallowed. She had no choice. One life for many.

"I offer myself." She dropped to her knees and bowed her head to her chest.

As much as she wanted to observe his reaction, she kept her gaze focused on the floor. His black boots crossed her vision as he circled her. An invisible clamp tightened around her stomach. If he refused, she had nothing to barter.

"What do you gain that you're willing to submit to a Raj?"

She jerked as his warm breath gusted against her ear. If she lied, he'd know. "A-a general's promotion."

"And for career advancement you'd surrender your body." He trailed a single finger across her shoulder and down her spine.

A million tiny starbursts exploded beneath the gentle pressure. The fact she couldn't see him only increased her response.

"For a rank, you'd risk death?"

The cool edge of his sword rested against her neck.

She resisted the urge to swallow. The slightest movement and the blade would slice her skin. "To save my sister and thousands of innocent people from an agonizing death, I would."

Sweat slipped between her breasts. Gentle waves meant to slow her pulse vibrated through her flightsuit. They didn't help. How could she relax when one swing would end her life? She closed her eyes and waited. The buffet of her heart against her ribs echoed inside her head.

"The UPF's decision to waste soldiers' lives isn't my concern."

The pressure against her neck increased. Damn him. "This isn't a war," she shouted. "Innocent people are dying."

"How?"

The new thickness in his tone concerned her more than the warm trickle of blood against her collar. Maybe he had a heart? "An aggressive virus, the Dark Sickness. It blinds its victims, then slowly eats away their eyes followed by," she forced the words past her tight throat, "their organs until they die."

The taut muscles in his legs stiffened further.

"UPF technology and their sterile environment can't stop it?"

"Not without Dragon's Eyes seeds." She glanced toward the blade perched on her shoulder.

"Be certain you have no need to cross a bridge before you burn it," he murmured.

He wouldn't help. She clenched her fists. "Do you care for no one but yourself?"

"If I didn't, no one else would," came the cold reply. "When are you scheduled to return?"

"Three days." Her barrette popped and her long hair fell down her back. What was he doing? She frowned.

"I'll sell you Dragon's Eyes seeds." He sheathed his sword.

Jade's muscles almost collapsed with relief, but she willed herself to remain upright.

"The price is eight million Solar Credits and twenty-four hours of your complete submission."

This time, her gaze shot up to his blue eyes. Thick clouds of desire swirled in their icy depths. His proposition went against every UPF regulation. A flutter of excitement sent her stomach into orbit. Jade pressed her palms onto the cool floor. The idea of submitting to this powerful man and his tactile world thrilled her in a way she didn't understand.

"You're awfully quiet, Captain Ahnat."

A pair of thick, hard thighs entered her field of vision. Moisture slipped between her legs. She struggled against shifting. Had her flightsuit malfunctioned?

"Or isn't a promotion enough reward to save the dying?"

"This isn't about my gain," she snapped. "I agree."

For one second, the Raj's eyes widened. "My men need twenty-four hours to load the cargo. During that time you are mine."

As fear and anticipation rocketed through her, Jade bit down on her lower lip.

"After confirmation of payment, you may leave."

She glanced up again. "I require personal verification of the contents before departure."

The corner of his mouth twitched. "You're shrewder than I expected, Captain."

"Jade." She cleared her throat.

Tiny creases crinkled the corner of his eyes.

"My name. Since we'll be on intimate terms, I thought you might want to know."

Hunger darkened his irises and penetrated her flightsuit.

Her nipples tightened. She still had a job to do. "I have one more requirement."

The Dragon crossed thick arms over his broad chest.

She hated how her position gave him a towering appearance like a great, dangerous beast. But, she didn't dare rise until bid. "I want to see your Dragon's Eyes plants and assure they're authentic."

The corners of his mouth sank. "Perhaps."

She had known the petition was a long shot. Her quads cramped. She shifted as best she could, without breaking her stance.

"Enough. Rise." He held out his hand.

Any other time she'd have refused, but the position had left her legs numb.

The Dragon ran his large hand down the length of her arm.

Immediately, her suit secreted a sheen of disinfectant.

"Did you feel anything?"

"Weight? Pressure?" She shook her head.

"You don't know if my skin is hot or cold, rough or soft." His sensuous lips curled at the garment.

"Unless I choose to learn the truth." Jade took a deep breath and reached for the release button on her left shoulder. A long, slow hiss of air jettisoned from the suit's bindings. She unfastened the catch at her neck, and peeled the material away from her skin until she stood clad in only her knee-high white boots.

Chapter Two

ꟷ

Cad stared at Jade's pale skin blanketed in the lanterns' golden light. His cock hardened at the sight of her exposed flesh. She possessed a rare boldness. As much as he admired her courage, he recognized her move as one for control.

"I didn't tell you to undress." He traced her smooth, delicate clavicle with his index finger.

Her pink tongue slid over her full lower lip.

Tiny explosions detonated in his chest and sent a shower of sparks all the way to his balls. "I will tell you when, where and how."

A fracture of fear broke in her silver eyes, but a gleam of excitement eclipsed the emotion.

He stroked a small, firm breast. Her eyes drifted closed as he rubbed the pad of his thumb against her taut nipple. With each touch the pink bud tightened further. Later he'd enjoy sucking them between his teeth as he drove her mad with the flick of his tongue. But not until she learned who was in control.

He'd build her need one touch at time, until her flesh quivered, her juices flowed and she begged him to take her. A feral growl clawed its way up his throat. He'd make her wait until she understood the agony of being at another's mercy.

The fires of vengeance burned just below his skin. He pulled a long, slow breath into his lungs as he massaged Jade's soft breast. Without her flightsuit, her body's natural ripe musk flowed from her pores. Cad caressed her rib cage.

She shivered.

His eager cock wanted to take her, but years of self-control subdued the impulse. He stroked the generous curve of her hip until his palm rested on the firm globe of her ass.

Uncertain silver eyes never left him.

"So you remember who's in charge." He brought his hand down against her skin with a sharp crack.

"Ouch." She rubbed her backside and glared.

"You do not act unless I tell you." He slapped the opposite cheek, careful to temper his strength. A light red flush spread over the area.

"Does everyone always do what you say?" Her breath quickened.

Anger, indignation and humility were his plan for her, not excitement. "Enough talk," he growled.

Cad yanked open his black, silk robe and stripped off his pants. "Take off your boots." He sat on the hard throne while she complied.

A pink hue spread down her neck to the tips of her breasts.

"Get down on your knees."

"You're kidding?" She let out a nervous laugh.

"No."

"Why?" She crossed her arms over her breasts.

He stared into twin swirls of liquid silver. "One, you want your Dragon's Eyes seeds. Two, you gave your word. And three," his voice dropped, "because deep down you want to."

A gasp tore from her lips.

Questions. Curiosity. The search for authenticity. He traveled the same journey and understood her quest for a life outside others' limitations. "You live in a cold, sterile world, where everyone is the same, and you hate it." The uneven rise and fall of her breasts confirmed his suspicions. "You want more."

Tremors shook her knees as she approached, her long, lean body gloriously naked.

His cock hardened at the roll of hips and how her breasts followed the same hypnotic sway. "You want to feel."

"Yes," she whispered.

"Everything they told you that was wrong, you want to know the reasons why." Emotions played over her delicate face as clear as a viewscreen. Astonishment widened her eyes while desire pushed down her thick-lashed lids. His balls tightened.

"Every day is about everyone else. Your crew. Their safety. Setting a good example." He crooked a finger and beckoned her closer.

"You're right." She swallowed and sank to her knees. "But even if you didn't have Dragon's Eyes seeds, I'd still want to know."

Cad let the lie pass. He had a beautiful woman with her full, pretty lips inches from his cock. The thought of her hot, wet mouth closed around his shaft and sucking him off almost made him come.

Jade's fingers shook as she stroked the tops of his thighs.

The light touch sent ripples down his calves. He closed his eyes and groaned.

Straight blonde hair fell past her shoulders. He twined the smooth strands through his fingers. Unlike most UPF women, she'd kept her hair long. A small expression of individuality in a homogenous world. She arched her neck as he combed through the soft strands. "Silk," he murmured.

Jade lowered her lips to his inner thigh.

Shallow quakes whipped through his muscles. Cad gripped the carved dragon armrests and wait for her next move.

A short row of light kisses up his thigh followed by a flick of her hot tongue brought her to the thick head of his cock.

His hips twitched as he waited for her to swallow him.

"Wait." She smiled and pulled back. "You didn't order me."

Cad's arms shot forward and he grasped her chin between his thumb and forefinger. "Do you want me to say, *Suck my cock*?" he snarled. "Does talking dirty excite you?" By the slight flush of her cheeks, he could tell he'd hit on another truth. "Or is it pushing my anger and the thrill of knowing I can kill you."

"No!" Fear flashed in her eyes. She tried to shake her head, but he held her head tight.

Before him was the humiliation and fear he'd wanted. But the thrill of vindication remained elusive. A lifetime of emptiness bored into his chest.

"I'm not the UPF." She swallowed. "Hurting me won't do anything to them." Tears pooled in the bottom of her eyes.

Cad had never felt more like shit. He should want her to fear him, but he didn't. And damned if he could figure out why. "Then do not test me." He released her chin and blew out a breath.

She sat back on her heels. "You don't really want to hurt me."

"I could." He leaned his head back against the carved ridges of his throne. One twist of her neck and…

"Not the same." Her shoulders lowered.

Warm breath gusted against his inner thigh.

He stroked the outer curve of her breasts, then along the smooth rounded underside and finally up the inner slope. They were perfect, firm yet pliable enough to mold to the shape of his palms.

Ten tiny nails dug into the tops of his legs. Her spine arched and thrust her breasts further into his grasp. She was beautiful with her lips half parted in an endless silent moan.

"Do you like this?" he asked as he squeezed.

She nodded.

"Tell me," he whispered.

"I like it." She swallowed. "I like the feel of your rough hands all over my skin."

He pinched each nipple and rolled the taut points between his fingers.

A small cry flew from her mouth. Her bottom squirmed against the back of her calves.

Damn, she was sensitive. The slightest contact and she reacted. He'd known too many women who had become numb after years without sensation, but the denial had the opposite effect on Jade.

"Touch my cock," he rasped. Sweat dripped down the back of his neck.

Limber fingers crept toward the plump head until she enfolded him in the palm of her hand.

Air fled from his lungs. Her grip loosened and tightened as she stroked him from base to tip. The varying pressure led him to the brink of release then pulled him back at the last moment. The hum of tension in his lower body grew louder.

The ends of her hair dusted over his cock like wisps of a teasing feather. She pressed her lips to his lower belly and laid a trail of kisses across his waist. Quivers rolled from left to right.

He rubbed the tightness pinching the back of her neck. He wanted her submission, but not her fear. "Have you ever taken a man's cock inside your mouth?"

Dark crimson flared in her cheeks. "It's not considered hygienic," she said in her most proper captain's voice.

He chuckled even as he throbbed for release. "Nothing good ever is." He stroked a finger down the length of her neck and the vale between her breasts.

Jade met his gaze.

"Do you have the strength to appease your curiosity?" He reversed his caress toward her throat.

Arousal hung in the heavy air and clouded her features.

"I want you to suck my cock, almost as much as you want to know the taste," he spoke softly.

The tip of her pink tongue flicked out.

"Open your mouth and swallow me. Use your lips and tongue to get me off." Cad gritted his teeth and waited. Years of battle had taught him patience over pain. Temptation held the key to her submission.

Tentatively, she lowered her head and flicked her tongue over the tip of his cock.

The wet heat was almost too much. White fire roared from the tip of his penis, scorched his belly and continued through his sternum. Need overflowed and pulled his hamstrings into taut cords.

She laved the flat of her tongue from the base of his cock to the head. The wet velvet caress made him even harder. He smoothed his hands over her shoulders.

At the same time, she massaged his balls, rolling the hard sac between her fingers. He let her magic touch overtake him as he had once allowed the hypnotic spicy smoke of Dragon's Eyes.

Pressure gathered behind his balls as she massaged the tight sac. With each roll between her fingers, they hardened to stone. "Jade." He gasped and flexed his hips upward.

She obliged and swallowed more of him. Her mouth sank down his length and then slid back to only his tip remained inside.

The force Cad had fought to contain exploded. He thrust deeper between her lips as the rush of cum surged from his balls, crested the length of his cock and poured onto Jade's tongue.

Body and mind fragmented. The cleansing fire of oblivion purged his painful thoughts. He gripped her shoulders. Band after band of ripples flowed through him. For as long as the sweet calm lasted, he'd remain in its coveted stillness.

As restlessness returned, he hooked his hands under Jade's arms and pulled her up. Never had a woman made him lose complete and total control. He didn't like the feeling.

"I guess the legends about dragons breathing fire are true." She smiled and licked her lips.

He bit back a groan as his spent cock sprang to life. She turned and took two steps before he caught her hand and pulled her back.

"Ahhhh," she cried and landed on his lap, her ass flush with his cock.

"I didn't give you permission to leave," he whispered in her ear and nipped at her lobe.

"You had your, uh, relief, and—"

"But you haven't." He reached around and once again cupped her breasts in his palms. Her head lolled against his shoulder.

"Yes," she breathed as he kneaded each firm globe.

Like a blanket, her soft warm flesh covered his. His fingers scattered the beads of sweat on her flat stomach and skimmed along the edge of the dark blonde curls between her legs.

Jade gasped. Her hips jerked off his lap and toward his hand.

The potent musk of her arousal filled his lungs. So thick and rich he could almost taste the flavor. "You want to come?"

She nodded.

He brushed his fingers over her pussy, enough pressure to induce sensation, but short of triggering relief. "I want to hear you say it."

She swallowed.

He stroked her thighs. This was how he'd show her who was in charge. He slid a finger along her folds, but refused to penetrate her. She squirmed, but he anticipated the move, and avoided giving further stimulation.

"Not until you say it." He coated his fingers with her smooth juices.

"I—" She gripped his wrist with her small hand. "I want to come," she blurted out. "Please. I—"

"Better." He nipped at her neck. "Now, tell me what you really want."

"I want to feel you inside me." Her eyes drifted closed. "Your hands touching my pussy."

Wetness pooled on his thighs where she rubbed against him. Despite his climax moments ago, his cock filled and lifted against her ass.

"And who do you want to come for?" He couldn't stop himself from pushing her boundaries. The woman had intense passion and emotions waiting to be set free. And he wanted to be the man who showed her the joy of freedom.

"You," she whimpered.

"Touch yourself. I want to watch your fingers sliding inside your pussy as you come for me."

Jade froze.

Cad wrapped his arm around her waist and held her in place before she bolted.

"I can't." The high pitch of panic punctuated her words. "I've never— Not with anyone looking at me."

The only way Cad knew to silence her was with his mouth. He took her lips and swallowed her protests. Her tongue tasted of salt and the tang of his cum.

With his right arm still wrapped around her waist, he threaded the fingers on his left hand through hers. "You can't know anyone else's passion until you know your own."

Jade sucked a shaky breath into her trembling body.

"Touch yourself for me." Cad waited for her to take the lead. His brief contact with her folds had revealed them wet and ready to part.

Finally, after what felt like light-years, she pushed their joined hands down her flat belly, and threaded their fingers through the curls above her thighs.

"Spread your legs," he whispered and used his knee to shift her knees apart. "That's right. Close your eyes and just feel."

Her torso relaxed against his chest.

The sight of her open and ready made him want to bury his cock inside. Her pussy shimmered with the slick tears of need.

She slid her fingers over her clit and against her opening.

Cad couldn't get enough of the thick plumpness of her folds, swollen and flushed a deep pink. Her heart and mind may not want him, but her body did.

Her eyes squeezed tight as she sucked shallow gasps of air through half parted lips.

"What does it feel like?"

"Incredible."

With anyone else, he hadn't cared, but with Jade the need to know bordered on compulsion. "Describe it to me."

"Like an itch. You scratch it and get a second of relief, but then the sensation comes back stronger. You need more."

"More what?" He groaned.

"Pressure. Harder."

He nipped at her lower lip. So, the captain wasn't adverse to a little rougher contact. The unexpected discovery sent a thousand new possibilities through his mind. "What else?"

"I'm-I'm thinking about your cock deep inside me."

"Like this." He guided one of her fingers along with his inside her pussy. Hot tight walls closed around him and contracted. His cock jerked at the knowledge of what lay ahead.

"More."

He helped her add a second digit and she squeezed tighter. The ache in his cock grew to a throb. But before he lost himself inside her, he wanted her submission, for her to know he could make her come in his hand if he chose.

In and out their fingers moved against her slick walls. Jade writhed on his lap, her back arching to take their fingers deeper. Before he lost all control, he reached up with his thumb and pressed the pad against the swollen bud of her clitoris. "Come for me now," he growled in her ear.

"Yes," she keened.

The sound echoed off the stone walls.

Her spine jerked as her pussy gripped and pulsed around their fingers. The sight of her lost in the ecstasy was more beautiful than any Dragon's Eyes vision he'd ever seen.

The buzz in Jade's nervous system dulled to a hum. Still, she didn't move. The blast of physical sensations shook her harder than a star's explosion. Textures and sounds sharpened. The sensitivity in the nerve endings throughout her skin heightened.

Her limbs lost their structure and melted against him. For once, she didn't care about germs or proper behavior for a UPF officer. And certainly not about any long-term effects.

His hands encircled her waist and set her on wobbly legs. She glanced over her shoulder as The Dragon rose behind her. He didn't say a word, but his earlier hunger had returned. The long cords of muscles in his neck stood out.

How could he be ready for more so soon? His carnal need should repulse her. Instead, anticipation coiled in her belly and sank lower. Her gaze flicked to his engorged cock jutting out from between thick quadriceps. A new surge of moisture flowed through her pussy.

He directed her down the dais steps and toward a pile of richly colored pillows.

"The inability to be satisfied is considered a weakness." She marveled at the scratchy crimson carpet beneath her feet so different than the dais' smooth, cool marble.

"Only to those without the strength of will to take what they want." His voice rumbled.

"A philosopher." The man was full of contradictions. One minute he acted cold and angry, the next he burned hot with passion. His pearls of wisdom were another inconsistency with his projected apathy.

She noticed a row of *real* paintings lined against the cave wall. How had she missed them earlier? Awe washed over her. Only once had she seen a piece of canvas artwork. Two of three paintings showed a sea of orange-red flowers with black bulbous centers. The center portrait contained mist-shrouded mountains. Dabs of thick paint stood out and made her want to run her fingers over the surface.

"Opium poppies. One of the plants crossbred to create Dragon's Eyes," he whispered in her ear.

His warm breath slipped over her skin. "They're beautiful."

"Their seeds too had the power to heal and to harm, before they were destroyed."

Like so many other things as she was quickly learning.

The Dragon set his hands on her shoulders and applied gentle pressure.

Jade sank to her knees in the sea of pillows. She turned to take him again in her mouth, but his body descended on top of hers. She flattened her hands against his chest. Muscle and sinew rippled beneath her palms. He slipped one hand beneath the small of her back, lifted her hips and slid a pillow underneath.

She glanced at his face, unsure of what he had in mind.

Everything she had experienced had been so intense she didn't know if she could handle more. At the same time, she craved the new sensations. Never again would she have this opportunity. Her muscles gave out.

"Are you going weak?" He dragged a single finger along the outside of her pussy.

"Maybe you're too full of yourself."

"You're right. I should fill you instead." With that, he thrust his cock inside.

Jade gasped as his long, thick penis breached her. Her pussy cried out as it stretched to accommodate his hard, filling presence. The head of his cock jutted close to her womb.

He held himself above her, bracing his weight on his muscular arms.

Before she could appreciate the long lines of his limbs, he moved inside her.

Each flex of his strong hips stroked his cock along her sensitive walls. A surge of unyielding hardness followed by retreat. The muscles in his buttocks constricted and stretched beneath her hands.

"Harder," she rasped, grasping his sweat-slickened torso and pulling him closer. She needed his strength against her skin, the coarse hair on his chest chafing her nipples, and most of all, the sensation of his cock inside her. Their combined musk and the spice of Dragon's Eyes filled her nose.

"Ask me to fuck you." He bit her neck.

Too far gone to think or worry about embarrassment, she complied. "Fuck me. Fuck me harder."

"Feel," he growled and stroked deeper.

Her hips rose to meet his driving pressure.

"Feel me inside you. Feel everything." With those words, he drew back until only the tip of his cock lay inside her and surged forward.

For one long second life stilled. She felt the heavy fullness of where their bodies joined. Cool satin beneath her hot, sweaty shoulders. The rough, solid muscles on top of her.

She pushed The Dragon's black locks back from his face. Bright pleasure and dark pain fragmented his blue eyes. The sweat of his effort rolled off his skin and onto hers. Explosions burst across her body, like a tiny, unprepared ship battered by an asteroid storm. Then, the culmination of every one of his tactile stimulations exploded at once.

Light flashed before her eyes. She clung to him as her inner muscles closed around his cock and pulsed. Jade screamed until there was no more air to force from her lungs. A jet of hot liquid seared through her channel as The Dragon shuddered and collapsed on top of her.

Chapter Three

ꟻ

Cad secured his rappelling harness. He glanced toward Jade, her back pressed against the cave wall. What had made him bring her here? Only a fool invited his enemy in twice. Heated anger, hotter than the thick clouds of steam from the field pit, rose in his veins.

Would Jade betray him too?

"*Cao*!" In his mind, she had gone from a UPF officer to Jade. The woman clouded his thought more than draughts of Dragon's Eyes smoke.

Jade's pale skin glowed in the black light. She tugged on the hem of the green silk tunic he'd given her.

After the past few hours, he knew she didn't have any concealed weapons hidden on her body. At least, none that would harm his crop. His cock jerked at the prospect of being buried deep inside her pussy again.

The pure want in her touch called to the desire to care for someone and be worthy of her care, and lo— He clenched his jaw. What did an unwanted orphan and warrior know of love?

He secured the cable line to the wall anchor. Jade had come to him for Dragon's Eyes seeds. Like everyone on Shilin, she was there for money and self-interest. He ignored the fact she needed his crop to save others' lives.

"Put this on." He tossed Jade a harness.

She caught the belt and eyed the field pit's shrouded rim. "This is the only way down?" She pressed further against the rough wall.

"Change your mind about looking into the Dragon's Eyes?" Now she'd prove all her talk about sacrificing for others was just that. Talk.

She rubbed her palms against her velvet trousers.

In an instant, he flashed back to how she had looked, with her thighs spread apart as their hands had moved in and out of her pussy. His cock fought the confines of his leather pants.

"Okay." She took a tentative step away from the wall. "Tell me how to do this."

"You don't have to go down." He was a bastard, a warrior, killer and a criminal, but he didn't lie.

"Yes, I do. I'd rather the agony of my own fear than the guilt of thousands of innocent people's deaths." With shaky fingers she gripped the buckle.

Few men outside Rajs had the courage to face their fears. Could Jade's unselfishness be genuine? Cad pondered the possibility as he instructed her on rappelling.

She dabbed at the perspiration already running down her neck. "I know the flowers need a dark moist climate, but how will I see what I'm doing?" A tiny tremor rocked her voice.

"From this." He took a palm-size ball from the pouch on his belt and twirled the sphere. Iridescent flames ignited within the globe.

Her eyes widened. "What is that?"

"A flaming pearl," he said as he dropped over the edge of the pit. "I'll go first."

She nodded.

"Start," he called as he passed the two-meter mark. The sheer, jagged gray walls bounced his voice through the cavern. He spun the fire pearl and waited. Had she given up?

As he prepared to ascend, Jade slipped over the edge. A smile tugged at his mouth. He battled back the feeling. A UPF captain in the middle of his illegal crop was nothing to be happy about. "Good. Don't look down."

She swiveled her head toward him and froze.

Cao!

"Concentrate on the rope," he barked. Millions of years of evolution and humans still persisted in staring in the direction they'd been told not to. She needed a distraction and at the moment sex wasn't an option. "What's your fascination with paintings?"

"An artist can take something beautiful," her voice shook, "and make it her own and share the beauty with others." She continued her downward progress as she spoke.

The passion in her voice mesmerized him. No one he'd known spoke with boundless love. An empty cavern yawned inside him. Just once, he wished someone could feel strong emotions toward him. Cad clenched his jaw and stared into the endless darkness below. Those wishes had died in the orphanage. Always, he'd been too tall, too short, too old, too young, too… He doused the memories. "Did you ever paint?"

"Virtual simulations, but it wasn't… It just didn't feel real," she panted.

"How would you know *real*? You can't have canvas, it's outlawed." And anything else that decomposed over time and bred bacteria. UPF fools. *Do not kill a river and bring drought because you fear deluge*. A lesson they never understood.

He unclipped the temperature monitor from his belt. Thirty-seven degrees Celsius and ninety-eight percent humidity. Perfect.

"Each year the highest-ranked academy student can choose any reward they want." She let out a long breath. "Usually the greenhorn slot on the top starcruiser. I got to paint, albeit in a full anti-contamination suit."

Cad bobbled the pearl. She might claim she wanted a general's rank, but her actions spoke the opposite. "A river cannot flow in two directions," he murmured.

The meteorology simulator thundered. The sudden jolt was a lot like Jade Ahnat, unexpected and unsettling. "I'd like—" To what? If he entered UPF territory to see her damn picture, he'd be killed. He stroked the rubbery blue-violet petals of a flower as he passed. Not even when he'd actually *chased the dragon* had his thoughts been so disjointed.

"Where's the painting now?" Meters of gray stone passed before she answered.

"Burned."

If not for the echo, he'd have missed her soft reply. Flames of rage swept through him.

"Canvas disintegrates and breeds bacteria." Her voice caught. "If it had to be destroyed, I wanted to do it."

UPF bastards. His admiration for Jade jumped. He plucked a dying pointed leaf from a bloom and crushed it. The small thorns sank into his palm.

Before he thought better, he unclipped his communicator. "Yinlo, find whatever paint, brushes and anything we have close to canvas."

Thunder rocked the pit as he reached the rocky floor. He set the flame pearl in a holder and unclipped his harness. A volatile gray sky roiled above the flower-filled ledges. Inside, his emotions churned with equal fervor.

"Stop," he shouted and undid Jade's rappelling line.

She stared at the ground a moment before a smile burst across her lips. "Thank you." She wrapped her arms around his neck and kissed his cheek.

He froze.

"You're a good man," she whispered.

No one referred to him as *good,* except as a fighter. An alien calm spread through his limbs. All his life he'd only known the burn of anger. What was happening? "I'm not good," he growled.

"You could have left me on the ledge." She stabbed a finger upward. "Why didn't you?"

"You'd sneak down here on your own. I don't need a dead UPF captain." He stalked down the first rows of Dragon's Eyes flowers.

"Liar."

He wheeled. A dense throb beat against his temple. Cad leapt over the blooms. "A wrongful insult is punishable by death." He grabbed Jade's arms and lifted her into the air. "Rajs do not lie," he ground out each word slowly.

"Not even to themselves?" Her stare locked with his.

He couldn't deny her accusation. He cared about her, and he didn't want to. Sharp breaths gusted through his nostrils. "How good a man am I? I bought you."

She didn't know him. She couldn't.

Thunder boomed overhead. The crash ricocheted off the cave walls.

"That's what you want." He jerked his head back toward the endless rows of blue-violet flowers. "Take a good look." He dug his fingers further into her flesh.

She licked her lower lip and shifted her gaze. "Yes, I need Dragon's Eyes and they are genuine." She swallowed. "But *I* agreed to our bargain, because I wanted to."

No, she was lying. She had to be, or he'd never slay the hope she'd somehow sown in him. He pushed her up against a wall between two clusters of blue-violet blossoms. "Shall I show you just how *not* good I am?" He pinned her soft body with his hard one. "Fuck you right here?"

Her heart thundered. The wild vibration passed through her firm breast and against his chest.

"You don't want this." Her warm sugared breath fanned his lips.

"Yes I do. And so do you." He pressed her harder against the wall and swooped down on her mouth. He thrust his tongue between her lips. The scrape of her teeth swelled his desire.

Her freed arms went around him. She kissed him back with matched ferocity.

Softness, generosity, want. His tongue lapped at the foreign flavors, unable to get enough. Her hips thrust against his pelvis.

"No." She pushed against his chest. "You're wrong."

"Now who's lying?" Cad ignored her attempts to free herself. "Tell me if I ripped your top off I wouldn't find your nipples tight and hard?"

"They—"

He palmed her breast through the silk and pinched her nipple. "Tell me they don't ache for me to suck on them," he growled and squeezed harder.

Jade gasped.

"You want me because I'm bad."

"No." She tried to turn her head.

"You want me because I give you permission to feel." He pressed his cock into her stomach. "Tell me right now your pussy isn't dying for me to fuck you."

Choppy breaths fanned his face.

Cad slipped a hand between their bodies and stroked her through her clothing. "Tell me if I had my hand between your legs right now, my fingers wouldn't be wet with your juices."

"I—I..." She writhed against him, rubbing her breasts along his torso.

"And if my fingers were inside your pussy and my thumb on your clit, you wouldn't come in my hand." He increased the pressure against the damp material barring him from her folds.

"I can't!" she cried.

With each second his control slipped. She wanted what he could give her, not him. And he would give her exactly what she needed.

Thunder cracked high above.

Sweat dripped down the back of his neck. "Ask me for it. I want to hear you say you want me to fuck your pussy." He bit at her neck as light raindrops pelted his head and back.

"I want you to fuck me." Jade's small hands tore at his shirt. "I want you to fuck me now."

The words were all Cad needed.

Thunder crashed and the rain turned to a downpour.

Cool water plastered their clothes to their skin. Steam rose from her neck.

He drank the liquid beads as they rolled over her closed eyes and down her cheeks. He ripped her top open and slid his hand over her rain-slicked breasts.

"Drag—"

"Cad." He ground his hard cock against her mons.

"Cad," she repeated.

The sound of his name on her lips with such tenderness unleashed a flood inside him.

"Please, fuck me, Cad." She reached for his pants.

Right then he had to bury himself inside her. All the water in the universe couldn't douse the burning need in his cock. He yanked off her trousers and slid his hand between her legs.

She gasped and gripped his shoulders.

"Spread your legs for me." He nudged her right foot with his. Rain and Jade's juices flowed over his fingers as he stroked the outer lips of her pussy.

As she ground into his palm, he slipped one finger inside and her muscles closed around him. She was so tight and ready. "You want to know what it is to feel? This is feeling." He grasped her hips and slammed his cock inside her pussy.

A scream. Sharp fingernails raked his shoulders. Wet heat surrounded him. Need as torrential as the water battering his skin tightened his muscles. Hunger sank from his belly into his cock. Nothing but the release of cramming deep inside her mattered.

"And this." He gripped her waist and pushed every inch of himself into her. The muscles from his buttocks down through his legs coiled tight and sprang forward as he thrust. "Is this what you wanted?"

"Yes!" She sobbed as he eased out of her channel and surged back inside. "I want all of it!"

Even if he'd wanted to, Cad couldn't have stopped himself from giving it to her. Her muscle spasms quickened with his pace.

She ground against him and wrapped one leg around his hip.

A tight gripping quiver rolled through her pussy and against his cock.

"Cad," she keened and clung to him.

The anger and emotions of the past few hours gathered in his tight sac and burst forward. Shock waves shook his legs. He surged into her pussy one last time and poured the truth, his feelings and fears into her womb.

Chapter Four

ഗ

"Thank you, Saree," Jade said as she wrapped a golden silk robe around her freshly bathed body. Her senses still hummed from the uncontrolled way Cad had taken her against the cave wall.

"You are leaving?" The girl collected Jade's wet clothes from beside the sunken tub.

"Tomorrow." A lump rose in her throat.

Saree's spine stiffened.

Was the girl Cad's mistress? Her fingers bunched in the smooth silk robe. "Are you Ca—The Dragon's *gui fei*?" She kept her voice even.

"No. I ask but…" She shrugged. "Raj Cad is not like other men." Her brown eyes darkened. "He pays us well, but never touches us."

Relief no sooner swept the tension from her muscles than astonishment froze them in place. How could Cad believe he was bad? "He-he is a good man." She smiled.

Saree nodded and shifted the bundle of wet garments. "Raj Cad never allows *guests* overnight." Saree leveled a pointed stare and disappeared through the steam.

Why had he permitted her to stay? The question rang like the soft tinkle of a bell as she entered the main room. A low fire burned in a grate to the left of the throne. Deep crimson and purple flames undulated toward one another, curling together. Each bent and bowed to the other as they rolled as one. Like lovers.

"A woman who finds beauty in danger," Cad said as she entered.

His deep voice licked down her nerve endings. "All good can produce evil, and all evil contains good."

"Careful, *General*, your UPF superiors wouldn't agree," he whispered and traced his lips over her ear.

Liquid pooled between her legs. She didn't give a damn what anyone else thought. Not when the pungent smoke and spice of Cad's skin surrounded her. "I'm not a general."

"Not yet."

A warm puff of air grazed her cheek a second before he stepped away. Immediately, she wanted the hard crackle of his energy back.

"Are you hungry?"

She noticed a sight hesitation in his voice. Cad had *asked* her. Jade padded to the small black table surrounded by pillows before the fire and joined him.

After their meal, Saree arrived with a black pot and two tiny cups balanced on a small tray.

Jade reached for the pot's wooden handle, but Cad had already poured the tea. She quickly covered her surprise. The man dined alone and likely was accustomed to serving himself.

"Your workers are very loyal." She accepted the tiny cup decorated with the same fierce dragons carved into Cad's throne.

"They're loyal to their pay," he said, matter-of-fact.

"Can't it ever be you, and not money?"

"What else is there?" He stared, his blue eyes hardened by pain.

So much more. But she didn't say the words.

Cad rose and disappeared behind the throne. He returned with a small, battered square box in one hand and a—

Air rushed from her lungs. Canvas. "W-what are you doing with that?" She held her voice steady even as her insides shook.

"Nothing. You're doing. I have business." He propped the canvas on the table and laid a box of brushes and paint beside it.

Joy filled her until she thought she'd burst. "Thank you," she whispered, unable to loosen her throat to say more. She placed her hand on the canvas. The tiny ridges tickled her fingertips.

Cad listened to her dreams and cared. He could name any reason he wanted for the gift, but beneath lay kindness. And she loved him for it.

Jade gripped the table's edge. Her gaze flew to Cad seated on his throne. A now-familiar flutter spread from her heart and through her chest at the sight of his long black hair and tall, powerful physique.

She had to return to UPF headquarters tomorrow. Ivory's life and thousands of others depended on the Dragon's Eyes seeds. She picked up a slender brush and rubbed her thumb over the bristles.

The rapid thump of her pulse slowed. Cad had challenged her to feel and she had—textures, her own desires and passion. The seeds must return to the UPF, not her.

She'd given thirty years to her family's dream. The rest of her life she'd dedicate to following *her* dreams.

Her gaze bounced between her sketch and Cad's repeated shifts in position. The flames in the grate threw bright light and shadows over the colored pillows at the same time. Like the fire inside The Dragon that gave him his power and strength, it also cast the darkness over his heart.

Cad switched his viewtablet from one hand to the other.

"You don't sit on your throne often, do you?"

"No, it's for show." The tiniest of smiles curved his lips.

Her heart did a three-hundred-and-sixty-degree roll. For the first time, he'd shared an emotion other than anger or lust.

"It's not as regal, but you could always join me." She patted the pillow beside her and held her breath.

After a moment's hesitation, Cad rose and settled onto a large blue-and-green pillow across the table from her.

She hid her smile behind the canvas. "Why did you become a Raj?"

"You read my file?" he snapped.

Jade refused to cower before the anger he used as a shield. "I saw a censored service record with more black than a black hole."

"You have your seeds. It doesn't matter." He rose.

"No, *it* doesn't," she shouted. "*You* do."

Cad's stiff jaw fell slack and he sat back down.

Every nerve pulsed with the echo of her heart.

He set the viewtablet aside and leaned against a stack of pillows. "No one has dared yell at me since I became a Raj."

"Then either you weren't acting like a stubborn ass, or they forgot no one has power over you unless you let them."

"I was always in trouble for fighting. When I was eight, I was sent to the Rajs." He shrugged.

"Wasn't your family worried?" She paused her painting.

"A tapestry does not miss the unwoven thread." He swallowed. A dark streak flashed in his eyes. "I never had a family."

Her insides cried for him. Her family hadn't supported her dreams, but they loved her. No one had ever loved Cad and at some point, he'd closed himself off so no one could. Every fiber in her wanted to hold his stubborn face between her hands, look him in the eyes and tell him she did. She gripped the edge of the table to stop herself.

He'd never believe her, not until their deal concluded. She sat back on her heels. "You don't talk about it much, do you?"

"Never."

Until now.

The fact he'd opened up to her said volumes more than any number of words.

"Tell me about the academy?" Cad asked.

She complied, and about her sister, and her Star Force assignments while she painted. After the third yawn, she gave in to fatigue.

Cad's head lay against the pillow with his eyes closed.

The sleeping dragon.

A flash of inspiration struck, and she forced her lids open. She snagged a fine-tip brush and sketched one more image on the canvas.

Satisfied, she crawled over the pillows toward Cad. Jade cupped his face in her palm and brushed her lips over his. "I love you," she whispered, curled up beside him and fell asleep.

* * * * *

Stiff muscles dragged Cad into the conscious world. What had he— A warm body shifted against him. His eyes flew open and his mind snapped awake.

He reached for his sword, but instead found Jade's slender form pressed against his. He stilled and stared at the sight.

Pink lips half parted and her arm thrown across his chest, in complete content. He'd been hard on her. Hell, almost cruel, and yet… She snuggled further into his arm.

His throat tightened. Never had he permitted a woman to remain after sex. He didn't want the pretence he'd meant more than a good fuck and money.

He ran fingers through his hair with his unencumbered right hand. Last night he'd planned to remain awake and avoid this exact situation. He let out a long breath. But now that he was here…it wasn't so bad.

Pleasant even, the feeling of her limbs threaded with his. She had come to him without force or demand. His cynical side reminded him she still needed the Dragon's Eyes seeds.

But maybe...for the first time since his days at the Shepard's Temple, he allowed himself to hope. He stroked her long, straight blonde hair.

Jade's thick lashes lifted with the slow grace of sunbeams at dawn. "Good morning." She smiled.

Cad held her, unsure of what to say. "You slept...well?"

"Yes." She caressed his bare chest. "You?"

"Sound." He frowned, unable to recall the last time he'd slept through an entire night.

She yawned and stretched her arms over her head. Her gold robe pulled tight against her chest, outlining her breasts and tight nipples.

Desire snaked through Cad's blood and collected in his cock. By now, he had usually grown bored with a woman. Not Jade. The need to possess her remained as strong as the moment she'd entered his chamber. She'd leave soon. The reality jabbed into his heart.

He glanced toward the canvas. "What did you paint?"

Pink bloomed in her cheeks. "It's not finished." She toyed with the beaded tassel on an orange pillow.

"Show me."

Her gaze swung the carved ceiling tiles while she pinched her lower lip between her teeth. "What if— What if it isn't any good and I just wasted a precious piece of canvas?" Her words tumbled out in a rush.

The uncertainty and fear struck a chord deep within him. "The dream must belong to the dreamer or it is not theirs."

"Ancient wisdom for 'pursue your own goals'." She smiled and stood.

Cad rose and walked toward the canvas. He could demand she show him. Instead, he found himself saying the one word he hadn't spoken in over thirty years. "Please."

Her pink lips curved into a small "O". She rotated the picture toward him.

Sketched on the canvas was— Him. He stared, unable to believe out of everything in the galaxy, she'd chosen him. Jade had painted him seated on his throne with a fire at his back and a bearded dragon curled around his feet.

"It's really rough." She touched the unpainted portions. "Most of the color still needs to be added, and—"

"It's amazing." The crop of bitterness inside him shriveled. "Why me?" His voice thickened.

"You looked so virile and beautiful." She slipped her hands beneath the front of his robe.

He closed his eyes as her palms slid up his chest. Hunger unfurled in his belly.

Tiny teeth nipped over his collarbone and up his neck to his mouth. Her lips hovered above his. "And because I wanted to paint you."

Relief from a lifetime of pain shook him. Blue fire flashed from his head to the soles of his feet. He crushed Jade to his chest. He had to have her. Right then. Right now.

Cad's mouth came down on hers. He feasted on her soft lips, biting gently on the tender, pink flesh.

She moaned and pushed his robe off his shoulders.

Silk and her anxious hands caressed his arms as Jade pulled the garment down his body. Tiny electric surges zinged to his fingertips.

He sucked her tongue inside his mouth. A hint of jasmine tea remained on her taste buds and added to her natural sweetness. As he cupped the back of her head in his hand, he circled her tongue with his, stroking and gliding.

Why Jade had chosen to paint him he didn't understand. All that mattered was *she wanted to,* and had done so of her own free will. Cad shuddered. She saw worth in him, the man, not his money. Acceptance washed over him.

Words could never express his gratitude even if he could've spoken them. All he had to thank her with was the one possession in the world that truly belonged to him, his body and soul. After years of lying dormant, his heart awoke.

With his single pull, the robe's sash fell limp at her sides. The golden silk folds parted the path to her body.

"You are so beautiful," he murmured, "all white and gold." He stroked her pale cheek and tucked a lock of long blonde hair behind her ear.

Silver eyes widened and shone in the muted lantern's glow. She pressed a kiss to his chest above his pounding heart. "You've never said something so kind to me."

No, he hadn't. He had made demands, spoken of sex and pushed her away. Yet, she had remained. The truth stilled his lungs and humbled him. A *man walking backwards only passes the present by*.

For all the miles he traveled from the Shepard's Temple, a part of him had never really left. Jade had brought him out of the past and shown him he was worthy of kindness and trust. Wild, intense emotions consumed him in a rush. He swooped Jade up into his arms and headed for the throne.

She yelped and held fast to his neck. "What are you—"

Cad set her in the magnificent carved chair and slid the robe from her body. Soft and smooth, he absorbed the sight of her firm breasts, dark golden curls glistening with wetness above her long legs. His muscles tensed and his cock filled.

He kneeled before her.

"I-I think we're in the wrong positions," she stammered.

"Then don't think." He relented to the smile on his lips. He ran the tips of his fingers up the back of her calves.

Her bottom squirmed in the seat.

"Feel." He stroked the sensitive spot behind her knees. "I'll prove you're exactly where you should be." He grazed his knuckles along her inner thigh. Muscles quivered in his wake. Watching her orgasm build gave him more pleasure than his own release.

"Cad," she gasped and grasped his shoulders.

"That's it." He leaned his chest against her stomach. Her softness contoured to his hard body. "Let me give you pleasure."

Jade nodded, eyes bright.

Passion had always been something he'd taken. With Jade, he wanted to give. Determination fired in his veins. He dipped his tongue into her belly button.

A giggle bounced off the hard, dark stone walls and once more she squirmed.

The sound of her joy and the knowledge he was responsible filled him with happiness he'd not known. He repeated the action and continued up her trembling stomach and over her sternum.

Tiny, sharp breaths whistled between her teeth pinched against her bottom lip.

He cupped her breasts in his hands.

"Oh, yes." Jade tilted her hips and wrapped her long legs around his waist.

"I take it you want me to stay?" He kneaded the small, firm globes.

"Well, since *you* asked…" She smiled.

Yes, he had, something else he had never done with anyone else. A shiver shot down his spine. Jade had changed him, but not by force. All along, he'd believed he'd held all the power when it had been she. Her soft strength had brought The Dragon to his knees.

He rolled a nipple between his thumb and forefinger. "So tight." The hard, pink bead continued to constrict under his attention.

Jade rubbed her hips against him.

Sweet juices moistened his stomach. He groaned. She was so wet *for him*. He stroked the backside of her hip and she jerked harder against him.

"Your pussy is so wet."

"And aching for you." She swallowed.

His cock hardened. The sudden jolt of her words threatened to release the explosion throbbing behind his balls. He closed his eyes and inhaled a slow breath. The promise of Jade's pleasure exceeded the pain of the wait.

"Not yet." He took her nipple inside his mouth and suckled. Too long he'd ignored the wanton buds. He circled her areola with his tongue while scraping its base with his teeth.

"So beautiful."

"More?" she panted and lifted her breast to his mouth.

With a growl, he laved her other nipple with the same slow torment. As he drew back, he noticed the red marks on her skin, where his stubbled face had irritated the delicate tissue. He winced and glanced up at her as he stroked the abused areas.

"I like it." She brushed her hand down his cheek.

He closed his eyes and soaked in the tenderness freely given. She understood him in a way no one else had. He spread her legs and slid down her body, determined to give her more.

After kissing her belly, he sank lower.

"Cad?" Her voice quavered.

"I want to taste you," he rasped. His cock was dying for release. The pressure inside throbbed through his length, in his temples and clenched muscles. "Let me taste your pussy."

"Yes."

The strength of her warm musk grew. He shuddered at the rich spice soon to grace his tongue and throat.

He stroked his tongue over her outer folds.

Her fingers sank into his hair as she jerked her pussy toward his waiting mouth. For once he didn't need her to speak to know she wanted him. The tip of his tongue tingled with the barest of her taste.

"So wet and sweet. I have to have more."

"Don't stop." Her fingers dug into his scalp.

Nothing could've prevented Cad from fulfilling her request. He parted the deep pink folds and circled her entrance. Fresh juices flowed and he caught them with his tongue. He groaned as he drank her ripe tang of arousal.

He nudged her knee and Jade quickly complied and widened her legs. He stroked her hips and belly with his hands as he ran the flat of his tongue up and down her pussy.

"Oh yes, Cad," Jade moaned.

After a few flicks over her clit, he raised his head. "What do you want?"

Jade stilled. Her silver gaze, swirled with dark ribbons of desire, met his. "Your mouth. You eating my pussy."

His scalded nerve endings flared. The unstoppable determination that had driven him to succeed and survive now focused on bringing Jade to orgasm. He thrust his tongue inside her. In and out he moved, licking her hot sensitive walls. The slick flesh rippled against him.

Jade ground against him, her hips mirroring the rhythm of his mouth. "Please, I'm so close," she panted.

Cad recognized the thread of need in her voice stretched thin and ready to snap. He wanted to break that tension. Nothing else mattered, but Jade. "I know, trust me."

"I do."

Her faith shot through him, stronger than anger and more gratifying than any battlefield triumph. He would not disappoint her. He sucked her swollen clit inside his mouth. He stroked the bead, and key to her pleasure, with his ardent tongue.

Tiny tremors grew to quakes. Her nails dug into his scalp while she bucked against him.

"Cad!" She cried his name over and over.

Moisture flooded his mouth. He drank every drop of cream she offered. Only when her flesh stilled did he relent and climb up her body.

Ragged breaths blew against his ear as she held him close. He fought down his own need, but just barely. The serenity of being held in her arms, his sweat-slickened flesh pressed to hers, was too precious to squander on impatience.

She kissed him on the mouth. "I never knew being eaten alive by a dragon could be so good."

He laughed, something else he hadn't done years. "Now you know the truth of the fate of all those story maidens."

"Who'd want a knight after that?" She smiled.

"What else does the maiden want?"

"You, inside me."

Cad couldn't wait. He grabbed Jade around the waist and flipped their positions so her legs straddled his cock as his length pressed against her hot, wet slit.

She rubbed her pussy against him.

He groaned. "I can't wait." He lifted her hips and speared his cock deep inside her. A silken river surrounded him. His eyes drifted closed and he thrust deeper.

"This is what I want. You. Your cock filling my pussy." She arched back, thrusting her breasts toward his mouth and sinking him deeper.

Her muscles squeezed the length of him. It was his turn to buck against her. He would give her what she wanted. "I have to fuck you now, Jade. I have to come inside you."

"Yes." She kissed him. "Help me." She kicked her legs forward and swung her toes above the ground. "Help me fuck your cock."

With a growl, he grasped her waist once more. He lifted her so she slid up until only the tip of him was inside her. Then he surged up. Her tight channel closed around him.

Jade ground down, rubbing her clit over his coarse hair. "Harder." She rocked.

As much as he wanted to prolong the sight of Jade and her skin dripping with the sweat of her effort, he couldn't.

Cad slammed inside her. Cramps seized his calves, but he didn't let up. He increased his tempo. His balls clenched and prepared to launch his seed.

"Oh god." Jade threw her head back as a chain of spasms wrung her pussy.

With a roar, Cad slammed his hips upward and his cock into the grasping walls of her pussy. Hot, sweet want surrounded him. Cad surrendered to the call as the explosion of his orgasm finally erupted.

Everything but the surge of power drawing the focus of his entire being to one center point disappeared. He was in the one place he had always wanted to be, with someone who wanted him. Clutching her close, he poured himself into her womb.

Chapter Five

ꟗ

Cad held Jade's naked body close. He never wanted to let her go and the knowledge scared him. In a few hours, she'd return to UPF headquarters. His muscles seized.

"Are you okay?" Jade pulled back, but remained seated on top of him with his cock buried deep inside her pussy.

He nodded and cleared his throat. "Would you like to stay and finish your painting?"

Her gaze strayed to the canvas and back. "The Dragon's Eyes seeds must be delivered."

"I, uh, meant afterwards." He ran his hands down her torso and held her tiny waist.

"Oh." She tilted her head. "Why?"

"I like the piece." He struggled for the right words. For once he didn't control the situation, and he hated the uncertainty the loss brought.

"Is that all?"

"You could paint, follow *your* dream. Don't tell me you want the damn promotion," he growled. Couldn't she see she needed to take a chance? That he needed her.

"How would I make a living?" She climbed off his lap.

He felt the loss of connection immediately. "I can help you find buyers."

"That might take time." She padded toward the small table to her left where her Star Force flightsuit lay.

An icy crackle of fear numbed him. "I'll pay you a retainer."

She paused halfway into the garment and closed her eyes. "I'm sorry. You can't buy me," she choked. "Not now. Not ever."

Old emptiness tore at him. The peaceful calm of the last few hours drifted away as quickly as Dragon's Eyes smoke. He had nothing left to offer. Nothing but…

Jade fastened the flightsuit's catch at her neck.

His heart battered his ribs. "Stay." He walked toward her. Dryness coated his tongue. "Stay because you want to." He swallowed. "And because," he took a deep breath and prepared to say the three words he had never spoken to another human being in all his forty-five years, "I love you."

Moisture glistened in her eyes. "I have to see to my responsibilities first."

Cad let his arms fall. Pain and rage far worse than anything he'd ever experienced exploded in his heart. He clenched his fists at his side. Everything had been about the seeds. How could he have been fooled?

"Your ship is loaded."

"Cad—"

"Leave." He wheeled and stalked out of the throne room.

"Wait," she called.

He didn't turn around. Nothing changed.

"Will you listen?"

No, he'd heard enough. His eyes burned as he headed for his private chamber. He squeezed them shut, but the pain remained. He let his head fall against his chest.

All his life he'd kept his emotions contained. But Captain Jade Ahnat had gotten to him. The last person he expected. If he could've torched the image of her rounded face and smile from his mind, he—wouldn't.

He loved her, even if she never returned the feeling. He pulled a tenuous breath into his lungs, but nothing could fill the emptiness.

Cad grabbed his sword, a clean pair of pants and headed for the field pit. Work didn't stop. If he focused himself, he could forget her.

For two hours, Cad examined the state of his crop, checked the undersides of leaves for fungus and snapped at his employees. All failed to distract him.

Yinlo waited at the top of the pit as Cad climbed out. "See the new seedlings are planted today, and the entire crop fertilized," he barked.

Yinlo nodded.

He ran a hand through his damp hair. "Did the UPF ship leave?"

"Yes, Raj Cad, but—"

"Deny all future landing requests." He stalked off before the turmoil inside him spilled out.

Jade was gone.

The dark emptiness he'd battled for the past hours claimed another foothold. He marched through the throne room and stopped at the unfinished canvas.

Why had she left it? He yanked his sword from its scabbard and held the diamond blade above the picture. Heavy breaths shook his chest. A part of him wanted to slice the image. He tightened his grip.

But the soft painted lines held their ground.

In his heart, he remembered Jade's tale of burning her first painting. The UPF destroyed great beauty out of fear and a lack of feeling. He'd lost his fear long ago. And now too, he'd lost his emotional apathy. Later, he'd have the canvas stored.

As he entered his bathing chamber, Cad sheathed his weapon. Clouds of steam rolled toward him. He unbuckled his baldric.

The outline of a woman's narrow shoulders rose above the edge of the tub. He stopped.

Damn Saree. She would pick today to try his patience. "What the hell are you doing?" He roared and shot forward to yank the girl from the water.

"Bathing. You invited me to stay, remember?" Jade swiveled to face him. Water lapped at the top of her breasts.

Cad's cock stiffened even as his first instinct was to lash out with anger. The smallest ember of hope sparked. Yet he held his emotions back. She couldn't be here. Yinlo said—"Your ship left?"

"Yes." She leveled a hard stare.

"I thought—"

"Dalton is flying the Dragon's Eyes seeds back to UPF headquarters." She smiled. "He'll make a much better general."

He let out a breath. "That's what you wanted to tell me." Old offenses had blinded him. "I thought you were leaving."

"Will you listen now?" A surge of water splashed onto the stone floor as Jade hoisted herself out of the tub.

"I'll try." His cock filled.

She pressed her wet, naked body against him.

Slick and hot, he wrapped his arms around her waist as she encircled his neck.

Tears pooled in her silver eyes. "I had to finish my old life before I could start a new one with you."

He nodded. It was time for him to do the same. The past did not die, but it need not rule his future.

"I didn't want you to wonder whether I'd stayed for the seeds or for you." She pulled his head down until their noses almost touched. "Never doubt the reason I'm here."

"Which is?" he whispered.

She cupped his face and their gazes locked. "I love you, Cad."

He closed his eyes and let his heart absorb the words. She loved him, not because of Dragon's Eyes, or money, but because of *him*.

"You're kind, strong, stubborn and—"

"And going to make love to you right now." He swooped her up in his arms.

"I wasn't finished." She smiled. "I want you forever."

The last of the bitter fire inside him died. "You have me."

"For eternity?"

He smiled and sank into the tub with her. "Longer."

About the Author

ꙮ

Megan Kerans began creating short stories long before she could read. Growing up, she traveled extensively and quickly developed a love of new places and cultures. If she wasn't reading about daring escapades, she was watching them in the form of Indiana Jones, Errol Flynn high seas swashbuckling films or Star Wars. Together they gave her a love of adventure, romance, and story telling.

After several failed attempts at penning category romances, Megan realized she might be on the wrong path after noticing her office decor resembled Tim Burton's Corpse Bride more than Cosmo. Armed with this knowledge and unique imagination, she switched to adventure and paranormal romance and the challenge of exploring sex hotter than the Sahara, along with timeless legends and exciting adventures. The risk led to several sales and she quickly became hooked.

A native Chicagoan with Wisconsin roots, Megan currently lives in Texas with her husband, an overly intelligent Abyassian and two flame point Siamese. The little time not spent writing or cat herding, she enjoys reading, making as many trips as possible to Walt Disney World, photography and graphic design, and listening to a variety of music.

Megan welcomes comments from readers. You can find her website and email address on her author bio page at www.ellorascave.com.

Tell Us What You Think

We appreciate hearing reader opinions about our books. You can email us at Comments@EllorasCave.com.

VIKING'S PLEDGE

By Melany Logen

Chapter One

Birka, Sweden

AD 917

ꟹ

Raynor's strides lengthened in anticipation of those who awaited his arrival.

Storr, his trusted friend, stayed in step with him as they made their way from the longship. Home. He'd been gone too long on this trip. He'd missed his young son, Advar. But most of all, he'd missed Mista, his thrall.

Her dark eyes had haunted him while he'd been gone.

He didn't know what had urged him to purchase the girl those years ago, but he had missed the little slave. Mista had been too young to be worthy of jealousy, but still his wife, Snorra, had hated her. *Nei*. It had been more than hate. And he could no longer ignore his fault in the matter.

Since the moment of Advar's birth, he hadn't been able to get her out of his head. Snorra's rejection of their son had compelled Mista to step in to care for Advar. From that moment, he hadn't been able to keep his eyes from the little slave.

No matter he'd denied himself the pleasure of fucking her once she came of age—Snorra's hate had grown with the girl.

He had never done anything but protect the little thrall.

His own mother had trained Mista when he'd brought her to his home. But she had feared him. Because Mista's eyes twisted his heart, he had been easy with her. They had talked, he had taught her...and grown to cherish her. In many ways he had begun to neglect Snorra, built a relationship with Mista where he had failed to kindle one with his wife. And as the seasons changed, the slave had come to trust him.

His stride lengthened further, hoping her life had been easy in his absence. Swinging up, he mounted his steed with an eagerness that surprised even him.

They were quiet as they traveled, giving him the time to wonder at the changes in Advar…and Mista.

Advar, only an infant when he had left, would be walking now, speaking some words. Mista had returned from his parents' home as a woman when his wife birthed Advar. His cock stirred to life. Every night while away, he had lain in his berth and remembered her smiling mouth, her dark eyes and the soft curves of her body.

Odin, he had enjoyed looking upon her beauty.

Storr took Raynor's mount once they reached the farmstead.

"How fare those within?" Raynor asked, his chest tight, his legs suddenly leaden on the path. It had been little more than a long season since he had left, and still the memory of her filled him with lust. In a moment, the memory would be real, touchable.

"All are well. You have a fine son. Mista seems to be—"

Raynor turned sharply. "What? She is well?"

Storr averted his gaze. "She is well. Only quiet. Gymir…while you were away…"

"What! The bastard what?" His fists balled, nails biting into his flesh. "Did he bed her?"

Storr moved to his side, clasping his shoulder. "The girl is fine. I stopped him in time. He'd tossed her skirts up, but he didn't stick her." He sighed, stepping back. "You've spoiled her rotten. She fought like a wildcat. I protected her when I could, as I promised you."

Raynor grunted. Good. He'd hope she'd fight if she didn't want to fuck. Most other thralls, male or female, would bend over for a price. "My thanks."

Storr nodded. "She's slept in your chamber while you were away as you requested."

His cock stirred to life.

"The other thralls talk behind her back. Say she's bewitched you." Storr glanced away. "I don't understand. You've kept her in your chamber for many snows and not taken her."

Storr collected the lead to his horse. He'd see the mounts were cared for. "Mista has been tending to Advar when Edda doesn't have her grinding corn and salt."

Damn the hag! Snorra's sister no doubt had Mista doing all the backbreaking tasks. Using a hand-quern… He closed his eyes, imagining what she'd gone through in his absence. Milking, churning and washing, among others.

"Edda didn't," Raynor growled.

Storr nodded. "Mista's been given twice the chores of the other thralls."

Up until the time he'd left, he'd kept her occupied with light chores. She'd taken up looking after his son all on her own. As soon as she'd noticed his mother ignoring him, she'd stepped in.

He should never have run from his wife's death. He had volunteered to take the voyage. He headed toward the longhouse, knowing it hadn't been his wife he'd run from, but Mista.

Nei.

He'd left for Mista's sake.

* * * * *

Advar climbed on Mista's lap, his little hands clutching her, one winding in a strand of her long hair. She winced at the pull, but didn't stop him from the cuddle.

"You're spoiling the boy." Edda's voice snapped harshly against her senses.

Mista bit back her natural response. Someone had to. God knew his mother hadn't. But she didn't want the slap she'd get from Edda to upset the boy.

Advar clung tighter to her, burying his head in her bosom.

Edda sneered. "You have chores to do. You'll be doing them into the eve again if you keep playing."

"I'll get my chores done." She rubbed her cheek against the boy's soft blond hair. He leaned farther into her. "'Tis all right, Advar. 'Tis all right. Why don't you help me with the hand quern?" She'd already done the milking. She stroked her palm across his soft cheek. Her hands, so rough from toil—they probably felt like the side of a rock.

They hadn't taken a step to leave the longhouse when a shadow fell across them.

Raynor.

Mista gasped. He'd been gone so long. She'd forgotten what a presence he brought wherever he came. He was the tallest man in the village, with the biggest shoulders. His kirtle hugged them tightly, the small fastener to one side of the high neckline. She'd made the braid around the edge of it for him before he'd left. Somehow, seeing him still wearing it warmed her all over.

"Mista?" His deep voice came out with strangled surprise. His eyes darkened as they slowly roamed over her from head to toe. His nostrils flared as his gaze lingered over her bosom. He took a step closer as if to touch her, making her blood race. His hands clenched into mighty fists.

"*Tá*." She smoothed down her fraying hangerock.

"Show your respect, thrall," Edda snarled from behind them. "Kneel before your master."

Mista's eyes shot to his. He'd never made her kneel before him before. Would he now? He had always talked to her kindly, like an equal.

Advar looked up at the giant man and, hearing the tone in his aunt's voice, cried. Kneeling, she pulled him to her side, rubbing her hands over his back to settle him down. When the boy calmed, she straightened.

"Edda, leave us. I must take time with my son…and my thrall." Raynor's baritone echoed in her ears. It sounded worse than any punishment Edda had ever meted out. His thrall? She'd always known it was her place, but she'd never had cause before to think he viewed her as such. That he would expect her to fulfill her duties as such.

She chastised herself for her foolishness. When she'd been brought here from Ireland so long ago, he'd seemed more friend than master. He had refused to let her call him anything other than his own name, much to Edda's fury. Even as her body had begun to fill out, he had not tried to claim her as a master would. She'd held on to the memory of the innocent nature of their relationship while he'd been gone. But apparently, she'd been wrong. Very wrong.

Edda narrowed her eyes. "I will leave so you can take your slave as a bedmate. Perhaps she will like you more than my sister did."

Raynor's gaze hardened. Edda skulked out of the longhouse, a smug look resting on her features.

Mista swallowed, clinging to Advar like a shield.

"You look well, Mista."

"It is good to have you home." She held his gaze longer than a thrall should her master's.

He rested his eyes on the little boy with features so like his own. "How is my son?" Advar shyly took a step back from Raynor.

"Your son is strong. A warrior." Advar beamed toothily at her. He looked so much like his father. Tousled blond hair. Blue eyes that saw into the depths of whomever they rested on. Nothing of that witch Raynor had been married to resided in their son. She'd often watched Advar and called to mind Raynor's features. Too many times.

"That is good to hear." His eyes blazed a trail over her woolen garments. She folded her arms around herself as Advar saw something that caught his eye and he toddled away.

"I cannot believe how you've changed." His voice carried that hoarse note again.

"You have changed naught." He hadn't. He was exactly as she'd remembered him. He still smelled of soap. He liked his time in the bathhouse. Her inner thigh muscles clenched. Her breasts swelled, her nipples hardening. His trousers rested so tightly against his hips, she could see the tightness straining there. The bulge had to be his erection. Her sex tingled.

She could not be attracted to this man.

Impossible.

She wanted her home back. Ireland. She wanted the people back she'd lost so long ago. Her father, oh God, her father. It had been so many seasons. He must think she'd perished long ago. She'd become determined to get back to him and decided the best way to do it was to talk—to ask of Raynor this one thing. He'd been her friend. Surely he wouldn't refuse her request to go home?

He'd never treated her like a bed slave, which was what her purchase had been made for. She'd known girls younger than herself who had been used as such. But Raynor hadn't touched her.

He grasped her hand, looking at all the scaly patches of skin and calluses.

Mista resisted pulling her hand back. What did it matter if he knew how hard she'd worked?

"Edda has worked you to the bone."

Mista shrugged. The work took her mind off her homesickness. Her favorite job had been looking after Advar—such a precious little boy. She'd miss him. "Not so bad."

His eyes looked as though he'd devour her. Like he would eat her like the finest delicacy of meat he could find. Her face heating, she looked away.

He'd said she'd changed.

When she looked back, his eyes hooded, clouding over. Advar had wandered some distance away. Raynor stepped closer to her. "Mista."

"*Tá*." Nervously, she reverted back into her native Gaelic as she'd done earlier. She looked up, misjudging how closely he stood. Her head banged his chin. "Oh! I'm sorry." She rubbed the stubbled jaw with her fingertips. So rough and scratchy against her fingertips. The contact seared her fingers like no poker in the fire could ever do. She shyly pulled her hand away.

He sucked in a breath, then lowered his mouth to hers. Their lips met in a rush of air followed by a sizzle. He softly explored her. His lips brushed hers, making a swipe across them. The touch tingled, shooting shivers to her already humming sex. The moisture pooled between her thighs.

His hand slipped down along her shoulder to rub against a breast through her usual aproned frock. Her gasp allowed him to penetrate her lips with his tongue, sliding in. He found hers and wound around it, twirling over and over. Her whole body shuddered. Pleasure swirled through her. She wanted to give over to the sensations.

Home. If he bedded her, she'd never make it back to her homeland. He'd never let her go.

She pushed away from him. His breath came in short puffs of air. His whole body stiffened. His cock jutted out from his body.

"What's wrong?"

She took a step back, her hand on her mouth. "Everything. Raynor..."

"*Já?*"

"I need to go home. To my people." Despite that part of her heart set against it, she needed to make her plea. Her body rebelled, wanting the act instead. It wanted the act of copulation with this big, strong, noble man. "I have to go home, Raynor. Please let me."

* * * * *

Mista wished to leave him. The time he'd given her had done nothing to change her thinking. Odin, but the time away had worked to change her. There was no denying the womanly curves. She now had hips to grab and breasts to nuzzle on a cold night.

At first glance upon the fully-grown Mista, every bit as perfect as he'd imagined, his knees had weakened. He could easily imagine her belly swelled with a babe.

His babe.

With a shake of his head, he cleared his mind. After what his wife had put him through, it was unthinkable. Then another memory taunted him. He pushed the image of the thrall lovingly caring for his son from his mind. It made no difference. She wished to return home.

Could he allow her to leave him without sampling the pleasures he could take with her? Raynor mulled over his thrall's request as he walked with Storr. Raynor's father had learned of his son's return and had sent Storr to collect him before he could say much to Mista.

"What?" Raynor asked suddenly. Storr had been speaking, but Raynor hadn't been listening. The man always talked. Raynor had too much to think about to listen to Storr spin tales.

"I have bad news," Storr repeated.

Raynor made a rough sound. "When have I returned home to anything but?"

Storr touched his shoulder as they neared the chieftain's longhouse. "Gymir is dead. I did not wish to tell you earlier. I figured it could wait."

Raynor stopped walking and groaned. His eldest brother—dead. He felt no remorse. No great pain of loss. Only a pang of guilt for not missing him. Gymir had been a vicious man, as vicious as their father.

And he had tried to force himself on Mista.

"Chieftain Kjarr bid me to bring you to him upon your arrival. But I knew you'd want to see your home first." Storr climbed up onto his mount. "He's been deep into the cups since the news came during *vetr*."

The winter had kept him away too long. The *sumar* season had warmed the lands for some time now. Raynor looked off into the distance. A trip to his father's longhouse didn't warm his heart the way thoughts of the little black-haired slave did. What would he do about what she'd asked of him?

* * * * *

Though he nodded to his younger brother Thord, Raynor had received no welcome when he'd entered his father's home. Only a headache. His mother hadn't dared to show herself yet.

"You must marry again!" his father roared, spittle flying.

Raynor gritted his teeth. Never again. He had already done his duty and produced a son.

"Gymir was promised as a peace groom. Now you will marry Noss." His father's eyes bore into him as if he didn't see him.

"*Nei*, Father. Have Thord stand in his stead."

Raynor's head snapped backward with the force of his father's blow. He wiped his bloody mouth and spat. Storr moved closer to his side, but he ignored his friend.

"Thord wouldn't know how to produce heirs if I stood over him instructing." Sneering, his father moved into Raynor's space.

Remaining mute, Thord tossed back his mead.

A tic pulsed in Raynor's jaw. Damn the old man. He had no desire to be pushed into another loveless marriage. He had done his duty by his people and had a fine son to prove it.

An image of sweet Mista surfaced behind his closed eyelids.

Raynor regretted not having made her his concubine before leaving. She was young, but no child. Others wouldn't have waited. In their lives, death could be but a breath away. And Mista had been born of a low class in a conquered land and then taken as a slave on a raid, while he was prince to his people. Advancing from mere slave to concubine would have been advantageous for her.

Perhaps he wouldn't find himself in the position he was in now. Forced to choose between doing what she'd asked and what should be allowed.

He had taken Snorra as a peace-pledge, a wife bartered in marriage to guarantee a truce. While he'd been good to his wife and shown her respect, she'd been unhappy, taking it out on his entire household—especially Mista. He'd known no peace since the wedding ceremony. Neither had Mista.

His father's meaty fist flung out, catching him on the jaw. "Listen to me when I speak!"

Storr pressed against his side, steadying him.

Raynor forced his head to clear.

"You haven't been the same since that bitch wife of yours died in childbirth."

Raynor's chest grew tight. He still felt guilt over the loss of Snorra and their daughter. After Advar's birth, he'd worked hard bedding his wife to birth more children. The thought that she might die bearing a child she hadn't wanted hadn't crossed his mind.

Odin. Once Snorra had started to swell, she'd taken pleasure in telling him how much she hated him and the babe she carried. Over every meal, she'd told him how she hoped the babe died—just as she had said while carrying Advar.

He was through siring children. He'd given his people an heir. His father had enough bastards running amok. Gymir had spawned as many bastards as their father, and though none of them could claim the position of Chieftain, they could fight over the clan once the noble line died out.

His fists clenched. "Father, it is Thord's turn to marry for peace."

He left his father's longhouse followed by slurs and shattering pottery.

* * * * *

Raynor's mood needed improvement. No denying it. Sunset had come all too soon for his liking. Mista had put Advar to bed long ago and had not come back into the hall from his chamber.

Men milled about drinking, and some played games. Others crawled between the thighs of slaves. He sighed. Before Mista had escaped into the bedchamber, he noticed many of the other thralls avoided her company.

As the night lengthened, the bunks that lined the walls filled, and pallets were rolled out.

Storr stood and glanced toward his chamber. "I'll see you in the morn."

"Did the trunk arrive?"

"*Já*. But, I think 'tis a mistake. To give a thrall such wealth."

Raynor grunted. He was presenting an elaborate gift to a thrall who would leave him. He rose, a bit unsteady on his feet.

Storr clasped his shoulder. "I've never known for you to take to the cups."

Raynor shrugged him off. He had needed the drink. Odin. If only Mista hadn't stayed in his chamber. But where else would she have slept? In one of the bunks with his trusted warriors?

Only at his death.

Storr helped him to his door as a slave scampered past to clean up after them. Raynor paused and Storr leaned toward his ear. "Go easy on her."

"You think I'd force her?"

"Of course not." His friend shook his head. "She's a fool to want to leave you."

"Did you get me the lard?" The decision to let her go hadn't been easy. Taking her home wouldn't be freedom for either of them.

"*Já*. I put it by your bed."

He nodded and opened the door before he could change his mind. A candle burned low. Snoring softly, Advar slept on a pallet in an alcove, covered by a fur blanket. Mista lay in Raynor's bed. She wasn't sleeping. Even this deep into his cups, he knew she didn't sleep. The ale hadn't dulled his lust either.

Once naked, he crawled in beside his thrall.

His.

His cock swelled thickly at her closeness. He rolled to face her. "Mista." He hoped his voice sounded calm. He didn't feel steady. His hand trembled as he caught her chin in his palm. "I know you do not sleep."

Her black lashes drifted up to reveal wide, captivating eyes. "*Nei*. I do not."

He released her and pushed up onto an elbow, causing her to roll onto her back. "You wish to go home?" His throat tightened.

She nodded.

He lowered his lids, hoping she couldn't see his sadness. A rush of anger balled his fists. He should keep her. It was his right to keep her. He blew out a rough breath through his nose. "I'll take you back to your people. But at a price." There, he'd said it out loud.

"What price?" Her mouth trembled.

He brushed her mouth with his thumb, trying to show gentleness. "At the cost of you giving yourself to me."

Mista's chest heaved.

"I want you to like everything I do to you." He needed her to enjoy the coupling. A tic beat in his jaw. He'd hated how Snorra had spewed slurs at him each time they'd finished. He'd not take them from Mista.

She opened her mouth, only to have him stop her. "*Nei*. Be still. I won't take your maidenhead. Your father will be able to barter you as a bride." He would still give her the treasure chest of jewels. She'd go to her husband rich.

Raynor's cock pulsed. It would kill him leaving her a virgin, but he would. She wanted to return home. He'd let her. He'd spent years with an unhappy woman. Mista more than any other, he didn't want to see unhappy.

"If I hurt you, you must tell me to stop." He looked her in the eye. "Do you promise me?"

She nodded.

"Remove your shift."

Shifting her weight, she pulled it over her head. Puckered nipples stood out from full, high breasts. His mouth watered as his gaze lingered over the flatness of her belly, the flair of her hips and the black thatch of hair at the center of her thighs.

Mista moved her legs to hide the treasure from him.

"I want you on your hands and knees."

Her eyes widened. "What?"

"I said I wouldn't take your maidenhead, but I'll breach your arse." He stilled, holding her gaze. "Do you wish to change your mind?"

"*Nil,*" Mista gasped. Raynor kissed her roughly, shoving his tongue into her mouth. He pressed into her when she clutched at his shoulders. He moaned, discovering her lips to be sweet and surprisingly eager. Nothing had ever pleased him as much as when her tongue played with his. Over and over, his tongue swiped, dueled around hers until her breath was ragged. Her breasts pressed into his bare chest. Scorching him.

Odin. How he wanted her.

All of her.

Chest heaving, he broke the kiss. "That's it. Enjoy me." He moved away, rolling her over and pulling her back onto her knees.

Mista's breath caught as he ran his hands up her thighs and hips. Leaning over her, he grabbed the bowl Storr had left for him. Positioning himself behind Mista, he used one hand to coat his thick cock. His other hand held her in place.

Mista panted. His breath matched hers as it rushed harshly though his nose. Setting the bowl aside, he pressed a finger to the rim of her arse and pushed.

"Raynor!" she breathed. "'Tis unnatural!"

His balls tightened. He'd never fucked an arse before. Storr had sworn that if she was relaxed, she could take him easily and without pain.

His second finger slid in as smoothly as his first. Her arse was tight and hot. He closed his eyes. So tight, and he wanted nothing more than to fill her sex instead. Plow her as deep as he could, and pray to Odin that he planted a babe. *Nei*! He shook his head to clear it. Something about her muddled his thoughts more than the cups did.

He shuddered. Would a babe with Mista be treated differently? Would his babe be wanted? His balls tingled at the thought.

"Raynor!" she rasped.

Removing his fingers, he grasped her hips. Her arse was so soft and round. He lined his thick cock head up against her opening. He pressed into the puckered hole only once before ramming himself to the hilt.

"Raynor!" He stilled at her shriek.

Her muscles squeezed him like nothing before. He pushed forward, refusing to be dislodged from her tight depths. "Relax," he ground out between his clenched teeth, "Relax. Give me this and you go home." He swallowed.

Mista panted, her hands fisting the bedding. Her body trembled.

Odin! Storr had lied. He had hurt her. He stilled, praying she didn't tell him to stop. Waited until he thought his heart would stop for want of continuing. "Shhh…relax. Don't fight me."

She was still for a moment, then arched her arse slightly toward him.

"That's it. I'll make this as good for you as I can." He pulled all the way out and sucked in a breath as he eased back into her, filling her completely for a second time. He swallowed. "Remember, I won't plant my babe in you this way."

They would have no ties binding them. Her future husband would never know he'd plowed her.

Raynor pulled out, gritting his teeth, then pushed back in deep. Twice as hard as before.

Mista whimpered. He froze, but she seemed to be easing herself toward him again. He noticed the quivering of her thighs.

"Raynor…" she whispered.

"Does it hurt you?" he rasped. "Do you wish me to stop?" It was too difficult to breathe, let alone speak. He neared eruption.

"You've split me in two," she said hoarsely, "but please don't pull away now."

His fingers bit into her hips as he held them in place and ground his cock inside her as best he could. He grunted when her arse pressed back into him, taking all of him.

Raynor began to fuck her in earnest. Sweat coated his body as he thrust deep and hard.

He could hear her breathing out his name on every stroke. His body was like a bolt of lightning as he thrust in and out. Her whispers pleased him like nothing before. He wished he had the strength to keep fucking her. He groaned on a final thrust as he flooded her arse with his hot seed. His body jerked, burst after burst.

Mista whimpered again when he didn't withdraw. Instead, he shifted until his cock was as hard as before. This time his strokes were slower. Longer. Teasing. This time, her hands fisted in frustration rather than fear as she began to match his thrusts. Over and over, he stroked in and out until his ears buzzed with pleasure.

Until his balls tingled.

Until Mista's legs quivered.

Raynor bit back a roar as he came the second time, thrusting deep, lifting her off the bed. He closed his eyes as his seed burst from him.

Leaning over, he kissed her shoulder and climbed from the bed. He cleaned his cock. She watched his movements with wide eyes. "Did I hurt you badly?" he asked her.

Her face bunched up into a frown. "I...'twasn't much pain... But Raynor, it's not the way of—'tis unnatural!"

Raynor lowered his lashes to shield his gaze. Unnatural or not, he'd enjoyed every moment of the act. His cock twitched. Mista hadn't said *nei*, hadn't fought him off as he had taught her to do should a man try to force himself on her. Instead, she had squirmed and panted as he'd plowed her back passage.

Pouring fresh water into the bowl, he moved back to the bed to clean her arse.

"*Nei,*" she gasped when he pressed his palm into her back. "I can clean myself."

He clenched his teeth as her arse wiggled beneath his hand. "Be still." He tried to use a gentle touch with her. It was difficult. By nature, he was a rough man.

Finally finished with the task, he set the bowl aside.

Once he returned to the bed, he rolled her over onto her back. She pulled her legs together, but he spread them with rough hands. "The night is still mine."

"Raynor, please…"

The look in her eyes was strange, both pleading and expectant. He moved down her body, settling himself between her thighs, and growled in satisfaction. Her passage, desperately wet and swollen, waited for his touch.

He didn't tease her. Instead, he sucked her clit into his mouth with a growl.

"Raynor!" Her hips bucked upward.

He shuddered. Odin. He liked how she cried out her pleasure. He suckled for a long time, drawing out her pleasure, earning cries of pleasure when she came in his mouth.

Unable to resist, he shoved his thumb into her sex. At her gasp of surprise, he began to pump his thumb in and out of her slick folds while he licked her swollen center.

His balls tightened when another climax rocked her pelvis. Abruptly, he rose, lightly rubbing his cock along her folds. Mista's arms came around his shoulders, holding him to her. Groaning, he shot his hot seed along her belly.

She whimpered in his ear.

Raynor held her close, feeling her tears on his cheek. "Shh… I swear by Odin, you remain a maiden."

Her hands tightened in his hair.

Before he could change his mind, he disentangled himself from her and sat on the side of the bed to dress with shaky movements. "I need a few morns to ready my ship." His throat hurt. "I won't bother you again." With Odin's strength, he wouldn't bother her again. He went to where his son slept and recovered him with the blanket. Back at the door to his room, he said to Mista, "Thank you." He didn't look back as he turned to leave.

* * * * *

Mista awoke in the once-safe haven of Raynor's bed. No one would dare approach her there, so it had become her sanctuary. It was a safe haven no longer. Now, it smelled of the man it belonged to. She stretched lazily, enjoying the scent. Her buttocks felt bruised and tired, hurting in places it couldn't be natural for a woman to hurt. Or to have taken a man.

She gingerly rubbed her bottom.

As she sat up, her sex gushed a little moisture. He'd brought her to her pinnacle over and over again. This wetness was the remaining fruit of his labors. And he'd kept his word—a maiden she remained.

Even if she'd now sit like she'd been riding a pack animal for weeks.

She shouldn't have enjoyed what he'd done to her. His staff going in her arse. His mouth going between her legs. His seed spilling onto her stomach.

Completely unnatural.

She'd seen women taken by men many times. In a longhouse, it was hard not to. But everyone ignored the goings-on of married folk and men and their thralls.

The arse was not where men put their staffs. Not hardly.

She swallowed, her mouth drying again. There'd been pain at first. She'd thought she surely must be splitting asunder. But then, everything had pulsated. She'd felt like she'd been lifted from the ground, like she spun around high in the heavens. His mouth had descended upon her, and he'd done wicked things with it. Her center dripped again, no longer because of pleasure gone by, but because of the pleasure she wanted to come.

She pushed a finger down into the depths of the part that ached for Raynor's touch. Never before had she explored it. She found a bit of flesh above the hole. Raynor had flicked it. Touching herself there lit her senses. But not like Raynor's lips and teeth. And his tongue had worked magic.

Nil. She took her hand away. No more pleasure of this kind. She was getting her wish, going home. She should be delighted he hadn't fought her. But then, she'd known he wouldn't.

"Missa?" Advar's small voice came from his sleeping alcove.

"I'm here, Advar." She pulled her shift over her head and went to retrieve him. She carried him to a chair, where he laid his tousled head against her breast. "Good morrow." She leaned down and kissed his forehead.

He sighed, snuggling into her. "Missa always here."

Her mouth opened and closed but no sound came out. She held him closer. "I won't always be here with you. But I will always love you."

"*Nei*. Missa always be with me." His arms hugged her tighter as if he could hold her there.

She swallowed the lump in her throat with difficulty. Leaving him would not be easy. His mother had already left this world. Not that she had done much with the boy. Now Mista would have to leave him at the mercy of his aunt. She shuddered.

It had to be done though. She had to go back to her people. Had to see her father and sisters again. She wanted a family, not an owner.

"Come, let's break our morning fast." Mista discreetly wiped her eyes.

Walking into the long hall, she saw Raynor in the distance. Her heart thumped in her chest, beating a rhythm like a celebration song. His blue eyes smoldered with boldness. Her womanhood tingled. She'd never experienced such feelings before.

It was like a burning in her loins. She looked to the floor. Her cheeks heated rapidly. How would she ever look him in the face after what they'd shared? And what she felt? He'd surely look at her and know.

Wanton.

Her thoughts and this longing had to make her wanton.

Raynor's people were much more open about sex than hers from necessity. The way they lived dictated it. She'd learned enough from her people to know she shouldn't feel this way.

It wasn't right.

Storr patted Raynor's shoulder in a hearty clasp, and Raynor's attention turned to the fair-haired giant.

Mista's eyes widened. Raynor had never taken her sexually before he'd gone away. When he'd come back, he'd taken her up the arse. That was the way men sometimes took other men. He and Storr had always been close.

Her eyes glossed over with unexpected tears. She swiped at them, wiping away the tears. Berated herself for being silly. She was a thrall and he was a chieftain's son so it wasn't as if it had been likely to happen anyway. No matter whose hole Raynor liked to stick it up, he would never take her as his wife.

Mayhap she wasn't unaffected by Raynor's presence, but feelings for a man who preferred men would bring her nothing but shame.

Good thing she would leave three days hence.

Chapter Two

ꘐ

Raynor's chest heaved as he threw his battle-axe. Storr was yammering away again.

"I'm in the right of it, and you know it." Storr crossed his arms and turned to face his friend head-on. "Keep her! You're a fool not to."

Raynor heard Storr grunt as he slammed into him, knocking them both to the ground. A good fight was what he needed. They silently exchanged blows. Neither cried a halt to the game. When at last neither could draw a breath, they wrestled to a stop.

Storr rolled away, flopping onto his back. "Odin, keep the thrall if it'll prevent more of these useless battles. She could put your energy to a more pleasurable use."

Raynor grunted, remembering how he'd plowed Mista. How he'd wanted to keep fucking her but had feared she'd be overly sore, not being used to coupling.

"She is yours, by right and by law. Keep her."

"By Odin! Leave off!" He closed his eyes. As much as he wanted to, he could not go back on his word. The coupling had been a bad idea.

Storr lumbered to his feet and helped him up. He grinned. "I think you're in need of a bath and massage. It'll help those sore muscles." With a wink, he added, "I know just the thrall to perform the duties."

Raynor groaned and followed his friend. So little time with her left. He'd take what he could from her. He'd never been a greedy bastard before but now, he would be.

* * * * *

Lust boiled hot in Raynor's veins, as hot as any battle rage he'd experienced. Mista's hands worked his body as she attempted to relax him. It wasn't working. Hadn't been working since she joined him on his bed.

Her breathing had changed since she'd begun her massage. He dared not open his eyes again. Her hair would be loose, her nipples hard, pleading to him to have a taste. Her face flushed as she paid attention to him.

He blew out a breath. A chore. She considered him a chore. Surely he only imagined her hands lingering over his body.

His cock pressed into the mattress, a hard ridge beneath him. Her hands roughly rubbed the hot oil into his shoulders and back.

Coupling with Mista wouldn't leave his mind. He had been rough with her, but after the initial taking she'd been eager for his cock. Her arse had been welcoming. Her breathless sounds would forever be trapped in his mind.

She had moaned for him. Him and no other.

Sweat broke out on his brow. He fisted his hands. His balls ached.

"Raynor?" Mista asked, her voice husky. She made long strokes from his shoulders to his hips.

He felt her hands tremble. He swallowed hard. "What?"

"You are not relaxed." She repeated the exercise over his back again and again.

Raynor was on the verge of pouring his seed under him like some young boy. "Leave off and go to sleep."

She sighed, but did as he bid. He tortured himself more by watching her undress. Teeth clenched, he rolled away from her to cool his lust. Only his cock didn't ease as he imagined Mista's belly swollen with his babe.

By Odin! His heart thumped.

"Raynor?"

He cleared his throat. "What?"

"Are you sure you don't want me to ease your chest muscles?"

He growled, unclenching his fists again as he rolled over to face her. Did she not know what she did to him? Was she teasing him? His cock stood straight out from his body. Surely she couldn't miss it in the dim light of the candle.

He reached out and touched her cheek. Such soft skin. Her breath quickened. Raynor had never kissed another just for the sake of kissing, but her red mouth drew his gaze, and when he pressed his mouth to hers, she didn't deny him her sweet taste.

His length prodded her soft belly. Groaning, he wrapped an arm around her, his tongue darting into her mouth to thrust savagely against her dueling tongue. The lust grew hotter in his veins.

Raynor trembled against Mista, his body so hot against hers. His mouth plundered, tongue sliding in to bind with hers.

She should stop it. Say *nil*. And she would. Soon. It was so hard to think with his mouth on hers. The heat flowed through her body, bringing all her senses to the aching wet need between her thighs.

His hand slid up under her tunic to cup a breast. Oh, how she fit in his hand. Briefly, he broke the kiss. He pulled the shirt over her head. A rough breath rushed from his teasing mouth to mingle with her own. His thumb flicked across a nipple. Her whole body clenched.

His mouth left hers, his head drifting back. "I won't take your maidenhead. But I must have you again." He groaned, his mouth dipping down to suck a nipple into his questing mouth.

Mista shook from the sensations overwhelming her senses. The pull on her nipple was such a small thing, but a big fray on her nerve endings.

She wouldn't stop it. God help her, she couldn't.

"Ohhh."

He switched to her other breast, nipping it and then drawing it deep into his mouth's warm depths. His staff rubbed her stomach. So hard. A little moisture grazed her middle under her navel, having rubbed off from his cock.

She wanted it inside her. Wanted it thrusting deep, taking her maiden's blood.

He slid up, his staff dangling between her thighs. She went rigid. *Please do it.*

Misunderstanding her stillness as something else entirely, he murmured soothing words against her breast. Her conflicted emotions warred within her chest. If he took her, she'd never go home. But she wanted the claim, shivered with the need for it. And the fear of it.

His hand slipped around and reached for the lard. He took a little on his fingers. His hand grazed her arse, sliding down the cheek. One finger pressed into her opening. She rubbed back against the digit. A second one followed, probing, experimenting. The whole time, his mouth did such wicked things to her breasts.

These feelings had to be unnatural. Wanton. And she didn't care.

"Please." Her whimpers followed the spoken word.

He took more lard, pushing some on the exposed hole and onto himself. He rolled her up and slid her down on his engorged staff. He helped her settle and guided himself into her.

She moaned.

Wider than a potato, it had to be. She'd been glad when their bodies came together so she couldn't see the reddened head of his staff. What would it taste like? The thought teased her so.

There was lots of pressure, but no pain this time. From this angle, she saw the sweat beading on his face, his teeth gritting. She caught the clench of his jaw. This cost him, having to take her slowly.

He used his hand to steady her, to go up and down.

His mouth found hers again. He tasted like mint and invaded her so fully, so aggressively. He caught her pants for breath and drew them into his mouth.

One finger flicked at the bundle of nerves at her center.

"Ooooh."

He did it again, stopping to slowly draw the hood in a circular motion. Her body tightened, muscles contracting.

Stars.

She could swear she saw the stars above, twinkling right around her. The heavens.

Slowly, she drifted back, going up and down on him as he pummeled himself into the tight hole.

His body went for one last thrust, one last clench, his climax teasing another one out of her. "Mista." Her name was loud on his lips. Loud enough to leave her ears ringing.

He collapsed under her, drawing her to his side and lying down with her.

"Sleep now."

She lay awake for hours, watching him slumber. Why now? With this man. When she was so close to getting what she'd always wanted—to go home. She had to harden her heart.

* * * * *

Raynor had no sooner finished his morning bread than Storr burst through the front door of his longhouse. "Your father is on his way."

Mista briefly caught his gaze from across the room where she sat mending his tunic. Advar played with wooden ships at her feet.

Raynor stood. "Stay here and keep the boy inside."

Remaining silent, Mista nodded. Raynor followed Storr outdoors. His father no sooner vaulted from his horse than he plowed his fist into Raynor's jaw.

He grunted and shook his head to clear it.

"If you think I'll let you take that whore back to her people!"

Raynor's fists clenched. His father walked a fine line with him.

"Odin be damned! I'll not have a *ragr* for a son!" His father's face turned red in his fury. "To a whore thrall, no less!"

Servants' footfalls slowed as they watched the scene. For the first time ever, he cared naught for what anyone thought. He took a step forward. "I will not marry in a peace groom offering." He knew the real reason behind his father's visit. The old man could bellow all he wanted. He would not change his mind.

Storr moved up behind him. He was grateful for his friend's presence, but it was unnecessary. He'd made his mind up. "I will not!"

His father's face turned an ugly shade. "We'll see about that!"

"Father, I've earned my place here. I've done our clan proud with Advar—"

Kjarr spat at Raynor's feet. "I sired six sons."

Já, but all but two were dead. Raynor glared at his father as the old man sneered, "You'll do as you're told for this clan, or *yours* will live to regret it!"

Raynor stiffened. Storr stepped into his space. He brushed past his friend to stand before his father. "Is that a threat?" he ground out between gritted teeth.

"By right, I can take all that you hold and banish you! Raise your son as my own! Give that little whore thrall to my men! And Storr…" His father's face twisted in an ugly snarl, "Storr knows what to expect from me!"

Mad. His father had gone mad since the death of his eldest son. The chieftain pushed angrily through the gathered crowd. Raynor turned to face Storr who shrugged. Turning toward the longhouse, Mista stood proudly in the doorway with his son on her hip. Advar chewed on his toy ship.

He nodded to her. His ears rang from his father's berating remarks. He needed some time alone to pray to Odin. He had decisions to make.

* * * * *

Mista rocked Advar in her arms, trying to send him back to sleep. His eyelids drooped and finally closed. Such a beautiful child. She didn't want to leave him, but leave him she must.

A sound skittered in the doorway.

Raynor's mother.

Tola stood watching her, head cocked to the side, her wavy hazelnut-brown hair flowing freely. She put a finger to her lips and motioned. They crept out of the longhouse.

"Good morrow, Mista."

"Good morrow, mistress." Mista smoothed at her clothes before clenching her hands. The woman had always seemed wise and acted gently toward Mista as she trained her in the ways of housework. "May I get you anything?"

"*Nei*, thank you. I am fine. You love my grandson, don't you?"

"I..." Mista's mouth wouldn't work. "I do."

Tola fingered some woodwork on the longhouse wall. "He needs you. No one else looks after him like you do."

"His father—"

Tola snorted. "A man. He can barely look after himself. And that witch he married wasn't interested in caring for Advar. All the boy has is you."

Mista swallowed. "I cannot look after him. Soon I will be gone."

"So the rumors are true, then? You will leave my son. And grandson."

"*Tá*. I want to get home to my people. Raynor has agreed."

Tola's eyes took on a shrewd expression. "My son agreed to send you home. No wonder Kjarr is in such a fidget. Raynor will be looked down on by many for this action."

Though she'd thought about what would happen when she left, it had never occurred to Mista how the other men would view Raynor over his thrall leaving with her master's permission. "I need to get back to Advar."

Tola nodded. "Advar will have a difficult time of it."

"You are his grandmother, surely you can—"

"What? I'm done raising my children, except for Kjarr. I am too old to take on a young one such as this."

"Someone will look after him." Mista couldn't meet Tola's eyes. Surely someone would take her place in Advar's life.

"Not like you. Ah well, 'tis a harsh life, and time the boy learned the realities of it."

"He already knows. He did lose his mother."

"Like the witch ever spent time with him during her days on this ground." Tola snorted again, her lined face contracting.

"*Nei*, he never knew her as anything but the shrew she was. You, he's known deeper."

"If you please, mistress. My mind is set." She continued to toy with her threads with shaking hands.

"To go home to your people."

"*Tá*." If only that had come out as emphatic as she wanted it.

"Sometimes, our people aren't always who we think they ought to be. You've been gone a long time. I best leave you now to your weaving. Good morrow."

"Good morrow."

Mista rubbed her face with her hands. Advar cried out in his sleep, and she raced to his side. Stroking his hair away from his cheek, she kissed it. He wrapped his chubby arms around her and squeezed. Her heart ached, making her chest and stomach hurt. She would miss this so much. He drifted back off into slumber.

She didn't have to leave.

Raynor might not want her as a woman, but he liked her arse enough. She didn't know if that would be enough. To be with him and yet not.

Could her heritage have changed? Could she become part of the people of this new home?

Her head full of spinning thoughts, she resumed her weaving.

* * * * *

Raynor and Storr made their way back to his home. It had been a long day of training. The warriors took pleasure in doing their best to beat him in matches. His body ached.

Odin give me strength.

"'Tis going to get worse," Storr said.

Raynor snorted, knowing Storr's words were the truth.

"I'm trying to understand you, but I can't. Why suffer so for a thrall?"

Their steps slowed when they turned the corner around an outbuilding and his father came into view. Not good. "Go to Mista. Make sure she is safe and stays that way."

Storr hesitated, before nodding. He cut back the way they had come.

"There is my son!" His father's lips were pulled back over his teeth. "String him up!" Raynor didn't struggle as he was taken in hand by two of the clan's older warriors. He didn't fight as he was tied to a pole. His father moved to his back, ripping his tunic to his belt. "I'll teach you to place a whore over your duties to me. You will be an obedient son!"

Raynor braced his legs. The first lash of the whip cut deep, but he'd felt this burn before. He clenched his teeth as the lash rained down on his back. Over and over, the fire ripped into his flesh. He concentrated on his father's harsh breathing as he fought to bring him to his knees.

He momentarily blacked out. His father beat him mercilessly. His back was now one live nerve. No doubt shredded for the benefit of the onlookers. In times like these, he tried to separate his father from the chieftain. It never worked.

His father finally ran out of steam and dropped the whip. His voice rough, he whispered, "Now you will yield to me." To his men, he bellowed, "Cut him down!" then turned to leave.

Raynor stiffened, hoping to stay on his feet. Odin. It had been many seasons since his father had punished him so. Surprisingly, his brother Thord caught his arm. "I've got you."

Raynor grunted.

"Storr asked for me to see to you. Brother, you have to keep the little thrall in her place."

His breathing rushed raggedly though his nostrils. "Mista wasn't born to be my slave. I want her by my side." His words slurred.

"You've lost your head!" Thord sneered, dragging him along.

Frowning, Raynor stumbled. Had he spoken aloud? The world blurred in green, blue and brown. His back pulsed. Hot fire rushed along his nerve endings.

"Listen wisely, brother. Fuck her. Keep her chained to your bed. But don't try to act as if she's more than a bed slave! Father will not permit it!" He grunted, steadying himself. "By Odin, don't attempt to send her back to her people. Father will banish you and keep Advar."

Raynor staggered, trying to walk on his own. "No one will keep me from my son!"

"Be still! Let me get you to your slave so she can tend your stupid arse!" Thord steadied him once again. Raynor didn't know how he made it to his longhouse. Sweat poured down his face and chest. He wanted the sweet silence of sleep to engulf him.

When Storr hurried out to help him inside, he tried to smile for Mista. She hovered nearby. Good. His son was nowhere in sight. Even as young as the boy was, Raynor didn't want him to witness this degradation in front of his people. He would suffer it again for Mista, but he still had his pride.

Mista's mouth worked. Groaning, Raynor slipped into the welcome blackness.

Mista watched as Storr helped Raynor inside. At first, she'd thought he'd been well into his cups. Then, she saw the bloody lash marks. She raised a hand to her mouth and worked it but no sound came out.

Raynor shook his head and passed out. Storr caught him, supporting his weight fully now.

"What in Odin's blood happened?" She blinked. She'd used their god's name. Not her own.

Storr growled, "His father. That's what happened."

"*Nil*. Why?" Her heart speeded up. Anger replaced fear.

"You."

She trembled. Her heart banged inside her chest.

Storr reached the bed, gently laying Raynor down. The warrior groaned. Storr straightened up. "Slaves should keep their place."

Mista winced. She had known there would be consequences for the huge favor she'd asked. But she'd thought Raynor would be able to quell whatever happened. He'd agreed, after all. Never had she imagined a father would do this to his own son. Mad. He'd gone mad. No sane parent would do this to one of his own.

She looked at the stripes marring his bloody back. Bile rose up in her throat. Nausea roiled her stomach. She stumbled, feeling faint. She had to get out of the longhouse.

Storr grabbed her. "*Nei*. You do not faint. Do not leave. You take a good, long look at this. Memorize the image. Because 'tis your doing." She closed her eyes, and he shook her. "Look. Don't close your eyes."

Storr made her stare at Raynor's wounded back for several seconds, not allowing her to comfort herself or deny her part in the bloody mess. When he released her, she fell to her knees.

Storr walked to a chest and pulled out a tin of salve. "Use this on him. Lots. Often. It will help him to heal and ensure sickness doesn't begin in the wounds."

"Aren't you going to clean his wound?"

"You will. You caused this. Fix it." He stalked out of the room.

Mista bit her lip. She didn't know if she could fix it. Grabbing cloth and water, she cleaned the wounds the best she could do. Then, she took handfuls of the salve and slathered it on his back. He moaned.

Wiping off her hand, she put a cool cloth on his forehead. "Shhh, Raynor, sleep."

"Mista?"

"I'm here. Be quiet. Rest."

He swallowed, his dry lips pursing.

She wiped them, then dripped water into his mouth.

"Do not go. Stay."

She closed her eyes. He'd never opened his, and a snore belting out from between his lips a second later told her he hadn't fully regained consciousness.

A tear snuck out past her eyelids.

She couldn't stay. She didn't belong here with these people. She belonged back with her family…didn't she?

What if her people had forgotten her? So much time had passed. Staying would mean she'd never get the chance to go home again. This was her one shot. If she didn't take it, she'd be here forever. Could she live with that?

"Da?" A voice made her turn. Advar stood nearby. He cocked his head to the side. "Da is sleeping?"

"*Tá,* Advar. He's going to rest." She stood between him and his father. She didn't want to draw up a sheet for fear of hurting the wounds, but she didn't want his son to see this. "Go play. Find your longship or your wooden horse. Stay in the hall." Raynor had made that horse for him. It was his treasure. He slept with the toy often.

"Missa make Da better?"

She forced her lips into a smile. "I will try, Advar. I will try to make Da better."

He grinned. "I know it." He dashed away, hair bouncing around his head.

Mista ran the cloth over Raynor's forehead, running her fingers over his sloping nose. More salve would soon need to be applied to his back. Could she make the situation better?

* * * * *

Raynor lay listening to the settlement come awake. Advar was asleep on his pallet. Mista had rooted up against his chest while she'd dreamt. He hadn't slept well since Storr had put him to bed. Hadn't slept at all since she buried her face into his throat. He dared not move, in fear of her waking.

This he could get used to. Before the voyage, he'd kept to his side of the bed. No more. Not since he'd taken her. Her head rested on his outstretched arm that had grown numb from tingling. He'd wrapped his free arm around her protectively.

Inhaling her scent, he brushed his mouth along her hairline. Odin, how could he ever let her leave? Using the beating he'd taken to keep her here longer tempted him. *Nei*. She wanted to leave. His pride wouldn't allow him to force her to stay.

Mista controlled a part of him he couldn't understand. Maybe the other thralls were right. Perhaps he was bewitched.

"Um…." she murmured.

"Shhh…sleep."

Mista's breath warmed his skin. "You do not sleep."

"*Nei*. I do not."

She squirmed. "You need to rest."

Raynor sighed, but released his hold on her. "I must rise soon."

"You cannot think to train today." She pushed up on an elbow. Her braid fell over her shoulder. He picked up the tip, toying with it. So soft. Not coarse like his own.

"I will. Then I'll finish readying for the voyage to your homeland."

Mista sucked in a breath. "*Nil*. I know your pride will not let you stay in bed. But preparing your vessel can wait. I have your word. I know you'll…keep it." Her voice had grown softer as his chest had tightened with every word. He was a man of his word. This his father could not take from him.

He thanked Odin when she rested her head back on him, her breath once again warm on his skin. "Mista, tell me what you miss most about your home?" His voice was rough. Tight.

"My father. We were close."

A father he could never replace. If she did consent to stay, he'd spend the rest of his days guarding her from his own father's sharp tongue.

"And your father like his father farmed for your clan?"

She sighed, snuggling closer. "You have a very good memory." Her hand roamed over his arm, to rest on his chest. "My sister is probably married…" She trailed off, her voice wistful.

Marriage. Lust hit his groin hard, and his cock sprang to life. Through the hours, he'd focused on his aching back with her in his arms. Talk of marriage… "Mista, I…" Odin. He bit his tongue, tasting blood. What he wanted to ask was unheard of. The son of a chieftain offering to take the hand of a thrall?

He could claim her in secrecy.

Raynor's heart thumped so loud under Mista's hand, he feared she'd notice it.

Secrecy. *Nei*. Given the chance to claim her, he'd rather have his people know. She deserved to be his wife, not his secret.

Growling, he rose up, dislodging her from her resting place. She gasped. "What is it?"

"The men are stirring." He swung his feet to the floor.

"Raynor, 'tis early. Please. Give me a moment, and I'll get you something to break your fast…"

He stood up, wincing at the pull across his back. "I must go. I'm not hungry."

"Not hungry?" Her hand clasped his bare thigh. He tensed. It would be so easy to turn around. Stepping away, he eased into his clothes. She sighed. His back to her, he listened to her settle back down. On his way out, he scooped up his sleeping son and placed him on the bed beside her.

"This way, he can wake up with you. He told me he likes that."

"Thank you." She cradled his little body close.

Raynor swallowed down the ache, liking the picture they made. He brushed the hair away from Advar's face and left them alone, closing the door behind him.

* * * * *

With the sun setting, Raynor sat on the bench along the front of his home. His back rested flat along the wall. Advar slept in his arms, his little legs spread over his thigh, his arms and head hanging over Raynor's forearm.

Odd, how the settlement had quieted like any other eve.

"'Tis ready." Storr blocked his view. "You do this, you'll be an outcast." Storr's face held shadows. Raynor stared. No one understood his need to see Mista happy. Not even him.

Would his father cast him out? Banish him for a year? Forever? He sighed. Whatever his father dealt him, he'd survive another day.

"I'm telling you, take her! It is your right!" Storr leaned down, picked up a stick and hurled it as he bellowed. "By Odin! You give some slave a fortune in jewels and cart her arse back to her homeland? It's unnatural!"

Raynor remained silent as Storr expelled his temper.

"Then tell me why?"

He shifted his son closer to his body. Why? He did not know.

The door opened, and they turned as one. Storr's face tightened. Raynor wanted to bash him.

Mista's hand fluttered to her belly. "Would you like me to put him to bed?"

"If you do not mind his wet pants."

Mista tsked. "You know what happens if he doesn't take care of his needs before he sleeps."

His knuckles brushed the full curves under her tunic when she collected Advar from his lap. "I'll clean him up and put him to bed."

He nodded his thanks, enjoying the sway of her hips as she left them. No one would ever care for the boy the way she did. No one would ever bring Raynor's lust to an animal pitch the way she did.

No one.

"If I ever meet a woman who ties me in knots in such a way…I'll use my own ax to castrate myself." Storr made a sound of disgust before leaving him.

Raynor's mouth turned up. Castrate himself, his arse. He stood up, heading indoors to clean his son's stench from his leg.

* * * * *

Raynor stood up from the bench that ran the length of the long table. He hoped he'd given Mista enough time to gather her few belongings. Their last night together had arrived. He remained quiet as he entered the room. Mista sat perched on the edge of the bed, braiding her raven strands. Lust lit his blood, thickened his cock. His fingers twitched to feel the softness one last time as he approached her. "Leave it down."

"*Tá*, if it pleases you."

"It does." He knelt on a knee and urged her hands aside as he gently unbraided the locks of silken hair. He caught her gaze as her hand clasped his wrist. Heart racing, he continued to work. Such long hair. Once done, he brushed it back over her shoulders. "Breathtaking."

Dark nipples pressed against the undershirt she wore. She wore no other clothes. Caving to temptation, he dipped his head sucking a nipple through the rough cloth. He tugged it with his teeth.

Lust burned hotter. He glanced up at her in the dim candlelight as he bit her other nipple. He groaned as she shivered, his palms running down over her waist and hips, along her inner thighs.

Raynor trembled as her legs parted for him. His hands caught at her feet to glide up along the outer line of her legs. Up and down, he caressed her. Mouth watering, he pulled her legs farther apart until she gasped and lay back on the bed.

Leaning forward, he sucked her sex into his mouth. Tasted. Toyed. And released. Mista shivered. He turned his attention to her curvy thighs. Clasping her right calf in his hands, he kissed and suckled from knee to her dripping sex. His tongue lapped. His teeth marked places along his path, earning satisfying cries from her lips. He repeated the laving on her quivering left thigh.

His breath rough and hot, he inhaled through his nose for control. His cock eagerly strained against his trousers. Whimpering, Mista pulled her outer lips back. His heart thumped. Tongue lapping at her fingertips, he flicked lower until he teased the cluster of nerves.

So hot.

Wet.

Inviting.

Nei.

She wasn't offering what he wanted. Grinding his mouth against her sex, tongue brushing across her swollen center, she burst under him. Tensing, moaning long and deep, Mista came apart for him. Raynor greedily sucked her sex, until she whimpered. She made a memorable picture, panting and limp.

Reluctantly, he pulled away. Kissed each knee. Standing up, he leaned over, placed his hands on each side of her, and pressed his mouth to hers in a kiss. Raynor jerked at the feel of her thighs cradling his hips. His knee pressed on the bed.

Such temptation. "Remember, I not once thought of you as my thrall." His throat grew tight. It was as close as he could get to telling her he'd miss her. Needed her beyond understanding. He pushed away from the bed.

Mista crawled up on her knees, looking more wanton than before with her wide eyes and trembling mouth.

Gently picking Advar up from his pallet, he carried his son to Raynor's bed. "I think he'd enjoy sharing his dreams with you this last night." He swallowed, briefly pressing his temple to his son's. "My mother has promised to collect him in the morn."

"Raynor..."

Straightening up, he turned away from temptation, and picked up a small chest from the corner. He set it on at the end of the bed. "This is for you. Have Storr bring it to the ship in the morn. I'll be there waiting."

"Raynor, wait...I..."

A groan rumbled up in his chest. Wait? If he waited he'd take her. Take her like a man takes a woman, his word be damned. His past be damned. And her future...

Nei.

If he took her in such a way, he'd never allow another to have her. He couldn't live with another unhappy and unwilling woman in his bed again. He closed the door with enough force to gain the attention of the whole longhouse. Ignoring the eyes watching him, he made his way outdoors.

* * * * *

Mista scrubbed out a wooden dish.

Her throat ached as she fought the tears that threatened to fall over her lashes with each move of her hand.

Morning. Time for her to depart.

This was what she wanted. Why cry?

Storr grumbled and ducked his head as he entered the longhouse. "Are you ready, thrall?"

She nodded. "Oh, Raynor wanted you to grab that." She pointed to where Raynor had put the chest.

"Did you look in it?"

"*Nil*. He didn't tell me I could." She'd been sorely curious, but had resisted the urge to peek. It had been important to Raynor to take this with them. He was being so nice to take her back to her family. She wouldn't do anything to jeopardize that. Not now. She was so close she could almost taste the air of Ireland. Only she couldn't remember what it smelled like. Not really. Only that Ireland was good.

Storr slammed the chest down in front of her. "Open it." His hard eyes flittered toward her as if daring her to act.

With trembling hands but a clenched jaw, she unclasped the latch and slid the top open. Then, she gawked. Gasped. There were jewels. Lots of jewels. She'd never seen so many before. "What is this?" Why would Raynor be taking this with him to drop her off at her home? Maybe he feared he might not come back here after all. Her stomach roiled. She didn't want to cause him pain. Or cause him to leave the home he loved so dearly. But she had to go home.

"Jewels for you. From Raynor."

"From Raynor?"

Storr nodded, leaning back against a wooden wall. Bending down, she reached out one finger to touch the top of it. She ran her hand along the wood, but refused to pick up such a lovely thing as a jewel. So shiny. They were not for her though. They couldn't be. She was only a thrall, not anything more to Raynor. Her heart pounded in her chest so loudly. "Why?"

"You can ask him yourself." He tapped shut the lid. "*Já,* ask him yourself. We must go meet the ship."

"Missa?" Advar's sleepy voice sounded.

She straightened to look at him. His apprehensive eyes soothed as they lit on her. Her nails clenched into her palms, digging in.

Mista bit her lip. She had wanted Advar to sleep through her leaving. "I'm here. Go back to sleep."

"*Já,* Mother." He drifted off before he finished speaking. His blond hair shone more than the jewels in the dawn's welcoming light.

The tears did seep then. Mother. He'd probably not remember saying it. But he'd called her Mother. For the first time. And she knew. She couldn't leave him. She couldn't leave them. Not because he'd called her Mother and especially not because of a chest of jewels, but because she cared too much to let them go.

She'd made a mistake.

So anxious to go back, she'd made an error. She'd forgotten something she shouldn't have.

Family was what you made it.

* * * * *

Storr led Mista onto Raynor's long boat. He walked ahead of her. The water sloshed against the banks. Gulls cried overhead.

How would she tell Raynor? Would he even listen with things having gone this far? She had to make him.

Raynor stood on a side, watching them. The men who would accompany them milled around, preparing for the voyage. The sail hadn't been unfurled yet. He took care of his sail above all things.

Shading his eyes with his hands, his back was straight like a tall tree. His hair blew in the breeze, which would be a good omen for a journey such as this.

She held her arms straight down by her side almost as true as he held his back. Didn't run to him like she wanted to or enfold him in her arms. She didn't know what his reception would be. He had to let her stay. To be a mother to Advar if nothing else.

She walked slowly over to him, taking her time to muster the courage that lay underneath her breasts. She savored the sight of him, so tense and sternly waiting for her to approach.

"Raynor."

"I'm ready to pull up anchor, Mista. We'll make the journey as comfortable for you as we can."

"Why, Raynor?"

"Why what?"

She licked her lips. He watched the motion and shifted on his feet. Maybe there was hope she could capture his attraction yet. Mouths didn't care about gender. Maybe that could be their pleasure. She'd use anything to tempt him. She licked her lips again, making a long swipe of tongue. "Why the jewels? For a mere thrall?"

"I told you… I've never thought of you as a thrall. You should have…something beautiful." He shrugged, making the action have less weight than it should have. Like it didn't matter. But it did. That he cared mattered to her.

She closed her eyes. Felt the rocking motion of the boat under her feet. Sex involved rocking against each other. Her sex leaked out its moisture. Bodies intertwined would be such heaven. *Oh Odin*. There again, she was referring to his religion. When had she started using his terms for her thoughts? She wasn't sure. She opened her eyes and faced Raynor head on as they moved to the front of the deck. A carving caught her eye at the tip of the ship's high bow. A woman.

"Raynor. I need to stay. Advar needs me. I've changed my mind." Her voice cracked, going higher than the seagull's songs. Advar had called her Mother. Maybe he'd repeat it when he woke. The word would always sound so sweet from his lips no matter if she heard it a hundred times. Or a thousand. This might be all she had if Raynor couldn't accept her as the sex thrall she'd been purchased to be. Long lonely nights… Surely he'd turn to her if she could make him decide to let her stay. Again, she licked her lips, letting her tongue make a slow trail around the outer edge.

His lips clenched together. "He'll get along fine without you." The words cut like a strap, only the pain was inside. She wouldn't get along fine without him. Or without Raynor.

"I know that I am…not who you are attracted to. But I…I'm your thrall. I was wrong. I don't need to go home. I am home." She spoke the last with the finality in her head. This was home. This place had been for a long time. She had refused to accept the truth, but now that she had she had to make Raynor see.

"You…you've changed your mind?" His voice hitched. Her hopes sprang up like a hidden spring. Emotion had shrouded his voice. She'd heard the inflection. Maybe he could care about her, even if he didn't want her.

"*Tá*."

"Because of Advar." He frowned, looking down at his boots upon the deck, not meeting her eyes.

"Mostly because of Advar." She spoke quietly, shifting her weight back and forth on the low ship. "I know I am not what you need for a lover. What you want for one. But I would like to stay and satisfy you as I can. And be a mother to your son."

"What do you mean not who I'm attracted to?" His face creased in puzzlement. His eyes met hers, full of questions. She'd never spoken of Raynor's desires to another person. How would she tell Raynor she knew about his preferences?

"I know…"

"Know what?"

She gulped. "That you lust after men."

"What?" Raynor roared, earning his crew's attention.

Mista, now wide-eyed, had taken a step back from him.

He took a step toward her, only to have her step back farther. He did not blame her. "By Odin!" He had heard wrong.

Her face flamed, and she lowered her eyes.

He clasped her face in his hands, forcing her to meet his gaze. "What nonsense is this?"

Mista's hands drifted up to grasp his wrists. "You do not want me in the way a man—" she whispered softly.

Raynor kissed her. His tongue thrusting, tangling with her smaller one, hard and deep, until he could no longer breathe. Until he could no longer think with her soft curves writhing against his body.

Breathing roughly, he broke the kiss. "I want you like I have never wanted another." His stiff cock pulsed between them. "I want you like I will never want another."

Mista whimpered and pressed her belly into him.

Still clasping her face, he kissed her once more. This time he was more demanding. He caught her every gasp. He ground his cock into her. His hand drifted to the back of her head, to force her head back so he could fuck her mouth with his tongue. The way he wanted to fuck her body with his cock.

Lust burned hot in his veins. Hotter in his loins. He braced his legs against the desire to take her to the wooden planks below their feet. Wrapping an arm around her to support her, he broke the kiss. Her mouth, swollen and bruised, held him captive. "I took your arse because in my greed, I could not let you leave me without having some part of you."

She opened her mouth to speak, then stopped.

He kissed her hard, his mouth grinding into hers, tongue delving deep.

Mista arched into him.

His chest heaved when he broke the kiss. "Be silent. 'Tis not easy for me to speak." He breathed into her panting mouth. "Mista of Ireland…I could not have you go away to hate me more for leaving a babe in your belly."

"Raynor…"

"Silence. I could not live with another unhappy woman. 'Tis why I was willing to take you home." His hand tangled in her hair. "Did you speak the truth before? Do you wish to stay now?"

"*Já*." Her darkened eyes held his gaze. "I wish to stay."

A shudder racked his body, and Mista whimpered. "I will keep you as mine. 'Tis not my son you stay for?"

"*Nil*. 'Tis not your son I stay for."

He briefly closed his eyes and thanked Odin for his blessing. His nostrils flared as he opened his eyes again. "I cannot give you a bridal ceremony." Raynor loosened his hold on her, knelt on one knee and clasped her hands in his. "I am pledging you my ring, my sword and my life. For neither state nor self, will I take another in your stead. There will only be you until my death."

Mista's mouth trembled.

"Accept his offer, so I can witness the claiming," Storr roared as the rest of the crew joined in.

Raynor held his breath until Mista's throat worked. "I accept all that you offer and I pledge my body and love to you until my death."

He rose unsteady to his feet to press a soft kiss to her mouth. Her arms slid around his neck as her tongue filled his mouth. Swinging her up into his arms, he carried her behind the sail to where sleeping bags were kept. Placing her on her feet, he quickly unrolled two and helped her settle down on them. She trembled. Undoing his belt, he let his pants drop and pulled his long tunic out of the way.

His cock stood out, engorged. Head buzzing, his hands were rough as he pushed her skirts up out of his way. Mista's sex glistened. He settled between her spread thighs. Claiming her mouth with his, he rubbed his cock along her slick folds, and braced on forearms, he whispered into her panting mouth. "I promise to make up for my speed when darkness falls. I promise to lick every inch of you. Now guide me to your passage and let me claim what is mine."

A trembling hand ran down his chest until she clasped his cock. She squeezed, and he jerked. He held her gaze as she brought the head of his cock to her wet sex. Raynor rocked his hips to push inside her grasping walls. She closed her eyes, and he shoved hard to arch in pleasure. Mista cried out, and he held still.

Her maidenhead.

His.

Raynor trembled. He could not be easy as much as he wanted to for her sake. He pulled out to enter her again. She gasped. Once more, he slid fully from her body to thrust back into her slick, tight sex. He rocked his hips into her so hard they would have moved along the deck if he hadn't been grasping her shoulder.

Her thighs clamped around his hips.

Mista panted beneath him as he grunted with each stroke of his cock. She clung to his shoulders when he rocked harder. Faster. The pleasure was so sweet he experienced Valhalla. Her sex eagerly clutched at his cock as she moaned long and deep in her throat, her hot clenching sex milking him. He roared as he came, filling her with his seed. Eyes closed, his body arched to jerk in release.

Odin, allow a babe to be planted, bonding us forever.

Still buried in her, he allowed the lower half of his weight to rest on her. He lowered his head to rest beside hers.

A cheer from his men rent the air. Raynor grinned as Mista buried her face into his neck. He enjoyed the feel of her legs wrapped around him. His cock swelled, growing hard.

"Raynor..." she whispered, still catching her breath.

He turned his head to face hers. "Mista mine, I will not fuck you again for my men to watch." He had claimed her as a wedding ceremony required of a couple.

She snorted. "Since I've arrived, I've witnessed all forms of debauchery."

"Not from me, you have not."

"*Nil*, not of you." She kissed him.

He gently untangled them, covering her with her dress. He grunted with satisfaction as he stood up, his cock showing signs of her maidenhead. He adjusted his clothing and helped her to her feet. "Come. Let us bathe before we introduce Advar to his mother."

Mista smiled.

Storr grasped him on his shoulder. "And you'll want to be the one to inform your parents of the claiming."

Raynor nodded and winked at Mista. "There is that."

Also by Melany Logen

ഇ

Torc's Salvation

About the Author

ഇ

Once upon a time, two little girls grew up hundreds of miles apart. They lived, they loved and especially, they read. Reading led them to finding each other and discovering a mutual love of writing.

We are two lucky people who have found a best friend and a wonderful writing partner online. We met writing fan-fiction and discovered a common bond in writing engaging characters. It wasn't long before we were branching off from each other's stories. We wrote together quite creatively, naturally, and sensually. We understood one another, we clicked.

Not only do we have a lot in common, we aren't afraid to criticize, guide and push each other. It seemed natural that we could take our association out of role-play and heat up the romance genre.

Melany Logen, an award-winning author, was born.

Melany welcomes comments from readers. You can find her website and email address on her author bio page at www.ellorascave.com.

Tell Us What You Think

We appreciate hearing reader opinions about our books. You can email us at Comments@EllorasCave.com.

TAKING IT ALL

By Cheyenne McCray

Author's Note

Taking It All incorporates only elements of Domination/submission and BDSM. It is not intended to accurately portray a true BDSM or Dom/sub relationship.

Trademarks Acknowledgement

The author acknowledges the trademarked status and trademark owners of the following wordmarks mentioned in this work of fiction:

Marlboro: Philip Morris & Co., Ltd.

Tonka: Tonka Corporation

Velcro: Velcro Industries B.V.

Chapter One

ᘓ

God, but she had to get a life.

Lisa Peterson slammed the door of her plain vanilla two-door car that went along with her plain, vanilla two-door life.

Door one, work. Door two, home alone.

She gripped the steering wheel in both hands, leaned back against the seat and tilted her head to look at the car's faded interior.

When did her life get so boring?

"More like, 'When has it ever been interesting'?" she grumbled as she lowered her head and looked at the nondescript, gray stone bank building she worked in as a teller. It was a warm Arizona early evening—she was one of the last to go home, always staying a little later to close up.

Boring, boring, boring.

Another day at work. Another lonely Friday night to head home to an empty apartment where she couldn't even have a cat or a dog to greet her. "Maybe I should get a bird. Or a goldfish. Yeah, that would be *real* interesting."

Not.

She could just see herself now having long, meaningful conversations with a goldfish.

Lisa put in so many hours at the bank that she didn't have time to see any of her old girlfriends very often. Besides, they were all married and rarely had time to go out. *They* had lives.

Yeah. She definitely needed to get one of those.

Grinding her teeth, she jammed her keys into the ignition and started the car. After a couple of chugs it thrummed to life, sounding like someone gargling through a bullhorn. Time for a visit to the local mechanic to get ripped off once again.

She gave a frustrated huff, threw the car into reverse, pressed her foot on the gas pedal and backed out of her parking spot—

And saw the man in her rearview mirror too late.

The car's bumper struck the man from his side as she slammed on her brakes. One second he was in her mirror, the next second he wasn't.

"Oh shit, oh shit, oh shit!" Lisa's hands shook as she put the car into park, turned off the engine and fumbled for the door handle. Her heart raced as she flung the door open and stepped out of her car, almost tripping in her high heels. "I'm so sorry," she said as she hurried to the man who was pushing himself up from the ground.

His back was to her, and if she wasn't so worried about him being hurt, she probably would have taken a better look at his powerful back and taut ass. His shirtsleeves were rolled up to his thick biceps and his muscles flexed as he got to his feet.

"Are you okay?" Lisa said as soon as she reached him. "Do you want me to call an ambulance? Take you to the hospital?"

The big man slowly turned to face her and her breath caught in her throat. Such incredible green eyes met her gaze that for a moment she lost the ability to speak. Clearly. In complete, understandable sentences.

"Uh… I'm… Please forgive… I'm… Uh… Sorry." Her face flamed as he cocked a brow and looked down at her.

And what a sexy brow it was. Dark brown like his ruffled hair that was cut short at the sides and only slightly longer on top. It had gold highlights from being out in the sun, which was obvious from the tanned skin she could see on his bare arms and face. His features were well defined and he was entirely too handsome.

Shit. She'd almost killed the Marlboro man.

His look was hard as he studied her, and she took a step back. Her heels wobbled on the pocked, uneven asphalt, and her short blue skirt ruffled in the wind. "Really, I-I'm sorry. I'll just get my insurance card—"

"Relax." His voice was husky, the sound of it rolling through her like spiced rum. He brushed off the backs of his thighs with his large hands. "You just knocked me on my ass. I'll live."

"I should have been paying attention." She clenched her hands as he approached her, suddenly towering over her in the almost-empty parking lot. "I just—I just... Never mind." She pushed her white-blonde hair out of her face. "I don't even know what I'm saying."

"Tell me." His sexy voice caused her to shiver as his words came out like a command. Like he was used to being obeyed.

"Uh, well—" Damn, was she articulate tonight, or what? "I was just preoccupied. It's stupid. Really."

He came dangerously close to invading her personal space. She swallowed and her gaze darted to the almost-empty parking lot. A trickle of relief flowed through her as a car drove up to one of the automated tellers in the drive-through. If she'd just backed into a madman she could scream for help. Her eyes returned to meet the possible madman's and this time his gaze captured hers and she couldn't dream of looking away from him.

"Tell me," he repeated, even more firmly.

"Boring." She threw up her hands. "My life sucks. No, let's correct that. I have no life." Which, including the times she'd been talking to herself, she'd now said for the third time.

The corner of his mouth quirked. "That's why you hit me? Your life is boring?"

Lisa blew out a frustrated breath. "I was feeling sorry for myself." The wind swiped several strands of hair across her face and with one hand she shoved the chunk of hair behind one ear. She sighed. "Hitting you is about the most exciting thing that's happened in my life in the past six months."

His lips turned up in a sexy smile. "Tell you what. Instead of showing me your insurance card, why don't I take you out for a drink?"

She blinked. That was the last thing she'd expected.

He could be a murderer.

But damn, he's sexy.

What if he's a perv?

Oh, I can think of lots of things I'd be more than happy to do with him.

Lisa wanted to slap herself upside the head. What? Was she crazy to even be *thinking* of agreeing to go out with him for a drink? Not to mention all the lewd, sexual acts running through her mind just looking at him.

Yeah, she was certifiable.

Well, what the hell. Hadn't she just been bitching about how boring her life was?

She cleared her throat. "When?"

His gaze still held hers. "Now."

Uh, okay. "There's a bar called Hannibal's around the corner. We can meet there in ten minutes." She gripped the door handle of her car. "But seeing that *I* ran into *you*, I'm buying."

He grinned and started walking toward one of the bank's automated tellers as he pulled a wallet out of his back pocket. "See you in ten," he said over his shoulder.

Wow. Her life had just gone from zero to sixty in the boring to not-so-boring department.

As she restarted her car it occurred to her that one, she didn't know his name.

And two, she was meeting him at a place with the same name as a serial killer.

Brad chuckled as he used his ATM card to withdraw some cash. The petite blonde with the sky-blue eyes and full lips might have bruised his hip and his ass a little, but he had a feeling that little love tap would be more than worth it.

He crammed the card and the cash into his wallet as he strode toward his king cab truck. The blonde had already left in her Tonka toy of a car. It was so small he'd probably done more damage to her bumper than her car had done to his ass.

Was she ever one sexy little package. Probably five-two in her bare feet, a good foot shorter than him. The way the strong breeze had pressed her white silk blouse against her skin, he could tell her breasts were small and perky. He definitely liked perky. Her short skirt had flipped up a little in the wind and he'd caught a nice glimpse of a toned thigh. No nylons, just smooth, bare, sexy skin.

He climbed into his truck and started the engine. His jeans were already strangling his growing erection as his mind inventoried all of her assets. While he drove his truck out of the lot, he thought about those pretty lips wrapped around his cock. He could just picture fucking her mouth before taking a flogger to her ass, making it a nice shade of pink and bringing her to the brink of orgasm again and again.

Christ. He'd never had such an immediate reaction to a woman as long as he could remember. From the moment he'd turned around and gotten a good look at her he'd found himself captivated. From the way she'd stumbled over her words to the way she'd said her life was boring, she'd looked so damn cute.

In the few minutes it took to drive from the bank to Hannibal's, he'd already had her stripped bare in his mind.

It was nearly dark, but as he pulled into the parking lot he saw her well-used little white car already parked and pulled up beside it. The car was small enough it could have fit into the bed of his truck.

He'd been to Hannibal's more than a few times. Nice bar. Cold beer. Hot waitresses. Great place for a good game of pool. Funny that the blonde had picked this bar of all places.

When he walked in, he searched the bar with his gaze. It wasn't exactly what you'd call a cozy place, but it was dim enough for some semblance of privacy if you picked a back booth—which was exactly what the cute blonde had done.

A waitress bumped into him and gave him a seductive grin. "Heya, Brad."

He slapped her on the ass. "Get back to work, Beth."

The tall brunette rubbed against his hip even as she held a tray filled with drinks. "I can think of what I'd *like* to be working on right now."

He winked and moved past her toward the very nervous-looking blonde who looked like she'd rather be any place than in that bar. The alternative rock was deafening, the roar of voices adding to the noise. Place was packed, the usual for a Friday night. Probably why the blonde had picked it.

When he reached her, he studied her for a second, letting his gaze linger on her lips, then those perky little breasts. Her nipples hardened beneath her silk blouse as he looked at them. He brought his eyes up to meet hers and his mouth curved into a grin at the pink that now tinged her cheeks.

Instead of sitting across from her, he scooted onto the seat beside her. Her lips parted in a surprised expression, but she moved over to make more room for him. He relaxed, his legs resting wide, his thigh pressing against hers as he kept his eyes on hers. Such damn pretty sky-blue eyes. His cock hardened at the feel of her soft skin against his arm as he took advantage of the small amount of room on the booth's bench to sit beside her, but at the same time tried not to crowd her too much.

She tilted her chin as if to not let him intimidate her. Good, she had spirit.

The top of her head came up to his chin. "What's your name, sweetheart?" he asked as he looked down at her, his voice raised so that she could hear him over the pounding music.

"Lisa." She squirmed in her seat, but stopped as she rubbed up against him. "What's yours?"

Master to you, babe. "Brad." He extended his hand and she took it. The soft feel of it caused his cock to ache. He could just imagine that hand stroking him…

She tried to draw her hand away, but he held on to it just a bit longer, already feeling possessive over her. Damn, but he knew a good submissive when he saw one.

Lisa cleared her throat and tugged her hand from his. The moment he'd slid into the booth beside her she'd felt fire shoot straight through her body to her belly and on to her pussy. Her thong was damp, and just the feel of his big hand around hers created a huge ache between her thighs.

Whoa. Just because her life was boring didn't mean she needed to jump all over the first man she'd run into. Literally.

Oh, but he wasn't just any man. Sexy, gorgeous and built like a truck. She could already feel the weight of his body pressed against hers…

Crap.

"What'll you have, Brad?" came a voice and Lisa's gaze shot up to see a beautiful leggy brunette with a cropped-top barely covering her big boobs. "The usual?"

"Yeah, on tap." Brad turned to Lisa. "What would you like, babe?"

She narrowed her gaze at Brad. "It's Lisa." She glanced up at the waitress who barely spared her a glance. "White zin."

"Figures," the brunette said before she smiled at Brad and jiggled her butt as she walked away.

"What figures?" Lisa said as she looked up at Brad.

He gave her that heart-stopping, sexy grin. "That you don't shoot whiskey or kick back with a beer."

"Hmph." Lisa straightened in her seat. "And how would she know that?"

Brad leaned close, his warm breath drifting across her ear. "You're not hard core. You're soft. And very sexy."

Okay. She could live with that.

Her heart rate had picked up as Brad leaned in close and she smelled his spicy aftershave. She liked the way he felt so close to her.

A perfect stranger.

And lord, what a *perfect* stranger.

She turned her face just a little, causing their lips to be so close they almost brushed against one another.

"Have you ever fucked a stranger, Lisa?" he said as she took her mouth off his lips and met his gaze, her eyes widening. "What would you do if I asked you to meet me in the bathroom? Would you let me take you up against the wall?"

Lisa gasped both in surprise and at the erotic image of the two of them. Their lips were even closer now, and she was afraid to speak.

"Tell me." He brushed his mouth over the corner of hers. "That would be out of the realm of boring, don't you think?"

Uh, yeah. Putting it mildly.

Her heart beat like crazy, her palms sweating, the tingling in her pussy increasing. Her chest rose and fell with every harsh breath she took. She was actually picturing it. Thinking about it. *Considering it.*

Brad moved his mouth to her ear and nipped her earlobe, causing her to let out a moan and to shiver all at the same time. "Have you ever been spanked, Lisa? Have you ever submitted to a man? Turned over control?"

This time Lisa's gasp was louder as she jerked her head so that she was looking into his eyes again.

He didn't wait for any kind of answer from her. He slid one hand into her hair and brought her mouth to his and kissed her.

At first Lisa couldn't move, she was so stunned. She'd gone from hitting a man in a parking lot to kissing him in a bar and considering fucking him in the back room.

And being spanked?

God, that turned her on.

And his kiss—she opened up to him and let his tongue explore her mouth. She let out soft little moans as he kept his grip on the back of her head with one hand and used his other to palm her ass and scoot her onto his lap, between his thighs. He was so big and strong, and she was so petite, that he had moved her before she realized what he was doing.

The kiss became deeper and Lisa wrapped her arms around his neck. His erection was firm against her ass. She wasn't wearing anything but a thong under her short skirt. It wouldn't take much to unzip his pants and free his cock, push aside the thin strip of cloth covering her pussy and let him fuck her right there in the corner seat of the bar.

He must have been thinking on similar lines because he slid his free hand up her thigh, and under her skirt, his hand moving up, up, up until his fingers stopped right at the juncture between her thigh and her pussy.

"Anything else, *Brad*?" came a voice that brought Lisa crashing back to reality as two thumps hit the table. The glass of wine and the bottle of beer.

Heat of embarrassment blasted Lisa's skin. She tried to squirm out of his lap as she jerked away from him, but he kept one of his hands cupping the back of her head and his other up her skirt.

"That'll be it, Beth." His gaze was on the brunette who was glaring at him, and his tone was dismissive.

Beth cast a snide look at Lisa then whirled away.

Brad acted like nothing had happened and moved his lips back to Lisa's. She drew back and he frowned.

"Old girlfriend?" Lisa asked, feeling a surge of jealousy that surprised her.

"I've screwed her a time or two, but I wouldn't call her a girlfriend." Brad's green eyes studied Lisa. She bit her lower lip and squirmed as he moved the hand he had up her dress and dragged his fingers over her damp thong.

"Wet. I like that." He smiled. "I think you'd be more than a good fuck. You're the kind of girl a guy could see himself wanting to keep around." He moved his mouth close to her ear again. "I'll meet you in the women's bathroom in two minutes," he said then slipped her off his lap and onto her unsteady feet beside the booth.

Her lips were parted as she looked at him, her mind spinning with what he was telling her to do.

"Go on now." His voice was a husky command. "I'll be right there, baby."

Chapter Two

ꝏ

She hadn't even had a damn thing to drink and her mind was spinning even more. Lisa stumbled a little, feeling tipsy, lightheaded.

Unbelievable. She was actually walking toward the ladies' room through the crowded bar. Obeying a man she'd barely met. A man who intended to fuck her in that very ladies' room.

Her whole body was on fire. Her nipples so hard they ached, her small breasts actually feeling heavy, her pussy positively soaking her thong. Fire licked her belly, a small firestorm swirling inside her and growing larger and larger.

Lisa squeezed through the crowds of people, their faces and the noise a blur in her mind. Neon lights edged her sight from the beer signs in the windows, and the stench of smoke, beer and sweat from so many bodies made her cough.

When she reached the ladies' room her cheeks burned red-hot as two women came out, both giggling and chattering over the loud music. Lisa's hand shook as she wrapped it around the metal door handle and pulled. She almost ran into another woman who was on her way out.

Lisa's heart pounded as loud as the music as she stood in front of the mirror. And looked at herself. Who *was* that woman in the mirror? White silk blouse, flouncy short blue skirt, bare legs and high heels. But it was her face, the face staring back at her in the mirror that she wondered at. Her white-blonde hair flowed over her shoulders and down her back, but was a little mussed. Her lips were kiss-swollen, her lipstick completely kissed off. Her cheeks were pink, her normally light blue eyes somehow darker and she had the look about her of a woman who wanted to get fucked.

A toilet flushed in one of the stalls behind her, and Lisa startled.

How did Brad think he was going to take her here, with women coming in and out?

What am I doing?

I can't do this. He's a stranger!

Not to mention it was a goddamned public place.

A woman slipped out of the stall and came to the sinks to wash her hands. Just so that she didn't feel stupid standing there, Lisa washed her hands, too, doing her best to avoid looking at the other woman in the mirror.

While she was drying her hands, the door opened and she shot her gaze toward it. Her heart beat like crazy as Brad peeked in and gave the other woman an apologetic look. He turned his gaze on Lisa. "Baby, you forgot your purse," he said as he held out her black handbag.

The woman brushed past him, but not without an appreciative head-to-toe glance first.

When she left, Brad slipped in the door, leaned his back against it and gave Lisa a sexy grin.

Fireworks exploded in her belly. God, he was hot. Faded jeans molded his athletic thighs and outlined his rigid cock. His muscular body and smoky green eyes promised nights of the best sex of her life.

"Come here," he commanded, and she found herself walking toward him. He handed her the black purse and gestured to the counter close to them. "Set it down."

She obeyed, her body shaking and on fire.

Why didn't she say "no" now?

Instead she turned to him and he drew her in his arms and kissed her. She melted all over again. He bit at her lower lip hard enough to cause her to cry out then thrust his tongue into her mouth. He tasted of beer and man. He must have downed some of his beer when she left.

At the same time he kissed her hard and hungry, he slid his hands up the backs of her thighs, under her skirt, and palmed her ass that was totally bare because she was only wearing a thong. With the fingers of one hand he skimmed the cloth that covered her pussy and she shuddered and moaned into his mouth as he slipped his fingers beneath the cloth and into her wet folds.

Lisa's mind turned to mush as he thrust his tongue into her mouth while palming one of her ass cheeks and rubbing her clit. In the back of her mind she knew there was some reason they shouldn't be—

Ah God, could the man kiss.

In the background she heard the pound, pound, pound of the loud music. Sounds of laughter and voices added to the cacophony, but it was all white noise as he claimed her, dominated her.

An oncoming orgasm began curling low in her belly the harder he stroked her clit and kissed her, and she started to shake. He raised his head, breaking their kiss and stopped the motion of his hand as he looked down at her. "Don't come without my permission, baby."

"Wh-what?" Lisa blinked up at him in her haze of lust, her body trembling for that orgasm she'd been so close to.

He brought his hand up and brushed hair out of her face. "You're turning control over to me, Lisa. You'll do what I say, and whatever I tell you to do. Understand?"

"Huh? I—what?" She was back to the kind of intelligent responses she'd given him when they'd met. Was it all of an hour ago?

Brad gave her an indulgent smile. "I'm going to turn you around, and I want you to place your hands against the door. I'm gong to fuck you from behind and you're not going to come until I give you permission."

The way he kept saying *fuck* was about to make her knees give out.

"Wait." She shook her head, trying to shake away some of the fuzz caused by all the lust that had built up inside her. "Someone—someone might come in."

"All taken care of." There was that sexy grin again. "And, baby, when I get through with you, you're going to want to scream so loud they'll hear you over all that loud crap they're playing."

Her whole body trembled as he took both of her hands in one of his and somehow turned her so that her palms were against the door, her hands beneath his, and she was bent over.

Still keeping her hands trapped against the door, he moved behind her. He was so much bigger than her that he did it effortlessly. With his free hand, he pushed her skirt up over her ass and rubbed his jean-clad erection against her, scraping her soft flesh. She heard the hiss of a zipper and felt his now-bare cock along the crevice of her butt cheeks.

Oh, shit.

"Condom," she said as she threw a look over her shoulder.

"Wouldn't go anyplace without one," he said and she saw he was already bringing a foil packet up to his mouth and tore it open with his teeth. Somehow he managed to get the condom out of the package and on his cock without letting her hands free.

Her eyes widened at the sight of his erection. "You—you're so big. I don't think you can fit that—"

"Spread your legs as wide as you can," he ordered her as he nudged her thighs with his knee.

Heart racing, Lisa obeyed and looked at his hand pinning both of hers to the door. It felt so surreal. All of it. She was in a ladies' room. About to get fucked by a man she really didn't know. A man with the biggest cock she'd ever seen. And she was so excited and hot that she couldn't wait to feel him inside her.

In the next second his hand landed hard on her ass.

She gave a sharp cry and looked over her shoulder again as her flesh stung. "What did you do that for?"

Brad rubbed the spot he'd just slapped. "Before pleasure, I've got to punish you, baby." He spanked her other ass cheek, harder yet, and she let out a louder yelp. "You hit me with your car in that parking lot. You need to learn a lesson in safe driving."

She'd offered him her insurance card, for Christ's sake. But instead she was getting spanked then fucked?

Lisa tried to wiggle out of his grasp, but he had a good hold on her. Tears stung at her eyes with every swat against her bare ass, but he rubbed the spot he'd slapped with his palm each time and the pain turned into a burning pleasure. Sweet pleasure that surprised the hell out of her. Somehow it was bringing her closer and closer to climax, and he wasn't even inside her.

His erection nudged the entrance to her pussy as he forced aside the bit of material of the thong. He spanked her one more time harder than any of the other swats. She tensed, waiting for another slap to her ass—then screamed as he drove his cock straight inside her.

Brad didn't even stop to let her get used to the size of him. He pumped his thick erection in and out of her, hard and fast. His flesh slapped against hers and he rocked her back and forth with every thrust.

Her vision blurred and she felt like she was spinning out of control with her oncoming orgasm. He felt so good inside her. Stretched her. Filled her. Reached deep inside her. His jeans rubbed against her sore ass making her feel even more tender, more on edge. He reached up with his free hand, sliding it under her silk shirt until he reached her bra. As he fucked her, he yanked down her bra then began pinching and twisting each of her nipples. Pain and pleasure whirled together and her cries grew louder.

Could she be heard? He said he'd taken care of it, but what if people were on the other side of that door? What if someone pushed at the door and tried to get in?

The thought of being caught drove her closer to orgasm.

Lisa pushed back against him, wanting more as he thrust hard and fast, in and out of her pussy. She was going to lose it. She was so close.

"Don't come until I give you permission, baby," he ordered her even as she felt her body start to spiral.

The combination of everything was too much. The fact that he was a total stranger… They were in a public restroom in a bar… He had just spanked her and turned her on beyond belief… They could get caught at any moment… He had the biggest cock she'd ever seen or felt…

"I can't stop—" Lisa's orgasm slammed into her so hard she screamed as loud as he had promised she would. Her body jerked as spasm after spasm of her orgasm racked her body, her pussy clamping around his big cock. It felt like flames whooshed up her body from her toes to her head and that even her hair was on fire. Tears rolled down her cheeks from the exquisite pleasure that was so intense it bordered on pain. It was the most incredible orgasm she'd ever experienced in her life.

He continued fucking her, thrusting hard and deep, and she found she could barely breathe. Spasm after spasm rolled over her, through her, and she thought she'd die from too much pleasure. She was so dizzy, her mind so clouded, that she felt as if she was in another place and time.

Then Brad gave a shout and slammed in and out a few more times as his cock throbbed inside her pussy as he climaxed. He grabbed her by her belly and held her tight to him as he rested his big body against her back, molding himself to her. She felt the rise and fall of his chest as he tried to catch his breath. Her channel continued to spasm around his cock with every inhalation and exhalationhe took.

Brad gave a low groan and nuzzled the back of her neck, causing her to shiver. "Oh, baby, I told you not to come without permission." He bit her shoulder and she shivered when he added, "Now I'll really have to punish you."

Chapter Three

ꟃ

When Brad led her out of the bathroom, she thought she'd die of embarrassment. There was a line of women waiting to go to the bathroom and a big bouncer blocking the doorway, keeping them out.

Oh. My. God.

The bouncer gave her a wicked grin—he'd probably heard her scream. Some of the women looked irritated, others snide and some amused. They knew. She had no doubt, they *knew*.

Lisa clung to Brad's hand, squeezing it in a death grip while she clenched her purse in her other hand. She avoided the gazes of the ten or so women in line, and everyone else in the bar, as if they knew, too.

She was barely aware of Brad leading her through the packed bar, squeezing through the warm bodies, dodging the waitresses and bursting out into the open parking lot. Lisa took big gulps of air, not only from the need to breathe after walking through all that smoke, beer and sweat smells. But then she got a whiff of something even worse—someone had puked their guts up by the door.

Lisa dry heaved twice, but stopped when Brad dragged her farther away from the bar and she drank in clean, fresh air. It was starting to cool off in the Tucson evening and she enjoyed the feel of the air against her skin after being amongst all those hot, sweaty bodies.

Before she knew it, she was at the passenger side door of Brad's forest-green truck. She tried to tug backward, but he had a firm grip on her hand.

"Uh, Brad." She looked up at him as the lights of the truck flashed and the door unlocked. "What are you doing?"

He opened the door, picked her up by her waist, and she squealed in surprise as he set her on the passenger seat. "Taking you home."

The fuzz started to clear from her mind. "Wait—" she started just as he closed the door. For a moment she stared at the door. Nothing was quite computing. She still felt full inside, as if his cock was buried inside her, and she tingled everywhere imaginable. She'd just been fucked by a stranger. In a ladies' room. In a packed bar. And he'd spanked her, leaving her ass a little sore.

Maybe it was time she came to her senses.

Just as she started to reach for the door handle to scramble out, Brad climbed in on the driver's side and grabbed her arm. She cut her gaze to him. He didn't look intimidating…just sexy.

He drew her close and kissed her again, his tongue slipping in through her parted lips. He tasted so, so good. And the way he kissed her… Sucking her tongue, moving his mouth over hers in such a dominating, controlling way that made her so hot her mind was turning to mush again.

A low groan rose up in his chest and he moved his lips to the corner of her mouth and kissed her softly. "Come home with me, baby. I promise you a night that will be anything but boring."

Lisa's words came back to her as he said them. She'd told him how boring her life was, and he'd fixed that in a hurry.

She sighed against his mouth. "I'm out of my mind." She looked into his eyes in the darkened interior of the truck. "I don't *do* things like this. I can't believe—"

Brad smiled and brushed his thumb across her lips. "You need this. You need us."

Us? That sounded so…intimate. Like it was more than one night of hot sex.

That one word did it. Crazy, but in that moment she decided she didn't care. He drew away, slipped the keys into the ignition and the truck's engine roared to life.

Brad's cock hadn't stopped aching since he met Lisa. Even after fucking her, he wanted her again and again. Something was different about the petite blonde that had his blood boiling. As he drove he glanced at her and saw how rigid she sat in the seat. As he pulled the truck out of the bar's parking lot, he draped one of his arms around her delicate shoulders and drew her as close as the center console would allow.

He kept his gaze on the road, but felt her start to relax beneath his arm. She tensed again as she said, "Where do you live?"

"In the foothills." He pulled up to a red light and stopped. "How about you?"

She shrugged beneath his hold on her shoulders. "Close to the bank."

Not the greatest of neighborhoods. The looks of her beat-up car, not to mention the sound of that engine, told him she either didn't have a whole lot of income or chose to spend it in other ways.

"What's your last name?" She gave a wry laugh. "I just let you take me in the ladies' room of a bar and I don't even know it."

As the light turned green, he laughed. "Akers. And you?"

"Peterson." She was clenching her purse in her hands when he glanced at her again. "What do you do?"

"Construction." He looked back to the road as they headed up to the foothills. "And I'm assuming you were either stopping by the bank for some reason, or you work there."

"I'm a teller." She turned her head and looked at the scenery as it sped by. "I've been working there forever."

"I'll have to start going inside instead of just visiting the ATM," he said, and she looked up at him and smiled.

Damn, he loved her smile.

It seemed to take too long to get to his house, but they finally arrived. He had a split-level home with a driveway lined with spotlights on his desert landscaping.

"Beautiful," she said, her voice a little breathless.

Brad went around to her side of the truck and helped her down then locked his vehicle again. He brushed his lips over hers and took her hand, leading her to the front door that he unlocked before letting them into the dark house and closing the door behind them.

"Nice," she said when he flicked on the lights. He released her hand and her heels clicked on the tiled floor from the door, past the formal dining and living rooms he never used, into the great room. "Obviously a male domain, but I like it."

He laughed as he looked around at the empty Chinese food containers on the coffee table and sports and news magazines strewn around. His work boots were beside the front door and one of his shirts was slung over the back of his leather couch. "I guess with this mess it does look like a guy's place."

While she studied his home, he moved up behind her, taking her by her slim shoulders and holding her still. He moved his lips along her collarbone, releasing one of her shoulders to push aside the long strands of her white-blonde hair that were in the way.

Lisa sighed and shivered. "You know your way around a woman."

He turned her around to face him and brushed his lips over hers. "I've had a few women over, but very few have seen my special room. I think you'll like it." Her eyes widened and he smiled. "Trust me."

"Uh-huh. Said the fox to the hare." But then she made her first aggressive move of the night and wrapped her arms around his neck and kissed him.

Jesus, she was sweet. He'd had her off balance all evening, and now he felt like she'd turned the tables on him. With his cock raging like it was, he had to fight the need to take her down to the floor, push her skirt up again, free his cock and ram into her.

She broke the kiss and he studied her flushed cheeks, her swollen moist lips and the desire in her eyes.

He brought her arms from around his neck and took her by one of her hands. "Time for me to show you my playroom."

Lisa raised her eyebrows, but didn't hesitate when he tugged her hand and led her to a side hallway, past the laundry room that was piled with his work clothes. When he pushed open the door to his "special room", he watched her eyes widen.

"You're into kink," she said, her cheeks staining a little redder than they were before.

"BDSM." He tugged her hand, forcing her to look at him again. Her eyes were wide, her lips parted. "And I owe you a punishment for climaxing before I gave you permission."

Lisa swallowed, her heart rate notching up and her skin prickling. She shifted her gaze from Brad's green eyes and took in the room and all the "toys". It was a nice room that could easily have been a place where he kept a pool table, air hockey and any number of guys' games. It was all polished oak, forest-green carpeting and green leather "furniture".

But instead of a pool table, there was a table with straps and cuffs on each corner, obviously meant to secure someone. She'd been to an elite lingerie and sex toy store before, so she figured out what some of the things were that laid on an oak credenza alongside one wall. And no doubt that black sling hanging from one corner was a sex swing—she'd heard of those. She recognized the huge X as a Saint Andrew's cross, but she wasn't sure why that would be in a BDSM room—until she saw chains and cuffs extending from all four parts of the X.

The more she looked, the hotter her cheeks grew. There were more things, including chains hanging down from a ceiling, that told her this guy was serious.

Her eyes met his. "Brad…I don't know about this. I only met you a few hours ago." Three, tops? "And this looks pretty…pretty intense."

He cupped her face with both hands and his palms felt so warm against her face. His expression was sensual, the look in his eyes promising he'd give her a night she'd never regret. How she could read so much just by meeting his gaze, she had no idea.

Must have been the hot sex in that ladies' room.

"Trust me." He brushed his lips over hers. "You have so far."

True. "Okay," she whispered against his mouth. "But what if you want me to do something I don't feel comfortable with?"

"You pick a safe word." He pressed his large, hard body to hers and she felt his rigid erection against her belly. She remembered how big he'd been inside her, and more moisture dampened her thong. "If you say it, we stop and I'll take you home."

For a long moment he held her gaze with his. "Piñata," she finally said.

He raised an eyebrow, amusement in his eyes. "My niece just had a party and they had a piñata." She couldn't help a smile of her own. "It's the first word that popped into my mind."

"From this point on, you'll refer to me as Master." Brad stepped away and his look became serious. "If you don't, you'll just earn another punishment."

She opened her mouth then closed it. Her whole world seemed to be tilting sideways and this was happening to someone else. Not her. Not Lisa Peterson with the boring two-door life.

He folded his arms across his chest. "How do you respond to me, Lisa?"

She frowned. "I don't know."

"*Yes, Master,*" he said. "Whenever I tell you to do anything, whenever you respond to me, that's what you say."

Ooooookay… Lisa swallowed. "Yes, Master."

Brad rewarded her with a sexy smile before turning serious again. "Strip for me. Slowly. But leave your heels and your thong on. And don't forget how to address me when I give you a command."

"Yes, Master." The words actually came easy to her—it must have been the way he was looking at her. The way he had taken total control of her sexually from the moment he walked into that bar.

Lisa eased her silk blouse over her head, taking her time like he'd ordered her to. She dropped it on the floor as his hungry eyes followed her every motion. The fact she could see how much he wanted her gave her a feeling of empowerment. She brought her hands up to cup her small breasts, then ran her palms down, along her sides, until she reached her flouncy skirt. Hooking her fingers in the stretchy waistband of the skirt, she shimmied a little so that it eased over her hips then dropped to the floor.

Lust flared in his eyes as she stepped out of her skirt and she was only in her blue heels, matching thong and bra. Keeping her movements slow and deliberate, she brought her hands up and unhooked the front clasp of her blue lace bra. She let it fall open and allowed the straps to slip down over her arms, to her wrists, and then it dropped to the floor. Her nipples were tight, hard nubs and she thought she could scent her own musk.

"Damn, you're gorgeous, baby." His husky voice sent shivers throughout her. "Have you ever been butt-fucked?"

She widened her eyes. "No—no, Master."

"Don't move." He turned his back on her, and she barely resisted folding her arms across her chest.

Nerves twisted her belly as she watched him. She wasn't sure she *wanted* to be butt-fucked, but to be honest with herself she'd always been kind of curious.

He moved with such masculine grace, his jeans molded to his taut ass, his large body so powerful beneath his shirt, his biceps flexing as he picked up what she knew was a butt plug. He took a tube of what had to be lubricant and squeezed some on the black rubber before spreading the layer of the gel.

Her belly twisted a little more as he turned and approached her again, holding the plug in one of his big hands. His eyes were so green, his gold-shot brown hair trimmed in a way that accented his well-cut features. His lips were sinfully gorgeous and his tanned skin made him even sexier.

When Brad reached her, he took her by one of her hands and led her to the green leather table. "Brace your palms on the edge and bend over so that your ass is in the air. Legs spread wide as you can."

"Yes, Master." Lisa's legs trembled as she followed him. Cool air brushed her naked skin and goose bumps prickled her arms.

When she reached the table she obeyed him, grasping the side of the table, bending over and spreading her legs wide. She couldn't help squeezing her ass cheeks together as he moved her thong aside and nudged her anus with the lubed plug.

"Relax, baby," he murmured as he slowly pushed past the tight ring.

"Yes, Master," she said even as she gritted her teeth and her eyes prickled with moisture from the pain. But try as she might, she couldn't relax. Her hole burned as he continued forcing it into her ass.

"Good girl." He thrust the plug the rest of the way in, causing her to gasp.

The sensation was strange. It hurt yet it felt good too. It filled her in a much different way than Brad's cock had filled her pussy. The conflicting sensations of pleasure and pain made her ache to be fucked again. Just like when he had spanked her.

"Mmmm…" He leaned over her back and palmed both of her breasts before squeezing her nipples hard. She moaned and he said, "How does that feel?"

She squirmed from the sensations of her nipples being pinched, his big clothed body bent over hers, and the plug inside her. "Different," she managed to get out.

"Different…" he said as though prompting her.

Thinking was nearly impossible at that moment, but then she realized what he was trying to get her to say. "It feels different, *Master*."

"That's better." He kissed the curve of her neck, making her shiver again. "I know exactly what you deserve for your punishment for climaxing without permission."

Lisa's heart started a pounding that was almost as loud in her head as the music in the bar had been. Brad helped her stand straight again and she almost squirmed at the feel of the plug inside her. It felt strange walking—no, make that bizarre—as he guided her to the chains hanging from the ceiling.

She held her breath as he took one of her arms and brought it high over her head then clamped a velvet-lined handcuff around her wrist. The pounding of her heart grew impossibly faster as her other wrist was cuffed.

"Spread your legs," he ordered and she looked down to see a pair of D-rings attached to the floor.

Her heels wobbled as she moved her feet apart and let her breath out in a harsh gust. "Yes, Master," she said almost as an afterthought.

"Almost earned another punishment." He secured one of her ankles with a velvet-lined ankle cuff. "I'm surprised at how good you're doing, Lisa." He moved to her other ankle and fastened it to the D-ring before slowly rising up behind her, his calloused hands running up her legs, over her bare ass and up to cup her breasts. "The moment I met you, I knew you were a born submissive," he murmured in her ear and she shivered.

She raised her chin and couldn't help the bit of irritation in her tone. "How did you come to that conclusion—Master?"

He moved around to face her, his expression a little darker. "Watch how you speak to me. I *am* your Master now. You're at my mercy. Mine to do with as I chose to. You turned over control when you gave me your safe word. If you want to change your mind, you'd better say the word now."

Spread out the way she was, her arms stretched high overhead, her legs splayed apart, a plug up her ass, and being basically naked in front of this fully clothed man—she was too turned on to think straight. All she knew was that she wasn't ready to end this. To let go of what the night might bring. She'd already felt his thick cock inside her once, and she wanted him again.

"I'm sorry, Master," she said and instinctively lowered her eyes.

He caught her chin in his hand and forced her to look at him. "I knew...just by the expression on your face when you came to my side. The way you stumbled over your words and the blush of embarrassment on your face. And how easily you obeyed me. I've trained plenty of women in the fine art of being dominated. But you—you were born to be a submissive."

Chapter Four

Lisa didn't have time to respond to Brad's statement that she was a born submissive. He had already turned away from her by the time all of his words had sunk in, and was walking toward the oak credenza that had too many unusual items on it to count.

When he picked up a paddle, she automatically jerked against her restraints. He was going to paddle her? Her breathing elevated as he approached and she saw the tough, black leather stretched across the paddle. When he reached her, though, she saw that the opposite side was lined with what looked like soft fur.

"Which would you like to feel *first,* Lisa?" His palm caressed the hard side of the paddle and then he flipped it over and ran his fingers through the fur on the other side. "Soft and sensual...or hard and painful?"

A sheen of perspiration broke out on her skin and she bit her lower lip as she stared at his hand and the paddle.

His expression firmed as he stood within a couple of inches of her. "Lisa...?"

She swallowed down a burst of fear—and excitement of all things. "Soft. Please, Master."

"Soft it is." He smiled and ran the furry side over each of her taut nipples and she moaned. "I love how perky your breasts are." He caressed one nipple with the fur and dipped his mouth down to suckle the other nipple.

A whimper rose up in her throat at the sensual feel of the fur and his hot mouth at the same time. He bit down on her nipple and she cried out and jerked against her restraints. The pain traveled through her chest, but as he licked the spot he'd bitten the pain expanded into pleasure that she felt all the way to her pussy and the plug in her ass.

Brad switched sides, suckling her other nipple while running the fur side of the paddle over the opposite one. Again he bit her, and again she gave a cry from the pain and then a moan at the pleasure that followed. He raised his head and kissed her as he slowly stroked her flat belly with the softness that notched up the desire in her body.

When he broke the kiss, he began to stroke her everywhere, the fur caressing her arms, her shoulders, her cheeks, her collarbone. Slowly and sensuously he lightly ran the fur along her sides to her belly, and then over her cloth-covered pussy. He knelt in front of her and nuzzled her mound, and she whimpered to have his mouth on her folds and licking her clit.

"This has to go." He set the paddle down and he gripped one side of her thong with both hands and yanked the seam apart with a small ripping sound.

"Hey, these are my favorite—" she started, but he'd already ripped the other side, pulled the cloth off her pussy and tossed it aside.

He gave her a hard look as his eyes met hers. "You just earned another punishment, baby."

"What?" She stared at him. "You just ripped *my* thong."

"Are you going for a third?" He slipped one of his big fingers between the lips of her pussy and all thought fled her mind. "You neglected to refer to me with respect both times."

Uh, yeah. Just put your mouth where that finger is and I'll agree to anything.

"Yes, Master," she said as he slowly stroked her folds. Words would barely come to her as she added. "I won't do it again."

"Good girl." He slid two fingers into her pussy and rammed them inside, causing her to gasp. "Maybe I'll go easy on your next punishment—after we're through with this one."

He pulled his fingers out and they glistened with her juices as he brought them to his lips. His chest rose as he inhaled and then he slipped his fingers into his mouth. Moisture made her folds even wetter as he tasted her on his fingers and she wanted his mouth on her so badly she wanted to scream.

A teasing glint sparked in his eyes as he picked up the paddle and stroked one of her legs with it, down to her high heel. She bit the inside of her cheek to keep from begging him to lick her clit as he caressed the inside of each one of her thighs with the fur.

Instead of doing what she wanted, the bastard nuzzled the trimmed curls of her mound before easing around her so that her back was to him. She shivered and tensed. Was he going to use the leather side of the paddle now to swat her? Just the thought brought forward the slight soreness of her ass from her earlier spanking.

But he gently ran the fur up each of her legs and inside her thighs again. She tilted her head back and relaxed into the sensations. Her arms were sore from being stretched up high over her head for so long, and her wrists ached a little from the cuffs even though they were lined with velvet. She was so exposed, her entire body naked now that she was only wearing her heels. The desire to come was so intense that she could imagine climaxing with him just touching her the way he was.

Brad brushed the fur against each ass cheek, crossing over the butt plug as he moved from one side to the other. She shivered as the fur tickled her lower back and her spine as he worked his way up to her back and shoulders. He pushed her blonde hair over her shoulder so that her neck was mostly bared and he stroked her there, too.

Lisa closed her eyes and relaxed into the feel of him running the fur-covered paddle over her skin. He took it up her arms again then brought it down her back again. She moaned softly as he brought her body to new heights. She had to come so bad it was killing her.

The leather side of the paddle struck one side of her ass so hard it jolted her out of her haze of desire and she screamed. "Time for your punishment," he said just before he spanked her other ass cheek with the paddle.

Again Lisa cried out and again. In between each strike of the paddle, he brushed her bare skin with the fur, then spanked her again.

Tears rolled down her cheeks as the combination of pain and pleasure fought for domination inside her. It hurt. Really hurt. But at the same time it was turning her on, making her pussy wetter, her nipples harder, her orgasm closer. She had to fight to keep from coming. She didn't want a third punishment. No way in hell. She knew she could shout her safe word at any time, but she didn't want her time with Brad to end. She wanted him inside her. And soon.

Abruptly he stopped spanking her and tossed the paddle onto the floor. It gave a muted thump as it landed on the forest-green carpet. Lisa sagged against her restraints, relief pouring through her body along with the heaviness of her desire.

Take me now, take me now! she begged in her mind.

As if in answer, she heard the scrape of Brad's zipper and a crackle like he was tearing open a package. She looked over her shoulder in time to see him roll a condom over his erection.

She expected him to plunge into her pussy, wanted it, needed it. But to her surprise, he drew the butt plug out of her ass and flung it aside. She didn't have time to think before he drove his cock into her ass.

Lisa cried out as he thrust in and out of her tight hole. The scrape of his jeans against her sore ass somehow heightened the sensitivity of her whole body. His thick cock filled her up, deeper and wider than the butt plug had.

"Do you like being fucked in the ass?" he asked, his voice raspy as he drove in and out of her.

"Yes, Master." And she did. God, she really did. The need to climax was so intense now that she couldn't help but beg. "Can I come now, Master? Please?"

Brad slammed into her one more time then stopped. "No, baby," he said as he drew his cock out and she almost sobbed. "That's part of your punishment." He kissed the curve of her neck. "You need to earn your pleasure."

She could just see it now. The man was going to torture her all night long, never allowing her to come.

He moved away from her, strode to a wastebasket by the table of toys and disposed of the condom. When he turned to face her, he tucked his cock back into his jeans and buttoned them.

Her ass was now stinging inside and out and her body crying for an orgasm, and she was so disappointed that he didn't strip out of his clothing so that she could view his naked body for the first time. All she'd seen was his cock, and she had no doubt the rest of him was just as impressive.

Brad walked back to her with his fluid, athletic movements. He knelt and unfastened the cuffs around her ankles. When he stood she moved her legs together and found she was sore in the crease in her thigh from being spread out so far. She moved and if her wrists hadn't still been cuffed, her knees would have given out. He released her wrists and brought her up close to him in his tight embrace.

Lisa sank against him, her sore body limp but comfortable against his large form. He smelled so good. Spicy and male.

For a moment he kept her secure in his embrace, then surprised her by scooping her up in his arms and carrying her to the large table in the center of the room. She was too exhausted, too sore, too filled with desire to care where he was taking her. She just needed him to be inside her in the worst way.

He settled her on the padded table and she gave a low groan as her sore ass met firm leather. As if reading her mind, he murmured, "Do you know how beautiful you are when your ass is all pink from my hand and my paddle? The flush on your face, the desire in your eyes. I can see how much you've enjoyed your punishment. Maybe too much?"

She bit her lower lip, but knew she had to respond in some way. "Not too much, Master."

He took her hands in his and kissed her knuckles before massaging her wrists. "One more punishment, baby, and then you'll earn a good fucking."

Chapter Five

ꝏ

Lisa met his gorgeous green eyes. Her thighs had grown slicker from his words—the way he said them made her feel like she could take anything he gave her. But no matter how good she felt right now, she really hoped no more spanking was involved.

Again he spread her arms and legs, strapping her to the table. Velcro straps secured her ankles and wrists to each corner. She watched him, her desire for this man increasing with his every movement. Now it seemed like she'd known him forever instead of—jeez, should she keep counting the hours?

When she was secured, he walked to the table and picked up two black silk scarves and a small red ball.

Brad pressed the ball into her hand. "If you want me to stop, drop the ball and I'll consider that your safe word."

She wrinkled her brow. *What*?

He seemed to be waiting for her to say something, so she hurried to respond, "Yes, Master," right before he brought one of the silk scarves to her mouth, raised her head and tied it securely. She widened her eyes as he gagged her and squeezed the ball in her fist hard. He took the other scarf and blindfolded her, taking away her ability to see, too.

Her belly tightened and she shivered as her other senses heightened. The cool air brushing her naked form, the soreness of her ass inside and out, the tenderness of her nipples where he'd bitten them… The scent of her musk was more obvious to her, and the smell of leather from the table met her nose. Her hearing became more acute and she heard Brad's footsteps on the carpet as he walked away. A panicky sensation rose in her chest, like a flock of birds ready to take flight.

"I'll be right back," he said, his voice sounding farther away.

Lisa only had a few moments to think about how crazy all of this was before Brad returned.

"Hi, baby." He brushed his lips over her forehead and she heard something clanking—like the tinkle of glass. "Now for your second punishment."

She tensed, her body vibrating from not knowing what he was going to do. Then she felt something icy-hot on one of her nipples and she gasped behind her gag. She gripped the ball tighter in her fist as a cold bead of water rolled down the side of her breast.

He was chilling her nipple with ice, causing her to shiver. She arched into it, her nipple so tight from the cold, but growing numb. He skated the chunk of ice along the curve of her breast to the other small globe and up to the nipple.

Lisa groaned behind her gag. Every touch of the ice cube made her squirm. The way she was strapped down kept her from moving too much, and the coldness was sheer torture.

He raised the now small cube from her belly and she heard the tinkle of the ice against glass. The next thing she knew he took the ice and teased her lips with it before leaning in and kissing her lightly on her lower lip, warming it. She wished she could kiss him back, but the gag, of course, made that impossible.

Slowly, Brad trailed the ice from her lips, down her cheek to her earlobe. She whimpered behind the gag. Water trickled along her the path the ice had made, adding to the chill.

The next area he chose was the curve of her neck to the hollow of her throat. He slipped the ice down the line from her chest to her bellybutton and she gasped again and tried to raise her head. She clenched the ball and her belly tightened as he dipped the cube inside. It was like her bellybutton was connected to her pussy, the way a fierce ice-cold sensation shot through her, making her ache even more to have him inside her.

With her sight taken away from her, the sensations of the ice against her skin were more intense.

The ice went away for a moment, and she heard the tinkle again, telling her he was getting a fresh piece of ice. She held her breath, wondering what he was going to do next.

She groaned against the gag as he took the ice to the inside of her thigh, starting at the crease between it and her pussy. The man was drawing out her torture by taking his time dragging the ice down to the back of her knee, along her calf and all the way to the pad of her foot. She pulled against her bonds at the tickling sensation as if that would make him stop.

Amazingly, the desire storming through her grew even stronger and she ached to climax so badly she was afraid she would. She didn't want another punishment—she wanted Brad inside her again.

After he got another piece of ice, he drove her even crazier as he rubbed the pad of her other foot, tickling it at the same time he chilled her skin. Then he moved up the inside of her calf to the back of her knee and reached the crease between her thigh and pussy. She shivered all over and goose bumps had broken out all over her skin.

"You're doing so good, baby," he murmured and his voice flowed over her in a way that warmed some of the chill of her skin. Again he retrieved a fresh chunk of ice—and this time rubbed it from her mound, over her clit and through her folds.

Lisa would have come off the table if she hadn't been strapped down. She cried out behind her gag and tossed her head from side to side. Tears rolled from the corners of her eyes from the extreme pleasure and pain she felt as he stroked her pussy with the ice. He played with it all around that area, from the sensitive spot between her anus and pussy, through her folds and around her clit.

God, he was going to make her come and she didn't know if she could stop it. She held back her orgasm with everything she had.

He lightly inserted the ice into her channel and held it there before drawing it out and taking the ice away from her body. Her chest rose and fell in harsh gasps as she tried to catch her breath behind the gag.

She felt his fingers, chilled from the ice, as he ran them through her hair, to the back of her head. He took off her gag and she filled her lungs with air.

His warm lips brushed hers and she moaned against his mouth. "I think that's enough of a punishment for now. Would you like me to fuck you, Lisa?"

"Yes, Master," she said breathlessly. *Yes, yes, yes*!

She wished she could see his eyes, his strong features, but he left the blindfold on. When he moved away from her, the loss of his body contact made her feel even needier for him.

Lisa heard the rustle of clothing and her heart rate sped up, a coil of excitement building in her belly. She felt his body warmth as he moved close again and untied her blindfold.

He was naked. And so damn hot that she squirmed against her restraints again, wanting to touch him. He was the perfect male specimen, his skin tanned, his muscles flexing as he moved to one of her ankles. From the side view she saw just how taut his ass was and the power in his thighs. His cock jutted out and again she wondered how something so big had fit inside her.

To her relief, he unfastened the restraints at her ankles and wrists, then sheathed his erection and climbed up on the padded leather table, between her thighs.

"I want to feel you wrapped around me." He brought his lips to hers and kissed her lightly before drawing away. "I want to see those beautiful blue eyes when you come."

Lisa swallowed hard. "Yes, Master," she said, not wanting to take the chance of him punishing her again before she had him inside her.

He smiled and placed his cock to the entrance of her core. She could barely breathe as she waited for him to slide into her. She hooked her thighs around his hips and dug her nails into his ass and saw the approval in his eyes.

Brad leaned in for another kiss and pressed his warm body against her chest, vanquishing most of the chill from the ice cubes. Heat started to suffuse her body as he drew away and looked down at her, desire in his eyes.

She cried out as he thrust his cock inside her. Damn, he was so big, but she was so slick that he rode her easily as she adjusted to the feel of him. He reached her so deeply and filled her up so much that the orgasm she'd been perched on all night threatened to overcome her.

As bad as she wanted to, she fought against begging, afraid that he would draw away. Instead, she concentrated on the feel of him and holding her climax back. She bit the inside of her cheek, dug her nails even harder into his ass and tightened her thighs and legs around his hips.

He fucked her long and hard and watched her with his beautiful green eyes at the same time. They captured hers and wouldn't let go.

Tears rolled down the side of Lisa's face as she continued to struggle against her orgasm.

"Are you ready to come?" he asked as he slammed his cock inside her, hard.

"Yes, Master," she said, barely able to talk as she concentrated on holding back her release.

Brad brought his mouth to her ear, his breath tickling her and adding to the myriad sensations swirling through her body. "Come now, baby. Come for me."

The command caused an instant reaction in her body. She cried out loud and long and her whole body felt like it had fragmented. Tingles burst through her, thrumming every nerve ending. Her sight grew fuzzy and she could barely see Brad's eyes. Her body continued to jerk and her core spasmed around his cock as he rocked back and forth, fucking her hard and deep.

He tightened his jaw and she could tell he was holding back from coming as he drew out her orgasm. She quivered around him, never wanting the moment to end, yet it was so intense she had a hard time keeping from screaming at him to stop.

His hips slammed against hers, hard, and then he shouted as his cock pulsed in her core. He thrust in and out several more times, then pressed his groin tight against her pussy and held it there. He'd never stopped looking at her. Seeing his face while he climaxed had been amazing. Feeling his cock throb inside her as her core clamped down on him—it was exquisite.

Brad groaned then took her mouth in a harsh kiss. When he raised his head, he said, "You're incredible, Lisa. I might have to let you run over me again."

Chapter Six

Lisa curled her legs under her as she flipped through a decorator magazine while she waited for Brad. She was in the living room of the house they now shared. He'd said he planned to take her somewhere special tonight, and she couldn't wait to see what he had in mind. He hadn't told her how he wanted her to dress, so she was waiting until he got home from working at the construction company he was a partner in.

She'd moved in with Brad six months ago, and she couldn't get enough of the man. They didn't live lifestyle BDSM, but did Brad ever know how to play. How to drive her crazy with one look, which one crack of his whip.

Smiling, she wiggled on the couch, her ass still sore from last night's play. She still worked at the bank, but was able to afford a new car now that she'd moved in with Brad. He'd insisted—he'd been worried her car would break down and strand her someplace. He wouldn't let her pay rent, so *she* insisted on doing all the cleaning and laundry.

The front door opened and closed and she looked up from her magazine to see Brad walking into the family room. He had such a smooth, masculine stride and he never ceased to turn her on.

To her surprise, he wasn't in his work clothes. He looked like he'd just gotten out of the shower, and was wearing black jeans and a black T-shirt. *Yummy*.

When he reached her, he scooped her up off the couch and she giggled as he held her so that her legs wrapped around his hips. The magazine she'd been holding slid across the floor. He looked at her like he couldn't get enough. He made her feel so special.

"What's up?" she asked with a grin before looking down at where his erection had already firmed where her pussy was pressed up against his groin.

Brad smiled and kissed her hard before settling her back on the couch. When she was seated, he sat beside her and gave her a serious look.

She cocked her head, wondering what he was up to.

He dug into his front pocket and held something in his closed hand. He took hers and set something cool on her palm.

When she looked, she saw what it was—

A diamond ring.

Lisa caught her breath as she stared at the large, faceted diamond. A carat at least. She looked up at Brad, not knowing what to say.

"Marry me, baby." His green eyes held hers as he took the ring from her palm. Her mind spun a little as he looked down and pushed the ring on her finger, before staring into her eyes again. "I want to know this isn't just another hit-and-run. You're mine for the rest of our lives."

Lisa flung her arms around his neck and buried her face against his chest. "Yes," she said, her voice muffled against his shirt until she drew away and looked into his eyes. "Absolutely, yes."

"Good thing." Brad grinned. "I wasn't planning on taking your insurance card or no for an answer."

Also by Cheyenne McCray

ꕥ

Blackstar: Future Knight

Castaways

Erotic Invitation

Erotic Stranger

Erotic Weekend

Hearts Are Wild (*anthology*)

Return to Wonderland 1: Lord Kir of Oz *with Mackenzie McKade*

Return to Wonderland 2: Kalina's Discovery *with Mackenzie McKade*

Seraphine Chronicles 1: Forbidden

Seraphine Chronicles 2: Bewitched

Seraphine Chronicles 3: Spellbound

Seraphine Chronicles 4: Untamed

Stranger in My Stocking

Taboo: Taking Instruction

Taboo: Taking On the Law

Things That Go Bump In the Night 3 (*anthology*)

Vampire Dreams *with Annie Windsor*

Wild 1: Wildfire

Wild 2: Wildcat

Wild 3: Wildcard

Wild 4: Wild Borders

Wonderland 1: King of Hearts

Wonderland 2: King of Spades

Wonderland 3: King of Diamonds

Wonderland 4: King of Clubs

About the Author

ꕤ

USA Today Bestselling author Cheyenne McCray has a passion for sensual romance and a happily-ever-after, but always with a twist. Among other accolades, Chey has been presented with the prestigious Romantic Times BOOKreviews Reviewers' Choice Award for "Best Erotic Romance of the Year". Chey is the award-winning novelist of eighteen books and nine novellas.

Chey has been writing ever since she can remember, back to her kindergarten days when she penned her first poem. She always knew one day she would write novels, hoping her readers would get lost in the worlds she created, as she did when she was lost in a good book. Cheyenne enjoys spending time with her husband and three sons, traveling, and of course writing, writing, writing.

Cheyenne welcomes comments from readers. You can find her website and email address on her author bio page at www.ellorascave.com.

Tell Us What You Think

We appreciate hearing reader opinions about our books. You can email us at Comments@EllorasCave.com.

Why an electronic book?

We live in the Information Age—an exciting time in the history of human civilization, in which technology rules supreme and continues to progress in leaps and bounds every minute of every day. For a multitude of reasons, more and more avid literary fans are opting to purchase e-books instead of paper books. The question from those not yet initiated into the world of electronic reading is simply: *Why?*

1. ***Price.*** An electronic title at Ellora's Cave Publishing and Cerridwen Press runs anywhere from 40% to 75% less than the cover price of the exact same title in paperback format. Why? Basic mathematics and cost. It is less expensive to publish an e-book (no paper and printing, no warehousing and shipping) than it is to publish a paperback, so the savings are passed along to the consumer.
2. ***Space.*** Running out of room in your house for your books? That is one worry you will never have with electronic books. For a low one-time cost, you can purchase a handheld device specifically designed for e-reading. Many e-readers have large, convenient screens for viewing. Better yet, hundreds of titles can be stored within your new library—on a single microchip. There are a variety of e-readers from different manufacturers. You can also read e-books on your PC or laptop computer. (Please note that Ellora's Cave does not endorse any specific brands.

You can check our websites at www.ellorascave.com or www.cerridwenpress.com for information we make available to new consumers.)

3. ***Mobility.*** Because your new e-library consists of only a microchip within a small, easily transportable e-reader, your entire cache of books can be taken with you wherever you go.
4. ***Personal Viewing Preferences.*** Are the words you are currently reading too small? Too large? Too... ANNOYING? Paperback books cannot be modified according to personal preferences, but e-books can.
5. ***Instant Gratification.*** Is it the middle of the night and all the bookstores near you are closed? Are you tired of waiting days, sometimes weeks, for bookstores to ship the novels you bought? Ellora's Cave Publishing sells instantaneous downloads twenty-four hours a day, seven days a week, every day of the year. Our webstore is never closed. Our e-book delivery system is 100% automated, meaning your order is filled as soon as you pay for it.

Those are a few of the top reasons why electronic books are replacing paperbacks for many avid readers.

As always, Ellora's Cave and Cerridwen Press welcome your questions and comments. We invite you to email us at Comments@ellorascave.com or write to us directly at Ellora's Cave Publishing Inc., 1056 Home Avenue, Akron, OH 44310-3502.

Cerridwen, the Celtic Goddess of wisdom, was the muse who brought inspiration to storytellers and those in the creative arts. Cerridwen Press encompasses the best and most innovative stories in all genres of today's fiction. Visit our site and discover the newest titles by talented authors who still get inspired - much like the ancient storytellers did, once upon a time.

ELLORA'S CAVE
ROMANTICA PUBLISHING